We Were Inevitable

KC McCormick Çiftçi

“It’s not that you don’t do good work, Melody. I just need to see more commitment from you. Do you really want to be here? Do you really believe in the mission of EduPowerment?”

Her mouth was totally dry as Melody Critchfield nodded her head. “Of course, Mr. Richards. It’s so important to me, what we’re doing here. I mean, creating opportunity for women around the world…that’s the dream, and I’m not exaggerating. I get so excited when I think about what we’re doing here that I can hardly contain myself sometimes.” She tried to stop herself from fidgeting as she stood in front of his desk. From the expression on his face, it was clear she was rambling. But she couldn’t stop, and she meant every word of it.

Mr. Richard’s lips raised at the corners, but the smile didn’t reach his eyes. “That’s great to hear. You know, we often have issues retaining our newer employees, especially the female ones—I’m not trying to be sexist, it’s just the truth. It’s refreshing to hear from someone who *gets* it as much as you do.” He settled back at his desk, the desk he had inherited from his mother along with her flourishing non-profit. "I'm just going to need to see that 'belief in our mission'—" He'd actually lifted his fingers to make air quotes when he said that. "—translate into your showing up at work on time a little more regularly."

"I understand, Mr. Richards, I really do." Now Melody's palms were sweating. Between that, the knot in her stomach, and her mouth that was getting drier with every word she spoke, she was experiencing the trifecta of an-authority-figure-is-expressing-disappointment-with-me anxiety. But she deserved it, and that's what made it even worse. "I left my apartment with plenty of time to make it to work, but I just...I should have checked the news. I didn't know that part of downtown was closed, even the sidewalks, but I should have left even earlier. I promise you it won't happen again." She'd sleep under her desk every night of the week if it meant avoiding another confrontation like this.

Mr. Richard's approximation of a smile deepened ever so slightly. "I'm glad to hear it, Melody. It might seem unfair, especially considering that the circumstances were out of your control...but it's about the principle of professionalism. Of committing to the task in front of us. We receive a significant amount of donations to do the work that we do, and it is imperative that we be blameless stewards with those resources. How would you feel if you donated a portion of your hard-earned paycheck to a charity, only to learn that their employees saunter in whenever they want and work only when it's convenient for them?"

Oh shit. She hadn't thought of it like that. On her detour that morning, watching the clock creep closer and closer to nine o'clock while she had to walk blocks out of her way had been bad enough when it was just her boss—and, of course, herself—that she was letting down. But thinking about the donors twisted the knife in her gut even deeper. Most of the donations EduPowerment received were small—a twenty-dollar bill mailed in by someone who had watched one of their documentaries, a tip jar walked over from the local café every month—and that made it even worse. It wasn't like she was letting down a massive corporation—not that Melody Critchfield would do that in good conscience, either—but she wouldn't be able to look any of her colleagues in the eye if she didn't make this right.

"I'll stay late tonight, Mr. Richards. And it really won't happen again. You can count on me."

He nodded. "I want to, Melody. Consider this a warning. Your *first* warning." He leaned in to the number like there wouldn't be a second. "You can go now. Don't want you missing any more work today."

Melody peeped out a "Thank you!" that could probably only be heard by dogs and darted from the office, across the hall and back in to her cubicle. She was surrounded by clicking keyboards and quiet murmurs as her coworkers answered calls and did the business that kept EduPowerment running. None of *them* were taking advantage of their donor's hard-earned money.

As her computer was coming to life, Melody removed the thermos from the cupholder at the side of her large, functional purse. Though EduPowerment provided coffee for their employees, she had brought her own every day since she'd started three years ago.

It was a good thing, too, because the last thing she needed on a day like today was to bump into Mr. Richards in
the coffee room after the conversation they'd just had. No,
today was going to be the perfect day for keeping her head
down and working efficiently. She already preferred to eat
lunch at her desk, but bathroom breaks would be kept to
a minimum today, too.

A squeak came from the cubicle next door, jolting
Melody upright and nearly spilling coffee down the front
of her light blue chambray shirt in the process. "Chloe? Is
everything okay over there?"

A blonde head popped up, wide eyes finding Melody's
own. "Better than okay!" she hissed. "Have you *seen* this
email from Jacqueline? I'm so flippin' excited!" She waved
her arm over the cubicle wall. "Come look at this email and
freak out with me!"

Melody sighed. "What does it say?" She nodded her
head towards her still-booting-up computer. She could
understand how cutting-edge technology wasn't a priority
item in the budget of a non-profit, but she did sometimes
wish for a slightly less ancient desktop computer. On her
wildest days, she even dreamed of one that would run her
design software without crashing every twenty minutes.

Chloe rolled her eyes. "That's why I told you to come
over here, silly! Just look at mine. It's the same thing that
was sent to you."

Melody was shaking her head as she ducked into Chloe's
cubicle. The two of them had been working side by side
since Chloe had graduated a year ago, and Melody was well
versed in her quirks. Including her very annoying quirk
of not taking no for an answer, even when all Melody

wanted was to work without interruptions. Chloe was a copywriter in the marketing department, working closely with Melody, who had graduated to the responsibility of running EduPowerment's marketing department.

"What am I looking at here?" Melody scanned Chloe's screen, where at least six different tabs were on display at the same time. There was an online thesaurus, a Pinterest board, a blank document with a blinking cursor, and...

"What in the—?" Melody mumbled as her eyes landed on the subject line in Chloe's email inbox. **Congratulations! You're invited to apply for EduPowerment's Generosity Exchange program.** As she continued to scan the body of the email, a few key phrases jumped out at her.

"Generosity Exchange year-long overseas exchange program...sharing talent with our sister institutions and schools...your exemplary performance...uniquely qualified...work with the marketing team at Deutsche Lebenshilfe in Dresden...instructional position at English-language university in Izmir...positions are competitive, respond with your order of interest..."

Melody looked at Chloe with wide eyes. "Are you shitting me? Is this a joke?" She glanced at the clock at the bottom corner of Chloe's screen. "It's not April Fools' Day, is it?" Shaking her head, she backed away from the desk. "No, there's no way. This isn't real, and even if it is, it's not going to happen. I'm not going to waste my time thinking about it, especially when there's important work waiting for me and I'm *already* late to get started."

Chloe blinked slowly, her jaw agape. "Are...are you doing an impression of a workaholic with no sense of adventure? Because if so, it's *spot on*, Mel. You're not even going to read it? Let yourself dream a little bit about spending a year in another country?" She took her mouse in hand, spinning the wheel to scroll through the email. "There are partner institutions all over the world, Melody. Surely *one* of them sounds like fun to you..."

Melody bit her lips between her teeth. The problem wasn't finding a location that called out to her. No, she'd known where she'd want to go—that is, if she was actually going to act on this foolish whim—the second she'd seen that city name cross her field of vision. That wasn't the problem at all.

The problem—and she felt awful even referring to it that way—was that she couldn't go, no matter how much she might want to. The projects she was working on here...who would take them if she left? What about her future at EduPowerment? Sure, this sounded like an exciting opportunity, like study abroad for the working professional set...but did you really come back from a year of studying abroad still on track for graduation? Racking her brain, Melody was pretty sure at least one of her college neighbors had needed to take summer classes to make up for the general education courses that hadn't been offered at her exchange school junior year. And what even was the equivalent of summer courses when you were already working full time?

Turning to Chloe and taking her hands in her own, Melody forced a smile. "It sounds like a great program. And I think you should definitely do it. I'll even help you with the application process or selection process, or whatever it is."

A frown crossed Chloe's face. "Are you really not even going to consider it?"

Melody took a breath, reminding herself that she knew what was best for her. She knew what this situation required of her.

*To get back to work and put away dreams of moving abroad, turn to **page 75***

*To think a little longer about applying for the program, turn to **page 117***

8

After work that evening, Melody followed Ben back to his apartment, a bundle of nerves settled at the base of her stomach. This was different. Different from any amount of friendly camaraderie they had settled into at work, and it felt unfamiliar. The intimacy of visiting his home, just the two of them...well, it had been a long time. A long time since she had been alone in a man's home—a date, a friend, or otherwise. That was probably why she was chattering with nervous excitement the whole way there, suddenly so full of questions that she'd never bothered to ask Ben before.

"We're going to your apartment, yeah? Where do you live? Any roommates?"

"It's just me," said Ben. "And I love my little place. It's very cozy."

"Ah," said Melody. "Isn't that the real estate code word for tiny?"

That got a laugh out of Ben. "Well, it is small, but it's at least not a studio. So no worries. We will sit at the table or the couch to drink our coffee. We don't have to sit on the bed or anything like that."

Now it was Melody's turn to blush. "Glad to hear you're not just trying to trick me into bed, then."

Ben wouldn't meet her eyes, shaking his head. "Ah, if we could just keep the conversation from going there, that'd be great, wouldn't it?"

Melody shrugged. "We can try, but it just seems to keep happening, doesn't it? It's okay," she said, reaching over to give him a reassuring pat on the shoulder. "You can relax. I promise I'm not flirting with you."

"Oh?" His expression was unreadable. "I appreciate the clarity then. That's uh...that's good to know."

"Mm hmm." She nodded. While she had thought that was going to ease the tension between them, if anything, it seemed to have created more. What the heck was going on here?

Whatever was developing between her and Ben was...complicated. And she could no longer deny that *something* was developing between them. She couldn't say what exactly it was that was brewing, but she could play it cool while she figured it out.

Only, Melody was racking her brain for examples of times when she had managed to be cool about *anything*.

She hadn't been cool about getting the job at EduPowerment. No, that time she had shrieked out loud when she'd gotten the email while sipping a latte at her favorite college cafe, and someone at the table next to her had poured her expensive drink all over her own lap in shock.

Thankfully, it had been iced coffee, so there had just been an embarrassingly positioned stain, a cold and caramel-scented crotch, and no third-degree burns to attend to.

No, Melody wasn't in the habit of playing it cool as a rule. Not when she got what she wanted, and not when she didn't. Time would tell how this would all unfold with Ben.

The walk to Ben's apartment was the dictionary definition of a beautiful autumn day. The leaves were still on the trees, though nearly all of them were deep into their color change, with far more reds and oranges visible than yellows or greens. A breeze was blowing that had Melody pulling her fleece jacket a little closer to her neck.

"Cold?" Ben asked, nodding towards her hunched shoulders.

She nodded. "Just a little. I'll warm up if we just keep the pace up."

"Say no more," said Ben, reaching for her hand as he started stretching his long legs further in front of them with each stride. "Let's book it."

Melody laughed as she fell into step with him, their hands parting ways soon after for the added momentum. She missed the warmth of his hand immediately, and not just because the two of them were now doing their best impressions of power walkers, arms bent at 90-degree angles and swinging forcefully at their sides as their legs just barely stopped themselves from breaking into a full-on run.

They stopped at the next intersection, a traffic light cautioning them not to walk into the empty street. Melody was glad for the break to catch her breath, but at the same time, it felt a bit silly to stand there and wait when there were no cars coming. She took one step off the curb but was stopped almost instantly by Ben's hand on her wrist, gently tugging her back next to him.

"What are you doing?" he asked, a quizzical expression on his face. "The light is red. We have to wait."

Melody chuckled, thinking he was making a joke, but abruptly stopped when he didn't join in her laughter. "You're serious? There are no cars on the street. We can just hop across, no big deal."

Ben shook his head. "Sure, there are no cars in the road, but what about the children?"

Melody raised an eyebrow. "Is this really a 'will somebody please think of the children' moment? Are you a character in *The Simpsons*?" When Ben didn't acknowledge her stellar joke, she continued with a different approach. "Sorry, what do you mean?"

"I mean...what about the example it sets for the children? If one of them sees you walk into the street, they might do the same thing and it could be very dangerous."

"I...I just..." Melody looked around her, finding not a child in sight. "I'm so confused right now, Ben. I don't see any kids and I have literally never heard that argument against jaywalking before. What is going on? Am I missing something?"

Ben shook his head, chuckling to himself. "I'm sorry. No, you're fine. It's definitely not you, it's me."

Melody cocked her head at him. "Are you the one making 90s pop culture references now? Because that's a classic breakup line if I ever heard it."

Ben's face paled as he shook his head fervently. "I didn't...no. No, that's not what that is. Not a breakup line, definitely not. I just meant the whole thing about crossing the street on a red light."

The light had changed to permit them to walk, so they fell into step again—slower, this time—and continued to talk once they were on the other side of the street.

"So what was that, then?" Melody asked.

"It's a weird thing," Ben began. "I think I discovered in that moment that I'm not as purely Turkish as I thought because that was possibly the most German thing I have ever said."

That got a laugh out of Melody. "Really? Is that a very German belief? That you shouldn't cross the street on a red light because it's a bad influence on the children?"

Ben nodded. "I heard it all my life. Not so much when I was a child, of course—"

"Right, because everyone was keeping it a secret from you that such a thing was even an option," Melody cut in, pulling a genuine smile across Ben's face.

"That's right," he nodded. "It was like a massive conspiracy carried out by the entire adult population of Dresden. It was only when I got a little older that they started to let me in on it. But if you're out late in the night in Dresden, even when it's just the partygoers heading home from the clubs and very few cars on the road, almost everyone will be waiting at the intersection for the light to change."

"I...I think I love it," said Melody, slightly awestruck at the idea. "There's something so wholesome about it."

"That's one way to look at it," said Ben. "A much more favorable way than a lot of people would, I think."

Melody shrugged. "Well, it's not hurting anyone. And if it's coming from such a good motivation, then who cares?" A thought occurred to her. "It's probably an especially good idea for those young folks who were out clubbing and are stumbling home in the middle of the night, too. Who's to say that just because they think there aren't any cars on the road that there actually aren't?"

"A very valid and intelligent point from Ms. Melody Critchfield," Ben crowed in his best sports announcer voice. Then, more softly, he continued. "I'll remember that next time someone needs some extra convincing that waiting to cross is the right way to go."

And just like that, her mood slipped right back to the uncertainty and sadness that had been waiting at the corners of her mind, not far enough away to be out of earshot or else they wouldn't have let themselves right back in at that moment. But the reminder that Ben would be explaining German traffic rules to someone else while she was far, far away stung enough to make her wonder what she was doing in that moment. Was it even a good idea to go to his house? To let herself get even closer to him?

"Come on!" Ben grabbed her hand and led her in a slow jog across the street just as the light changed, and Melody allowed herself to be swept along, to forget her questions about the future for a moment and just enjoy the evening ahead.

Ben's apartment suited him so perfectly that she couldn't help but laugh when she stepped inside. It was nice and tidy, she was pleased to see, and it smelled just as good as he did—fresh and clean, but in a way that seemed to come from a forest and not from a bar of soap or a bottle of cologne.

His apartment also had touches of Ben's heritage everywhere she turned. There were spices on the counter, books on the coffee table, and photographs in frames that all spoke to the "different in magnitude but equally important" roles that his German upbringing and Turkish ancestry played in his life.

Ben made himself busy right away, pulling open cupboards and drawers. "I figured we would have coffee and cake first, dinner later, so you don't have your caffeine intake too late in the evening. Is that alright with you?"

Melody had brightened at the word "cake," and she was already nodding repeatedly. "I had no idea cake was on the table. I mean...not literally, since no, there's no cake on the table yet. But...um...yes, please. Cake sounds great. Coffee and cake? Even better."

"Is that not a typical combination for you?"

"Not really. Cake and ice cream? Sure. Coffee and a doughnut? Absolutely. But I can't say I've ever actually had coffee and cake before and now I feel like I'm missing out."

"Hmm." Ben pursed his lips. "I'm realizing now that this is a very German thing to do. *Kaffee und Kuchen.* Well, have no fear." He lifted a covered tray from the top of the refrigerator. "I made this yesterday, and you're going to love it."

As he lifted the top off the tray and revealed what Melody could only describe as an apple tart (not that she'd ever tasted one of those, either), her mouth watered and her jaw dropped open—a dangerous combination that nearly had her drooling on her shirt. "I...wait. What? You *made* that?" The perfectly arranged apple slices, arranged in concentric circles and surrounded by a crust that looked like it was made of buttery shortbread, were beautiful. It looked so good she barely stopped herself from pulling out her phone and taking a photograph of it.

"I did." Ben didn't even seem proud of himself. He was just stating it like it was a fact. *What sort of wizard is this guy, anyway?* Melody wondered to herself.

He had taken a small copper pot out of the cabinet, along with two canisters, one she could now see was full of sugar and the other...

"Is that the Turkish coffee?" she asked, leaning forward to catch a whiff as Ben opened the jar.

"It is." He nodded. "So, who wants to learn how to make Turkish coffee?"

"Me! Me! I do!"

Ben smiled. "I'm glad you want to learn. I was going to offer that you could sit on the couch and wait, but it's a lot more fun this way."

He took the small copper pot and handed it to her. "This is called a *cezve*. We use it to cook the coffee."

"You *cook* the coffee?" She shook her head. "Why does that sound so weird? I mean, there isn't that much of a difference between brewing and cooking, I guess. Still. It's like when someone says, 'Drink your soup.' Just sounds weird, I guess."

"But you *do* drink soup, don't you? Is it considered eating when there's nothing to chew?"

Melody shrugged. "You've got me. I think it's just that it's a meal and I don't believe in drinking meals. But a smoothie could be a meal, too, I guess, and you definitely drink those." She frowned in thought. "But I'm getting us way off topic. So, are we going to cook this coffee, or what?"

Ben measured the finely ground coffee into the *cezve*. "How sweet would you like it to be? We'll cook it with the sugar in it, because it doesn't really work to add it later."

"Just a little? I don't know, how do you drink it?"

"I usually go for the 'medium' option. Not *no* sugar, and not sugary, but medium."

Melody smiled. "Are those really the options?"

He nodded. "*Sade* means plain, *şekerli* means sugary, and *orta* is medium, middle."

"Middle it is, then."

Ben added a spoonful of sugar to the pot, then filled it up with water and stirred it. He positioned it carefully on top of one of the burners of the stove, then turned the gas flame on below it, stirring at the beginning and then just watching.

Melody used the waiting time to peruse Ben's bookshelf, running her finger down the spines with their unfamiliar titles.

Ben continued speaking. "I really appreciate you accepting my invitation. I've really enjoyed getting to know you."

She lifted her gaze to meet him, eyes wide. "Really? Because I feel like I've had some moments that were anything but delightful."

Ben tipped his head to the side as if weighing her words. "Who hasn't? It's not as if you weren't under more than your fair share of pressure. It can be a stressful environment, the office."

Melody pursed her lips, chewing at the corner of her mouth. Was that what this was going to turn into? Another conversation about work and boundaries and every-thing she already heard more than enough of from Chloe?

"I feel some of that stress and pressure, too," said Ben. "Or I have...more...in the past."

"What changed?"

He looked thoughtful. "Well, at the beginning I believed so much in what I was doing that I was always willing to do more. Anything else that I had going on in my life, any personal commitments or plans I'd made with a friend or even just promises I'd made to myself, like...promises to exercise or read a book or see my parents for dinner on the weekend. All of those things could be canceled if there was a need from my boss, from work. Luckily, I was fortunate enough to work for someone who recognized that. Who stopped me in my tracks and said something I'll never forget."

"What did they say?"

"That I was on a one-way path to nonprofit burnout and rapidly accelerating. That if I didn't make a change, I was only going to hurt myself and the mission that I so desperately cared about."

Melody pulled her lips into her mouth, stopping your-self from speaking as she continued to listen to him.

He shrugged, his attention still focused on the pot that he was periodically stirring and watching closely. "Af-ter that, I made some changes. Set firmer hours for my-self. Took my work email off my phone. Made plans for evenings and weekends that I wouldn't let myself cancel."

"And did it work?" she asked.

He looked up then, smiling at her. "Yeah," he said. "It did. I still love what I do. But I love my life, too. Like this moment right now. We wouldn't be doing this if I was the person I used to be."

"You mean someone more like me?" she asked, a hint of bitterness creeping into her voice.

Ben shook his head. "I didn't say that. If you recognize that in yourself, then that's for you to work on. I'm here to be your friend. I'm not here to tell you how to live your life."

Melody sighed. "If that's true, then that's a relief." He gave her a puzzled look, and she continued. "I just mean I already have enough people giving me unsolicited input." She held up a hand to stop him before he could say something. "And I know where you stand. Your position is clear. But you're right...this is my life, my choices. And what I'm doing right now works for me."

Ben nodded. "Then that's all that matters."

Melody came closer to watch from above. "The pot seems so full. It won't boil over?"

Ben smiled. "Not if we do this right. That's part of the challenge, though. If you get distracted and walk away, it'll boil over and you'll have a giant mess. Coffee cooked right onto your stove."

Melody pulled a face. "We don't want that. We prefer to drink it, don't we?"

"Absolutely." He pointed down at the pot. "Do you see those little bubbles forming around the edge?" She nodded. "It's almost ready."

The rich, earthy smell of the coffee made Melody's mouth water. She watched, impressed, as Ben removed the *cezve* from the heat and smoothly poured its contents into two waiting cups. The cups were small, patterned with blues and reds weaving together, and they were—like the pot before them—nearly filled to the brim. Each cup was placed on a matching saucer, then on a tray. Ben added two small glasses of water, two plates, a spatula, and two forks, before nodding towards the cake and picking up the tray, heading towards his couch.

Melody picked up on his lead and carried the cake behind him, depositing it on the coffee table next to the tray. As Ben placed a cup of coffee and a glass of water in front of each of their seats, she used the spatula to slide a slice of cake onto each plate. When she took her seat next to Ben, she didn't know what to taste first. Between the buttery crust and sweet apples of the cake—or was it a tart?—and the aroma of the coffee that smelled like a lazy Sunday morning yet somehow even better at the same time...it was a sensory overload in the best kind of way.

Ben lifted his coffee cup to her, and Melody raised hers to meet it, lightly clinking the two together. "Thank you again for being here," he said, "And for sharing your first Turkish coffee experience with me. First of many, I hope." He lifted his cup to his lips. Melody felt the briefest flash of envy, the barest wish to be where that cup was, pressed ever so softly against Ben's lower lip. Just for a second, just for a taste.

Melody took a small sip of the liquid that was somehow thick, smooth, sweet, and bitter at the same time. It was delicious, like nothing she'd ever tasted before. "That's really good," she told him, delivering her verdict. "I normally don't like black coffee, but it's...different, somehow. There's a taste to it I can't quite place."

Ben murmured in agreement. "There are extra flavors in Turkish coffee sometimes. This one, *damla sakızı*, is my favorite. I think it's mastic gum in English?"

He was watching her face for a reaction, as if to confirm that he had said the right word, but Melody only stared blankly back.

"Gum?" she asked. "I mean…is there *gum* in this? Like chewing gum? Trident?"

Ben chuckled, shaking his head. "It's a tree. Or something that comes from a tree. I promise it's perfectly natural."

"So if I swallow it, it won't stay in my stomach for seven years?"

It was Ben's turn to look confused. "Seven years?"

"That's what they told us as kids, to discourage us from chewing gum. That if we swallowed it, it would stay in our stomachs for seven years. Or else, we would blow bubbles out of the wrong end." She slapped a hand over her mouth, as if to stop herself from talking. "Please ignore me, now that I have started talking about farting gum. It's only downhill from here."

Ben laughed, a hearty sound that seemed to surprise both of them. "Sorry," he said, gesturing to the drips of coffee that had spilled over the edge of Melody's cup onto the saucer at the sudden sound. "I just…well, I feel really comfortable with you. And I was hoping you were feeling that way, too, wondering how I would know for sure." He shook his head, an amused smile playing at the corners of his lips. "And then you dove right in to talking about farts and now I know for sure just how comfortable you are feeling."

Melody could feel her cheeks flush with heat. "Ah. So...it's a good thing then? I don't need to rein in my potty talk?"

"No, you don't need to tone a single thing down or stop yourself from saying anything on your mind." Ben shook his head, his eyes finding hers. "I like it all. Everything you share, everything about you, in fact."

She smiled at him, feeling relaxed in his presence and more comfortable in his home than she would have expected. "Thank you. Thank you for all of this...for inviting me here, for sharing everything with me. Your snacks and your coffee, I mean. You certainly didn't have to do that.."

He nodded. "I know. But I welcomed the chance to get to spend a little more time with you. Is that okay?"

"Of course it is," she said, busying herself with another sip of coffee, rather than trying to figure out what he meant by that. Was he just lonely? In need of a friend? She could relate to that. But if there was an implication of something else, she didn't know what to do with that.

After their Turkish coffee experience, things were different between Melody and Ben. When she no longer had to wonder how he felt about her, it freed up her mental capacity to examine how she felt about him. And the more time they spent together, the more they shared laughs and eased each other's stresses and sat in companionable silence to share meals, the easier it was to see that she enjoyed being around him and that there was nothing wrong with that.

It wasn't as if spending time with Ben or thinking about Ben was taking away from her ability to get her job done. And it wasn't as if there was a problem with enjoying this other part of her workday.

And yet, she did feel some guilt, in particular one day when she and Ben were laughing in the kitchen after having refilled their coffee cups and a colleague walking by had given the two of them a look that bordered on caustic. Melody sobered immediately, the smile melting from her face as she turned 180 degrees and made a beeline back to her workspace.

"What's wrong?" Ben asked, lengthening his steps to catch up with her.

She shook her head, dropping her voice. "We can't talk about it right now. We need to get back to work."

"Is it about Phillip giving us a nasty look back there?" He asked. "Don't worry about him. He's just one of those unhappy people who can't stand to see anyone have a good time."

She shook her head more fervently this time. "It's not just that, though, is it? We're wasting time and we're not getting paid to flirt with each other on company time."

Ben's eyes widened. "No, indeed we aren't. I'm glad to know that's what was going on there, though."

Her cheeks were on fire now, not just with the embarrassment of being caught slacking off at work but also with the awareness that she had just showed her full hand of cards to Ben.

They made it back to her workspace first, and she ducked right inside, settling on her chair as her hands flew to the keyboard. She heard a lengthy exhale from over her shoulder and turned to find Ben standing there, looking at her with an unreadable expression on his face. "Is there something I can help you with?" she asked. "I really need to get back to work. You probably do too."

He just nodded. "That's true. But there is something you can help me with."

She raised an eyebrow. "What's that?"

"I'd like to take you out on a proper date this evening. Does that work for you?"

Stunned, she nodded back.

"Good," he said. "Then it's settled. I'll pick you up right here at...how does five o'clock sound?"

She nodded again, still unsure of her words.

"Great. Then it's a date."

Once he was gone, Melody continued staring at the computer screen for another few minutes before shaking herself and regaining the power of speech. "Back to work," she reminded herself.

On her lunch break—and not a moment sooner because she had already missed enough work in the kitchen that morning—Melody fired off a frantic text to Chloe. "First date with Ben this evening," followed by a wide-eyed emoji that conveyed just a fraction of the stress she was feeling.

Chloe responded almost immediately. "OMG, this is News! Tell me more. Where are you going? What are you doing? What are you wearing? How are you feeling?"

"I don't know the answer to any of those questions. He just asked me a couple of hours ago, and it's happening right after work. So I guess I'm wearing whatever I'm wearing right now."

"Hmm," wrote Chloe. "Well, that's okay. You can save the fancy clothes for date number two or number three. What about the most important question - how are you feeling?"

"Pretty nervous, actually. Like...what if it all goes wrong? What if it's super duper awkward and then we still have to work together for the rest of this program?"

"That's unlikely. It's not as if the two of you don't know each other pretty well by now. And it's not like you don't spend time alone, you know?"

"Yeah, but that's all just been coworkers, maybe even friends, hanging out. This is a Date."

"Good. I'm glad it's got a proper label. That's the only difference. Because the two of you spending all that time together with no one else around, having fun, sharing personal stuff, all the things you've been doing....baking cakes to impress each other, for crying out loud. That all seemed pretty date-like to me, too."

"Really? But it can't actually be a date unless you call it a date...right?"

"I think that's a technicality. Sometimes I'm in the middle of a date before I realize that's what it is. These things aren't quite as cut and dry as they may have been in the good old days."

"Ah, you mean when you had to bring a chaperone along?"

"Precisely. But anyway, you will be just fine and those nerves you're feeling...that's not anxiety, it's excitement. Because you're going to have fun and I'm going to be waiting for you to tell me all about it when it's over."

"You want me to call you tonight? No matter how late it is?"

"Let's plan to talk tomorrow," wrote Chloe. "There's some big meeting this afternoon. The supervisor of the Generosity Exchange program is coming in to talk to us, and I'll probably go out with some friends after that."

"Oh, interesting. You can tell me a little about that tomorrow, too."

"It's a date." Chloe's last message had a winky face and a face with its tongue stuck out that made Melody roll her eyes.

"Asked out on two dates in one day...what, is she trying to kill me?" she mumbled to herself.

At five o'clock on the dot, Ben appeared outside Melody's cubicle, a shadow falling over her monitor to announce his presence.

"Alright then," he said, "I believe it's time for me to pick you up. It's not as good as picking you up at the bottom of a long staircase where you've just made a dramatic entrance, but it'll do." He shrugged. "And maybe we can get the staircase for next time."

Melody finished switching off her computer and closing her monitor, then turned to greet him with a smile. "The staircase is a classic, isn't it?" she asked. "It's always the part where he finally sees just how beautiful and magnificent she is, you know? He goes silent and just stares in awe, losing his train of thought in mid-sentence because he's just...you know, overcome."

The expression on Ben's face could only be described as adoring, as if he were hanging on her every word. "It is a classic scene," he said, "but I don't need to see you walking down the stairs to know that you're beautiful. Believe it or not, that's never been a question."

She looked away, busying herself with packing her things in her bag, but he continued speaking.

"Even before we had spoken, you had gotten my attention. And then it only grew from there. So what I'm saying is that this date is a long time coming. So long, in fact, that it doesn't even feel like a first date. It feels like it's just a regular workday evening and we're about to go out for dinner like we do a few times a week."

"Oh?" She schooled her expression into one of playful ignorance. "Just a few times a week? And what am I supposed to do the other evenings?"

His smile spread impossibly wider. "Well, it's good for new couples to spend some time apart, of course. Have their own hobbies and things like that. But also, I cook for you sometimes too. We don't go out all the time...we work at a nonprofit after all, remember?

That got a laugh out of Melody. "We sure do. And it's not exactly in the budget to go out for a four course meal every other day. Even once a week is pushing it for me!"

"It may have been a slight exaggeration." He held out his hand to her. "Are you ready for some fun?"

The butterflies in her belly were back in full force, no doubt in response to that twinkle in his eye, the slight hesitation in his smile. He was feeling vulnerable too, putting himself on the line, but he was doing a much better job of being clear with his feelings and intentions than she was. The least she could do was ease his concerns a bit. "Absolutely." She took his hand and let him pull her to her feet. "And I have to say, I've been excited about this all day." She looked at him from beneath her lashes, feeling suddenly shy. "You made it hard for me to focus on work today, because I was so excited about this."

Ben widened his eyes comically. "Melody Critchfield distracted from her work? Now I've really heard everything."

She chuckled softly to herself as she let him lead her out the door. The hand that had found hers to help her to her feet hadn't let go since then, and they were now walking, hand in hand, through the office door and out onto the street. It felt ridiculous to even think it, but something about the world outside looked different now that she was holding Ben's hand, looking at it through the eyes of someone who was somehow attached to him.

He'd made it sound like they were already a couple, but that couldn't be the reality, could it? It had been a minute (or two) since Melody had been in a relationship, but she was pretty sure there were conversations that needed to happen in order to make the transition from single person to one half of a pair. Did you have to make it official on social media? Or did one of you have to do the embarrassing job of actually asking the other one to be their significant other?

She shuddered at the thought, brushing it off as a shiver when Ben looked her way. If he wanted to ask her to be his girlfriend, that was one thing. She knew how she would answer that question, and she knew exactly how happy she would be about it.

But that didn't mean she wanted to speed things along by asking him to be her boyfriend. It was too much, and far too vulnerable, for her to let herself even imagine.

"So where are we going?" she asked Ben. "Or are we just going to wander around, play things by ear, see what sounds good?"

"As much as I love a spontaneous plan, believe it or not I did actually put some thought into our first date?" He led her to the nearest intersection, waiting for the light to change before they crossed towards the busier section of the city.

"Oh?" She quirked an eyebrow in his direction. "Is that what kept you so busy today? Planning a date when you were supposed to be working?"

Ben shook his head. "Believe it or not, I've been thinking about this for a while. All I had to do today was call and make a reservation, so now we're all set." He checked his watch. "And at this rate, we'll get there just in time. Are you hungry?"

Melody nodded.

The restaurant Ben had chosen was further from the office than they normally ventured on a weeknight, but the time passed quickly as the conversation flowed between them. Melody felt herself relaxing in his presence, eased by the knowledge that they were on a proper date, while at the same time the anticipation of what that meant had a grin plastered across her face that wouldn't budge.

They came to a stop outside a small Italian restaurant, one Melody had never noticed, though she had been in the neighborhood plenty of times. Ben held the door open for her as she made her way inside, where they were seated at a cozy, candlelit table near the fireplace.

"Are you nervous?" Ben asked, as she focused her attention on the menu.

Melody gave him the slightest of nods, along with a small smile. "A little," she admitted. "It just feels different, you know?"

He reached across the table for her hand, his eyes kind and warm. "It doesn't need to. It's still just me...just you. I like you just as much now as I did yesterday. The only difference is that now you know about it."

Her smile was weak at the edges, her nerves refusing to leave her alone. "Right." She nodded once, gesturing to the menu. "So what's good here?"

"Everything? I've never met a pasta I didn't like."

That got a soft chuckle out of Melody. "Same here. Should we order two different ones then and share them?"

"Perfect." Ben pointed at his menu. "I think I'll order the chicken pesto, if that sounds good to you, too."

"Love it. I'll get the salmon tortellini."

It was strange—and at the same time not strange at all—how easily they slipped into the rhythm of a couple. Sipping a glass of wine as they waited for their meals, which they shared from across the table just like they had done it a million times before. Melody could almost let herself believe that a state change had happened, that they had gone from nothing to Something (with a capital S) without having to talk about it...but only almost.

"I have to ask you something," Melody blurted, once they were outside the restaurant. She pulled her jacket closer against the cold fall wind.

"What is it?" Ben's forehead wrinkled in concern.

"What are we?" she asked. "I mean...I know this was a date, and I get that a date is somehow different from just hanging out, but..." She sighed. "I don't want to play games like the cool kids do or whatever. I don't want to wait three days to text you or make you think I'm texting other guys to figure out how serious you are about me or anything like that."

"Good." Ben took both of her hands in his, pulling her closer. "I don't want you to do any of those things. And I don't want to play games, either. If you would like to be my girlfriend, my partner, well...that is what I would like you to be. Of course, it's your choice. If it's too fast, or—"

"No, it's perfect." Melody interrupted him before he could finish his sentence. "That's what I want too."

Ben's eyes dropped to her lips and then back to her eyes. "So we agree." He gave her a devastating smile then, pulling out all the stops.

And her own grin matched his, just before she grabbed the lapels of his coat, tugged him closer, and met his lips with hers. Pure electricity flowed then, from one to the other and back again.

• ❤ • ❤ • ❤ • ❤ • ❤ •

Melody woke the next morning with a smile that couldn't be stopped. Last night hadn't been a dream, but a very, very sweet reality. She was in a relationship with Ben Kaya, he was just as crazy about her as she was about him, and in every way that mattered, it felt like life couldn't get any better than it was in that moment.

She practically skipped from her bed to the kitchen, where she drank a glass of water while she was brewing her morning coffee. "Look at me," she said out loud, "feeling like such hot shit I'm even hydrating before I caffeinate. Who *is* she?"

She chuckled at herself, retrieving her phone from where she had left it on the table the night before. As a brand new girlfriend, she was pretty sure that texting her boyfriend a good morning wish was the standard protocol, and the fact that she got to do that with Ben now created a fresh wave of tingles.

As she swiped the screen to wake up her phone, she smiled at the sight of unread messages waiting for her. There were two from Ben, one she hadn't seen last night telling her how happy he was that she was in his life, and one from just a few moments ago wishing her a good morning.

But before she could open the conversation with Ben, the message from Chloe caught her eye and her stomach dropped.

"Shit. Shit. Shit. This isn't good. I need to talk to you ASAP."

Melody's fingers were already flying to video call Chloe, without even bothering to check the time first. Chloe answered almost instantaneously, her face illuminating the screen from the bedroom of her London flat, a flurry of activity happening behind her..

"What's going on, Chloe?" Melody asked, her inner alarm immediately registering the wrongness of the situation.

Chloe's face was the picture of stress, her cheeks looking hollow and the circles under her eyes darker than Melody had ever seen them. "It's over, Mel. All of it. The whole freaking Generosity Exchange program. You haven't heard this yet?"

"What? What are you talking about? No...no, that can't be right. Why...how would you know that?"

Chloe shook her head. "I told you about that meeting we had scheduled, right? With Madeline, the director of the program? I guess they told us about it first because the London program is the biggest, but..." She gestured with her hand, miming a slicing action across her throat. "It's finished. They sent us home after the meeting, and we're getting booked out on flights within the next few days. It's such a mess, Mel." Chloe sniffled, a hand darting across her cheek. "And I'm so freaking mad and sad and disappointed about all of it. This wasn't supposed to happen."

"Why *is* it happening? Did they say?" Melody's mind was whirring a mile a minute. Were she and Ben about to be parted? She didn't want to be a bad friend and make this about herself, but the concern was there at the back of her mind, pounding to get her attention.

"Believe it or not, they didn't exactly give us all the details." Chloe's expression was sardonic. "There was some talk about budget cuts and the efficacy of the program, and, like...yeah. It's probably all pretty much the concerns you had at the beginning. Too many people treating it like spring break and it not ultimately being worth it to the non-profit partners. Some of the bosses probably don't feel like they're getting their money's worth, even if most of us are working just as hard in our new roles as we did in our old ones. If not harder, even."

Melody thought of the ways she had let her work slide, the fact that Ben had picked up the slack for her more than once, and she couldn't confidently say the same thing. She gave Chloe a weak smile instead. "At least this means we'll be reunited sooner than we thought, right? I know it doesn't seem like it now, but I have to believe this is for the best for all of us. If the program is creating bad work ethic and habits, then it's better to cut it short than keep it going just for the hell of it."

"I knew you wouldn't get it." Chloe's sigh was exasperated and her tone was shrill. "Don't you even care that this is going to tear you and your new guy apart? I know I haven't even asked you about how your date went last night, but if you can't tell I'm a little busy over here. And a little heartbroken myself, if I'm being honest. I'm not ready to be done with London. I don't know if I would have been at the end of a whole year, and I'm definitely not ready now. It's too soon."

Melody couldn't let her façade crack. Of course, the thought of being separated from Ben made her sad. But if a relationship and her work couldn't coexist without one of them suffering, then it wasn't ever going to work out. "I'm sorry, Chloe. I'm guessing they're going to tell us about this today, too." She shrugged. "Maybe when I know more and you're feeling less freshly wounded about it, we can talk more."

Chloe rolled her eyes. "Way to make it sound like I'm being dramatic and overreacting, Mel. That feels awesome, in case you were wondering."

"You're not overreacting. I know it hurts, but I'm just trying to look on the bright side. We'll talk soon, okay? I'm sure I'll get some more answers today, too."

It felt strange to leave things that unsettled with Chloe, but Melody didn't need someone else's emotions crowding her mind when she was already feeling the stress of an impending bomb that was about to destroy everything in its path. She believed—she *knew*—that everything had to work out for the best, and she was going to trust that outcome, even if it caused her some temporary heartbreak.

Because all heartbreak was temporary. That's what it meant that time healed all wounds, wasn't it? If she and Ben were suddenly ripped apart by an ocean, it would be out of her control and there was no choice but to believe that it was for the best. That they wouldn't have made it. That it was better for things to end before either of them got too attached. That it was better for both of them to go back to the work that they were best at and to stop being so distracted from that work by each other.

Of course, it was still possible that none of this was real. Chloe may have misunderstood what was shared at the meeting. Or, maybe it was just the London program that was closing down. That would be sad for Chloe, and Melody would do her best to support her...but it didn't mean that things were changing for her, too.

"That's the spirit," she said out loud to herself as she got ready for the day. "There's no need to grieve something that hasn't happened yet. Let's wait and see if this is even real before I start trying to figure it out."

Of course, it wasn't easy to put aside a potentially life-changing stressor, to pretend it didn't exist when the day had literally begun with a confrontation of it. But Melody did her best. She slipped on her headphones, listening to her "for a special occasion" pump-up playlist to keep the good feelings from last night's date going despite the very real possibility that everything was about to fall apart.

Against her better instincts—and every promise she'd ever made to Chloe to stop thinking about work so much outside of office hours—Melody checked her email on her phone as she slipped out the door. And there, right in front of her eyes, was the conformation that something was very, very wrong and that everything was about to change.

The message that caught her eyes was from Mr. Richards, and the few lines that showed up in the message preview had her stomach bottoming out.

> *"Now that the Generosity Exchange program*
> *is extinct (as it should have been all along),*
> *I will need your 100% commitment to a few*
> *additional projects..."*

"Well, shit," Melody breathed, padding down the hallway of her building and making her way to the office.

She arrived to chaos. It seemed that everyone else had been similarly informed about the Generosity Exchange program's demise, either from those like Chloe who had attended the London meeting or from their bosses to arrange the end of their stays abroad and return to work as soon as possible.

All around her, cardboard boxes were being packed with belongings and entire desks were being swept clean into the recycle bin. There was a frantic look in the eyes of everyone impacted—and it wasn't just the participants in the program, either. There was travel to be arranged, work responsibilities to be redistributed, and a whole mess of loose ends that needed to be tied up.

Ben found Melody first, taking each of her arms in one of his hands and looking deeply into her eyes to read the expression there. "You're here. Good," he said. "We need to figure out what we're going to do. You heard about the program, right?"

She nodded back at him, holding his gaze. She had spent the journey to the office weighing the situation ahead of them, trying to see through to the other side of it, and she had come to only one conclusion. One that she needed to share with Ben now, so that he wouldn't get his hopes up of things working out differently than they possibly could.

"I heard. Mr. Richards was in contact this morning, and Chloe told me about the meeting with Madeline yesterday."

Ben shook his head. "It's such a mess. Zeynep gave me the inside scoop since she's involved with the leadership committee of the program." He pulled Melody into his cubicle, out of the fray. "It seems like your Mr. Richards was the ringleader behind all of this. He approached her to try to sway her opinion about the program, get on board with this whole—" He gestured to the chaos around them. "—mess. I mean, closing down a program that's barely even made it to the middle? I can't even imagine the complaints he must have lodged to get them to take it seriously, but it's appalling. Complete mismanagement of everything."

"He must have had his reasons, though, right?" Melody looked at the room around them, the emotions and stress evident on the faces of all their colleagues. "He wouldn't do something like this just to be a jerk. I know you don't know him that well, but I just know that can't be it."

"Really?" Ben gave pointed looks at their surroundings. "Because this seems like some pretty classic jerk behavior. And that's why we need to figure out what our next steps are going to be. You can't keep working for this guy, Melody. You know that, right? I know you care about your job, but this...this goes against everything you believe."

Melody crossed her arms over her chest. The one thing that did *not* make a stressful situation better was someone—even someone as good as Ben—telling her what she needed to do. "Does it? Because it looks to me like he may have discovered that this program was a misuse of funds...or that it wasn't as effective as it could have been since everyone was acting like they were on spring break rather than doing their freaking jobs."

Ben recoiled. "Are you seriously defending him right now? I know you care about EduPowerment, but this is actually ridiculous. You *have* to see that. No matter how ineffective a program might be, you don't just drop it cold turkey like this. And what, are people just supposed to fly right back to their old jobs and pick up where they left off? So much work is going to be lost, so much time..." He sighed. "And that's saying nothing about the personal uprooting. I'm sure you and I aren't the only ones with something personal at stake." His eyes searched hers. "What are we going to do, Melody? I just got you into my life. I don't want you out of it already."

She steeled herself. It was for the best for both of them if she didn't give him a reason to hold on to hope. It would hurt less in the long run, and it would spare them both the pain of trying to figure out a way to stay together or to try doing things long distance...none of that would work, she was sure. "I think, maybe...we need to accept this, Ben. I know it seems like the timing really stinks, but...well, maybe the timing is meant to tell us something." Her laugh was hollow. "You can't deny that there's a certain dark humor to our whole world falling apart the morning after we go on our first date. Seems like maybe it's just not meant to be, you know? Or at least that's what the universe is trying to tell us."

He shook his head. "You don't mean that. And you don't *know* that, either. The whole universe doesn't conspire to keep people apart, Melody. And explaining this that way rather than explaining it with your boss's backwards manipulation is some impressive gaslighting you're doing to yourself."

"I can't believe you." She felt her gaze harden as she stared at him. "Since I got here this morning, you've done nothing but tell me how I'm supposed to feel about this, what I'm supposed to think. How are you any better than Mr. Richards then, ignoring my perfectly valid feelings to get me to think and behave and act the way you want me to?"

"This...this isn't real, is it? This thing that's happening right now?" His arms were on her shoulders now, his eyes darting between both of hers. "We don't have to be against each other, Melody. I'm sorry if it sounded like that, I...I'm just frankly terrified of losing you. I thought you'd feel the same way, and I thought we were going to figure this out together. Is that what you want? Or..." A horrified expression crossed his face as a realization dawned on him. "Or do you want this to be the end? To go back to your job, your boss, your old life, and never think about me again?"

It hurt to see him feeling that way, so much so that she wavered in her convictions.

To proceed with misunderstanding things between them, turn to **page 124**

To clarify, and actually communicate what she's feeling rather than what she thinks is best for both of them, turn to **page 306**

40

"I'm sorry," Melody blurted, jumping to her feet. "I never do this, but..." Her mind scrambled for the most innocuous invitation she could make, the thing least likely to sound the alarm to Ben that she might, in fact, be interested in him in a *non*-professional way. "Coffee? Er...I mean, would you like to join me for a cup of coffee? Would that be nice?" *Would that be nice? What kind of question was that?*

Ben didn't seem to mind her question, though, offering her a wide smile in response. "That would be lovely. No better way to start the day, is there?"

"I agree."

They fell into step side by side, and for the briefest of seconds, Melody had the delicious feeling that this was what it would be like. What it could be like, always, if Ben also felt the electricity zapping back and forth between them. How could he not?

"So...tell me about yourself," she began. "Where did you grow up?"

Ben nodded. "Interesting question to start the day with. Born and raised in Germany, but my parents are from Turkey, so I kind of feel like I'm from there, too."

"Oh wow, I had no idea." *What a dumb thing to say,* she chastised herself. *You barely know this man. How would you have any ideas about him at all already? Don't forget, just because you feel like there's some magical connection between the two of you does not, in fact, mean that he feels the same way.* "Ben doesn't sound like a Turkish name to me," she offered instead. "Not that I know much about Turkish at all...apart from Turkish delight and that '*aslan*' means lion. You can thank *The Chronicles of Narnia* for that vast knowledge of the Turkish language of mine."

Ben laughed then, a beautiful melodic sound that came along with his head thrown back, a clear view of his neck and Adam's apple. It was a good neck, too. Not that Melody had known she was a neck appreciator, but this one just couldn't go unacknowledged.

"Well, first of all, I'm very grateful that C. S. Lewis awakened so many young children to the magic of Turkish delight. And *aslan* is a good word to know, too, although he didn't exactly get the pronunciation right."

Melody felt her ears turning hot—and most likely pink to match—at the difference between Ben's "*aslan*" and hers. His sounded refined and powerful, a name befitting the noble beast of the lion, both the character in *The Lion, The Witch, and The Wardrobe* and the one that roamed the savannahs of Africa. Hers, on the other hand, mostly consisted of nasal Midwestern "a" sounds and sounded more like the duck from the Aflac commercials.

But it wasn't a language lesson Ben was offering, apparently. He continued, answering her other question. "Ben isn't a Turkish name, you're right. It's actually my parents' own little joke, I think, giving me 'Ben' as a middle name." Off her quizzical expression, he continued, explaining. "In Turkish, *'ben'* means 'I.' So even though they gave me a Turkish first name, which is Yunus, and naturally a Turkish surname, too— that's Kaya...they gave me a more German middle name I could use to blend in more, if I wanted to. Of course, they just happened to pick the name that also meant something in our language, too." He shrugged. "I like it. It's kind of my little secret, you know? Like I can introduce myself as Ben and people just think I'm this German guy who's using the abbreviated version of Benjamin, but it's actually more like *'Ben Yunus Kaya.'* Which, of course, means 'I am Yunus Kaya.' I like being just Ben, though."

"That's really interesting," said Melody, genuinely fascinated by every single detail Ben was sharing with her. She pushed the button to start the single-serving coffee machine. "I wish I had something unique to tell you about my name, but no. It's just Melody. No secret meaning."

Ben raised an eyebrow at her. "That can't be true. A melody is a song, right? Or, like...a mixture of fruits, you know? You get one of those little cups full of peaches and pears and they call it a fruit melody?"

Now it was Melody's turn to laugh, and Ben's eyes sparkled with delight at the sound of it. "That's a medley, actually. But you're right about the song."

"Ah, I knew I was close." He shrugged. "You got the better end of that deal, though. You're not 'just Melody' then, you know? You're a beautiful song, like something a Disney princess would sing to call the birds to come sit on her hands."

She knew her cheeks were coloring with heat again—how could they not be, when he said sweet things like that?—and she didn't care. Still, a shyness came over her. What was she doing, wandering away from her workspace to spend time with this man she didn't even know? This man who was supposed to be a mere coworker, not someone she actively sought to spend more time with?

She handed him his cup of coffee before restarting the machine to make her own. Thanks to his influence—or was it just his presence?—she was even drinking office coffee, rather than the thermos she had brought from home. That was going to cut into the money they had available for programs, something she had been lobbying against. If all nonprofit employees just brought their own drinks and snacks from home, that discretionary money could be funneled to their in-country programs, and wouldn't that be a better use of those funds?

And yet here she was, thoroughly enjoying the smell of the coffee dripping into her cup, watching Ben as he stirred a splash of milk into his own mug. The coffee she brought from home was fine, but there was something comforting and homey about the smell of freshly brewed beans. It made her feel warm and cozy and just a little bit more comfortable taking up space in the office.

Of course, some of that warmth and coziness could be attributed to the man who was currently smiling at her with his eyes over the rim of his coffee mug. He raised his eyebrows at her in an unspoken question, and she looked away. What was even happening right now?

"So what, uh...what questions do you have for me? About work stuff, I mean?" she fumbled. She finished doctoring her own cup of coffee and then the two of them made their way back to their desks.

"Admittedly, I don't have a lot of questions about the work," said Ben. "I do actually have one question, but I feel like it's not totally appropriate."

Melody's pulse picked up. Either he was about to say exactly what she was feeling...or she had totally misread the situation and he was about to harass her or tell her she had something hanging out of her nose. "Okay..." she prompted him, reaching up surreptitiously at the same time to wipe her nose.

"I was wondering if you were available after work and if you wouldn't mind joining me for something then."

Okay...that wasn't exactly either outcome that Melody had prepared herself for, not unless 'something' referred to a carriage that used to be a pumpkin picking her up to squire her around the town.

She wouldn't know unless she asked. "I may be free after work, but that is going to depend on what you mean by 'something.' It's too mysterious as it is, and I don't want to agree to it until I know what I'm committing to."

"That's fair," said Ben, a brush of color appearing on the apples of his cheeks. "I didn't mean to be mysterious, but I didn't exactly want to be too clear about my interest in you in case it scared you away." He shook his head in dismay. "But now I've gone ahead and referred to it as 'my interest in you,' and that has definitely escalated things to such a level that I can't pretend I didn't just say that."

"Your...*interest*...in me?" Melody asked, mouth agape.

"Yeah." Ben looked sheepish. "I'm sorry about that. I know it's totally unprofessional to say something like that in an office and to someone I just met. I swear I didn't mean it like that, though, and also that this isn't something I would normally—*ever*—do." He ran a hand through his already messy hair. "It might sound like a line, but I promise it isn't. I just felt this *zap* when I first saw you, like I had been waiting for you or something. And it made me want to spend more time with you and get to know everything about you and...I know it's ridiculous. We've shared one cup of coffee." He looked down at the nearly full mug in his hands. "Okay, not even one full cup of coffee yet. And somehow, I still want to spend the whole afternoon with you and just walk all over the city...it's too much, I know. I'm sorry."

"No!" Melody protested. "Don't be sorry. Everything you said, it *does* all sound like too much. Like it's too good to be true and it can't possibly be real. And yet, I felt the same kind of thing." She shook her head, remembering Chloe's words. "My friend who's in London now, she wished something like this would happen. That there would be someone hot and fun and we would have crushes on each other or something. I don't remember all the details of what she said. And I dismissed her, told her that would be a major human resources issue and dropped it." She shrugged. "And yet here we are on our first day in the office and I just want to pull my chair over next to yours and ask you what your mom is like."

Ben's grin got impossibly wider. "I would love that, and I can tell you that my mom is actually the best. In fact, I *will* tell you all about her…later?" His eyebrows climbed with hope, with a question.

Melody nodded. "Absolutely. I'm all yours after work."

She traveled the remaining few feet back to her desk and dropped into her chair, stunned. Nothing that had just happened felt like it had happened to her…she felt like she was watching a movie or possibly dreaming. In real life, Melody Critchfield would not befriend an attractive new coworker or agree to spend time with him after work, and she *certainly* wouldn't admit to feeling a spark between them. Was this all some exhaustion-induced alternate reality? Had Chloe pulled some magic trick or made a wish with a genie to add some more excitement to Melody's life?

"Psst." Ben caught her eye. "Are you actually able to focus on anything over there? Because I'm struggling over here, and I don't think it's just waiting for the caffeine to kick in."

She shook her head, laughing softly through her nose. "Well, you're just going to have to figure that out, mister. We can't very well duck out of the office just to go chit chat." Her expression sobered up then, as a thought occurred to her. "Actually, when I find it hard to focus, I always think of the important work that we're doing in the world and how I get to play my part in that." She shrugged. "And honestly, I sort of feel like I'm stealing from those who receive our services if I'm not totally focused on my responsibilities."

That made Ben's expression get serious—and quickly—too. "Ahh, yes. Good point. Okay, then." He saluted.

"I'll leave you alone then so you can get to work. As long as I definitely will get some of your time once the work day is over?"

Melody nodded. "You certainly will. And I'll even finish working at five today, just for you."

A look of concern flashed across Ben's eyes. "You don't normally leave at five? Is that, like...normal?"

"I'm pretty sure it's just me who does that. There's not much excitement waiting for me outside of work, and I like seeing the difference I can make with our projects and beneficiaries."

"Okay. Good to know." The corners of Ben's eyes lifted ever so slightly, suggesting that the half of his face she couldn't see had a small smile on it. "Catch you later, then!"

Admittedly, it felt more than a little strange to shut down the chance to keep chatting with her handsome new colleague, especially when he was *right* there, but Melody's loyalty to her work had to take priority. In the three years she had been working at EduPowerment, she had seen too many colleagues run out of steam, lose their drive to show up every day and do their best work. Whether it happened because they were frustrated not to receive a raise or because they had gotten bored with the repetitive nature of their job or because they had gotten distracted by a shiny object, she was determined that would not happen to her. Even if whatever was brewing between her and Ben turned out to be a relationship, she would continue to prioritize her work. Time with Ben could fill her evenings and her weekends, and she could even enjoy seeing him around the office...but she would not let herself get distracted from why she was here. Why she did the work she did in the first place.

On that note, it was time to dive in. She had plenty to keep her busy, along with whatever was waiting for her in her email inbox—Mr. Richards and his top-priority projects were the one constant in her life.

Melody slipped in her earbuds, queueing up her favorite focus playlist—classical tunes really helped her dial in to the task at hand—and lost herself in her to-do list. She was vaguely aware of Ben getting up from his desk, leaving with a wave, and she was almost sure that she had returned the pleasantry but couldn't be positive. Such was the reality when she was in the zone.

At some point, she felt a soft touch on her shoulder and nearly shrieked. Ripping her earbuds from her ears, she spun around, shoulders dropping when she saw it was Ben, hovering in the entrance to her cubicle.

"Sorry," he said, looking sheepish. "I didn't want to interrupt you since you were so focused, but..." He glanced down, then back up. "You've been sitting there for a very long time and I thought it might be good for you to have some lunch?" He gestured with his head back towards the kitchen. "There's a bit of a 'getting to know each other' lunch going on today. Do you want to come join?" He looked at what was on her screen. "I mean, *can* you? I don't want to disrupt if you've got something important there, but I also didn't think you would want to be left out."

That was sweet of him. With time, he would proba-bly—no, he would *definitely*—learn that Melody usually *did* want to be left out. Especially when it came to cliquey office gatherings and forced socialization. "Actually," she began, pulling a face. "I should really finish this up. I brought some snacks from home, though, so I promise I won't go hungry." She smiled at Ben.

"Alright, then." He smiled back, though a bit of disappointment shone through. "We're still on for five o'clock, though, right?"

She nodded in response. "Absolutely."

At five o'clock on the dot, a gentle tapping interrupted Melody's flow, pulling her back to the present. "Are you ready to go?" Ben asked, staying just a few feet back, hesitant to interrupt whatever might be taking her attention.

Chloe would be so proud of me, Melody thought to herself as she stood and nodded, closing her laptop as she did so. She started to reach for the computer to slip it into her bag to take home before she thought better of it. Not only did Ben not need to see her bringing her laptop home and giving him the wrong idea about her workaholic tendencies, but she also didn't need to be carrying it all around town.

I'll just come in a little early tomorrow, she told herself, as she gave the laptop one final, reassuring tap on the lid.

"Did...did you just say goodnight to your laptop?" Ben asked, a smile in his voice that brought a matching one to Melody's face.

"Something like that," she responded. "Like, a 'see you tomorrow,' I guess. Sometimes I bring it home with me, so I guess I just needed to reassure it that it will be okay here at the office all by itself."

Ben gestured to the cubicles surrounding them. "It's hardly 'all by itself,' though, is it? Seems to me like there are plenty of other computers and office supplies here if it gets bored, needs someone to talk to."

"You're right." The image of all the computers and copy machines coming to life and having a *Toy Story*-esque adventure while all the humans were away popped unbidden into Melody's mind, making her grin. "Come on, then. Let's leave these guys alone." She nodded towards the door and Ben fell into step with her as they made their way outside.

Once the door closed behind them, Melody stopped in her tracks, taking a deep breath of the fresh air that had greeted them when they walked out. It was easy to forget what she was missing in the world outside her office when she was in the zone working on a project, but the smell of a fresh breeze never failed to force a moment of mindfulness and appreciation.

She glanced to her side and saw Ben doing the same, eyes closed and a serene expression on his face. "It's beautiful today," he said when he reopened his eyes to smile at her. "It was a hot summer, but this is just perfect weather." He looked around at the early fall colors, the sun still shining even if it was tracking lower in the sky. "Walking around outside with no jacket in September is the dream come true."

"Sure." Melody nodded, then gestured to the large bag she had slung over her shoulder, which was expanding even bigger than normal under the force of the jacket she'd halfheartedly stuffed inside. "Always a good idea to carry an extra jacket or sweater, though. You never know when it's going to change."

Ben shook his head. "Nah, I'll be fine. You don't survive German winter without developing a certain hardiness when it comes to cold weather." He paused, looking thoughtful. "Though I suppose I do have Turkish blood, too, which is not necessarily that equipped for cold days. So, on second thought, maybe let's be prepared to duck indoors if it gets chilly. Where to first?"

Melody gestured to the sidewalk leading away from the office towards the downtown area. "Let's walk."

"Walk and talk?" Ben asked the question with a smile. "I love the sound of that."

Melody and Ben soon found themselves in a quaint café, a small independent coffee shop with a used bookstore attached to it. They took a few minutes to browse through the selection of used books before heading to a small table in the café. Melody ordered an herbal tea and Ben opted for a cappuccino.

"So..." Melody smiled, not entirely sure where to begin this particular conversation. The instant connection she had felt with Ben earlier that day had felt so tangible, to the point of being undeniable. And yet, here they were, out of the office, with no other distractions around, and all she felt was her own anxiety warring against the butterflies she'd been feeling all day. Which one would win? Would Ben look at her with pity, dismissing her feelings outright? By some miniscule chance of fate, would he reciprocate them? Or would he play along, pretending to feel what he didn't, just for the hope of finding someone to pass the time with for a while?

"So." Ben smiled back, a sheepishness playing at the corner of his mouth. "This...is unexpected, right?" He gestured between them. "I certainly didn't think this year had anything like this in store for me, but...I'm not mistaken, am I? There's something here?" A shadow passed over his face, something akin to horror. "Wait...don't tell me. Did I make this whole thing up? Or rather, did one bad night's sleep make this whole thing up?"

Before he could get up from the table and run away—because the situation suddenly did seem to be just about that dire—Melody placed her hand over his. "You're not making it up. I feel it, too, and I can only hope that you still *do* feel the same way once you've had a few nights of decent rest and there's no chance that insomnia is steering your thoughts in a mistaken direction."

Ben shook his head vehemently. "That won't happen. To be honest, I just offered that suggestion to save face. If anything, things like extreme exhaustion just get us to be more honest more quickly." He shrugged, unbothered by his honesty. "It's harder to bullshit when you're too tired to keep up with pretending or playing it cool. I like you, and I can't find any reasons why it's a bad thing for you to know that."

Melody's smile widened, despite any of her own attempts to play it just a bit cooler. "I like you, too," she said. "I don't even know how to explain it, since we just met, but...yeah. I do. Something felt like it clicked into place today, like it made sense in a way that...well, that honestly I can't even explain." She shook her head, laughter sneaking out as she did so. "Where did you come from, anyway? And why does it feel like I didn't even know I was looking for you and yet here you are, filling what feels like the most important vacancy in my life?"

Ben was quiet long enough to make Melody wonder if she'd said something wrong.

"Was that too much? Come on too strong?" She shook her head at herself. "I never know when to stop."

His hand came across the table, landing warm and comfortably weighty on top of hers, his thumb running up and down the side of her hand. When she brought her eyes up to meet his, they were kind, unguarded, as if he didn't care how deeply into his soul she looked.

She raised her eyebrow in a question, but she didn't speak. It still felt as if she had said enough, as if he needed to be the one to steer things from here before she embarrassed herself more than she already had.

"It's not too much. And you didn't come on too strong, either. It's just...you expressed what I was feeling, too, and it all felt so surreal. I don't know what to say. I don't know how to talk about it or even how to trust that it's real, what we're feeling." His expression sobered, earnest eyes darting back and forth between hers. "It's not that I don't think it's real...I just...I don't know—"

"You don't know how to trust something you've never experienced before?" When Ben nodded back at her, Melody let herself smile. "We're in the same boat then. And I'm not sure we're going to figure it out, not without going through it."

"You mean actually giving this thing a try? Rather than just talking about it and trying to figure it out?" Ben's cheeks were flushing with excitement. "I'm all for gaining practical experience over theoretical knowledge. What do we do now?"

Melody shook her head with a chuckle. "Well, for starters, we don't need to treat a crush like it's a science experiment. Because that's what it is, right? A crush?"

"I think it's a little more than that, but I maybe don't know enough words to tell you what it is." Ben shrugged. "Maybe we should make up a more appropriate name for it, since the English language seems to be failing us here."

"I like the sound of that. Any ideas?"

Ben's smile was sheepish as he shook his head. "I was hoping you'd have a suggestion, given that you're the one with English as a mother tongue. If we were trying to think of something that worked in German or Turkish, I'd have some more suggestions to offer."

"Okay, then..." Melody paused, contemplating. "What if we call each other a pet name like...Pumpkin? It's cute, it's fall appropriate...not too serious, but hopefully also not the cheesiest thing you've ever heard."

Ben smiled. "No, not the cheesiest, even if it's...well, it's close." He gave hear a reassuring nod. "I like it. Until we have something more...official...to work with, Pumpkin it is."

For the rest of their journey, Melody couldn't stop smiling, even as part of her was flaring up with caution. This wasn't normal. This was too much. It wasn't safe to feel this way about someone, let alone about someone she had met so recently. How did she even know she could trust Ben?

But it wasn't just that she was shoving those concerns aside—after all, she'd never been particularly gifted at convincing herself *not* to think about something that was causing her stress. It was also the fact that Ben was so easy to be around and that the time they spent together felt comfortable in a way entirely unfamiliar to Melody. It was comfortable, like hanging out with Chloe was comfortable, except that where there were no sparks between her and Chloe, there was an electric current running up Melody's arm every time it brushed up against Ben's.

They walked, and they talked. It was partly getting to know the city, or at least the district where they worked. The best cafes, the shops with the best produce, restaurants with the best views for future long shared meals.

Eventually, it was impossible for the excitement of getting to know Ben to hold its own against the exhaustion Melody was feeling. It had been a long day—for both of them—and as much as her mind was wide awake, stimulated by the company and the conversation, her body was just about ready to curl up on a grassy spot at the side of the road to take a little nap.

Melody stifled a yawn, about to call it a night and make plans to see Ben again soon.

"Tired?" he asked, his hand flying to his own mouth to cover the response to her yawn. *Proof he's not a sociopath*, thought Melody, as she nodded. *Not that I thought he was one...but it's always good when the cute guys pass the contagious yawn test with flying colors.* "We should get home then. I mean, to our respective homes, obviously."

"Agreed." Melody looked around to regain her bearings. As luck would have it, even though they had walked around and around, racking up quite a few steps for the day, they had ended up just a few blocks from her apartment. "Where are you going?" She gestured vaguely back towards her apartment. "I'm just that way, not far at all."

Ben pulled a face. "Lucky." He gestured in the opposite direction. "I've got a little further to go myself." He shrugged. "I mean, it's about a twenty-five minute walk but I don't mind it. I'll enjoy the fresh air, maybe listen to some music." He gestured in the direction of Melody's apartment. "Let me walk you home first, and then I'll be going."

"No, it's okay. Really." Melody shook her head. "Seriously. I know you're tired, and it's just going to add on to your walking time." She waved around them at the twilight, the people bustling around on the street. "I appreciate the chivalry, of course, but I promise it's perfectly safe and I'll be fine. It's still light out, there are plenty of people around, and I've done it before."

Ben didn't look happy with her response. "What if it's not just chivalry?" he offered.

"What do you mean?

"I mean, that of course I'd like to know that you've gotten home safely and I believe it's good manners to escort a woman to her home if you find yourselves out in the evening together. You can call me old-fashioned for that."

"You're old-fashioned." Melody smiled at him. "But if you're going to be old-fashioned in any way relating to gender roles, that's probably a good one."

Ben nodded. "I figured as much." A faint pinkness spread across his cheeks. "But as I said, it's not just that."

"Right." Melody paused. Was this the moment the bubble burst and Ben revealed himself to be a creep who was following her home in exchange for pictures of her feet or so that he would know where she lived and be able to creep on her through the windows? *Wait,* she thought. *Why would I even wonder* that? *It's not like I'm a character in a horror movie who leaves her curtains open while she's changing her clothes...*

She shook the invasive thought away. "So, what's the other reason?"

He shrugged. "Could you believe I just want to spend a little more time with you? I know I'm going to see you again at work, but...that still doesn't mean I'm ready to call it a night yet."

She softened immediately at his words. "So it's like that, is it? You're not following me home in hopes that I'll be so grateful for the gesture that I invite you inside or give you pictures of my feet?"

Ben recoiled in horror. "Is...is that the kind of thing American guys do? Because *truly,* that thought would never have crossed my mind."

Melody laughed, her head falling backwards as the joy and hilarity bubbling out of her magnified. "It's not. Or at least I don't think it is. That's just what my brain came up with. The worst-case scenario, I guess."

"I guess I'm glad the worst thing you thought I was capable of was having a foot fetish. Alas, I do not. Not that there's anything wrong with it."

"Oh, right." Melody was quick to agree. "Some people love feet, and that's great for them. It's really the idea that you would feel *entitled* to pictures of them that would have been the problem."

Ben reached for her hand, his fingertips playing lightly across the back of her knuckles. "Let me assure you that when it comes to you, to this day that we spent together, the word 'entitled' is the farthest thing from my mind. Fortunate, yes. Lucky as hell, of course. Blessed beyond my wildest imagination, clearly."

Melody's cheeks were warm, and she was grateful for the respite from the intensity of the feelings flowing between them when Ben turned in the direction of her apartment, her hand still in his, and began to walk slowly.

And then, too soon, they were in front of Melody's apartment, saying goodbye. Despite the fact that she would see him on Monday, Melody didn't want the night to end. She had to stop herself from sitting down on the curb to keep the conversation going at least a few more hours.

Finally, she reached up to put a hand on his shoulder, nodding as she did so. "We've got to call it a night, Pumpkin. Save some of the topics we *haven't* covered yet for next time, or else we'll have nothing to talk about."

"Not possible," said Ben, "But I agree that we should call it a night, get some rest. Are...are you free at all tomorrow?"

"I mean...yeah. I was just going to do some work, try to get ahead of it for next week, but that can't possibly take all day." Melody chuckled, downplaying just how seriously she took her job.

Yet Ben still looked alarmed. "You're working on the weekends, too? Pumpkin, that's too much. You need a break. Some fun. To think about something besides marketing strategies."

Melody shrugged. "Maybe. But it doesn't feel like work to me. I like what I do, you know?" *Most of the time,* she thought, immediately feeling guilt wash over her.

Ben nodded. "I like what I do, too, but that doesn't mean I do it for free when I should be, I don't know, going for a hike or drinking a fancy coffee."

"So you're a fancy coffee drinker?" Melody relished the opportunity to change the subject away from her work habits, to learn something about Ben in the process.

Ben held up a hand at the look on her face. "I'm not talking about a double triple caramel vanilla two pumps whipped cream whole milk coffee drink—"

"That's good, because it doesn't exist. You just made word salad out of a whole bunch of different ways to add sugar to caffeine."

A grin spread across Ben's face. "I guess that proves my point, that I don't know what I'm talking about. But I do enjoy the caffeine, though. Sometimes even a bit of sugar." He shrugged. "I'm not ashamed to admit I don't drink my coffee black, but that doesn't mean I go for the full sugar bomb either."

"So what is it, then? A latte? Cappuccino? Mocha?" Melody asked, a frown then wrinkling her forehead. "...and I'm out of coffee words now, too. You got me."

"Cappuccino when I'm out at a café. But I make Turkish coffee at home."

She felt her eyes widen with surprise. "You know how to make Turkish coffee?"

Ben laughed, a full body laugh that had him throwing his head back with unexpected glee. "Of course! Why? Is it so shocking that I would possess such a basic skill?" He crossed his arms in mock affront. "You know, there's a whole tradition in Turkey that when a young man and woman are deciding to get married, the woman makes Turkish coffee for him and for their parents."

"It's like a test of her ability to make Turkish coffee? Why? Is that considered an essential skill in a happy marriage?"

Ben shrugged. "It's probably partly that." A mischievous grin crossed his face. "Of course, it's also a test of the young man's character, too."

"How so?"

"Because she usually makes his coffee with salt instead of sugar."

It was Melody's turn to laugh. "And he just has to drink it along with everyone else and keep a straight face? I like that tradition!"

Ben smiled at her, drinking in her laughter. "I'll make Turkish coffee for you sometime."

"With sugar, or with salt?"

"Sugar, of course."

"Then I'd like that." She reached to give him a hug, her heart pounding wildly at the contact between their bodies, forcing her to pull back quickly, barely two seconds into it. "Okay, then." She gave an awkward wave, stepping back. "I'll see you tomorrow, I guess. Maybe in the afternoon sometime?"

Ben nodded. "That sounds perfect."

Over the next days and weeks, the time Melody spent with Ben was the highlight of her days. She had found her way around the city through his eyes, enjoying a picnic in the park, hikes on the nearest trails they could find, rainy afternoons spent comparing the skills of baristas at different local cafes.

So quickly, so seamlessly, he had become a fixture of her days. While at the beginning, they tentatively asked each other if they were free to hang out the next day, that had shifted into questions of what activity they wanted to do the next day, instead. And even if part of her was flashing the warning lights, telling her it was all too easy, all too good to be true, and that she should pump the brakes, she didn't want to.

And so she didn't.

She was allowed to have fun with Ben, especially if it wasn't coming at the expense of her performing her work with excellence. But Melody knew herself, and she had never once let her desire to spend time with Ben keep her from getting her work done.

If anything, the opposite was more likely to happen, and she occasionally had to cancel on Ben or push back their meeting time because she needed to focus on a project.

One Tuesday afternoon, when they were due to watch a movie at the local theater, Melody put her head down, determined to finish up a project that Mr. Richards had sent her way. Melody barely stifled a groan as an email notification popped up on her screen, Mr. Richards's name in the sender line.

Melody,

This isn't going to cut it. We need two more options if we're going to make a decision about which direction to go.

I need it first thing tomorrow morning. Richards

The groan came out in full force as she read the message, clapping her hand over her mouth with guilt as soon as it escaped. The project they were working on—a cooperative learning initiative across a few different service locations—was important. It was one of the most unique campaigns that had come Melody's way, and the messaging for how they presented it to the world to attract donors and volunteers was a high priority task, no one could argue that.

But couldn't Mr. Richards have given a little more direction than to say he didn't like her current strategy? How was she supposed to know what other directions she should offer as alternatives? She dropped her head down on her desk, feeling the briefest glimmer that this wasn't how things were supposed to be. That it might be nice for a boss to say "please" and "thank you" and offer constructive feedback and even the occasional compliment. That there was no escaping the nightmare that it was to work for Mr. Richards.

Guilt immediately consumed her, jolting her upright. "Too harsh, Mel. It's all about the mission. The mission is what matters," she reminded herself. "And the mission is good. I'll do *anything* to support the mission. This is how I make a difference in the world."

And so she lost herself, again, in striving. Sure, she might not know exactly what was expected of her in order to see this project through to completion. But that didn't mean she couldn't still knock it out of the park. If Mr. Richards wanted two more options, then she would give him four more. One of them had to be the right answer.

The flow state came easily for Melody; that was one of the ways she knew she was in the right field, how easy it was for her to lose herself in a project, all concept of time slipping away as she brainstormed, drafted copy, and played with concept art. She was so focused that a soft tapping on the entrance to her cubicle jolted her back to awareness with a start.

"Hi," she said, rubbing her sternum with one hand to calm her racing heart. "What can I do for you?" As she swiveled her chair to face the entrance, her eyes landed on Ben and a smile spread across her face. "You." She felt warmed from the inside out. "I'm glad it's you."

He smiled back at her. "I'm glad it's me, too. You were expecting someone else?"

Melody shook her head. "Just fell into a wormhole thanks to one of Mr. Richards's projects. That could have been anyone—Dame Maggie Smith herself—knocking on the cubicle door to bring me back to reality."

"Makes sense."

"Does it?" Melody chuckled at herself. "I'm not sure anything about this makes sense, but then again I'm still halfway in the world of brainstorming."

"Well, then." Ben rubbed his hands together. "Time to get all the way out of that world, isn't it?" He glanced at his watch. "We've got about an hour until the movie starts, but I thought you might want to get some snacks to sneak into the theater—"

"Ben," Melody interrupted, biting her lip with chagrin.

"What?" he asked. "I know technically you're not supposed to bring your own snacks in, but it's not *that* big a deal, is it? If you're not comfortable with it, we can buy overpriced popcorn and candy. I'm okay with that, too."

Despite herself, Melody chuckled. "Believe it or not, it's not the snacks that are giving me pause." She looked back at her computer, scrolling through the work she had completed, the work she still had to complete. "It's just...I'm not done with this. Not really. It still needs my attention, my energy, and I won't feel good about it if I quit now."

"But Melody. Your work day is over." He glanced at his watch again. "In fact, it ended nearly an hour ago. The fact that I am still here, waiting for you, is a great testament to just how much I enjoy spending time with you. But come on. Mr. Richards can't expect you to stay here past closing, and if he does...well, that's completely unreasonable of him, isn't it?"

Melody shook her head. "You don't understand, Ben. It's not like he's thinking about me and how I spend my time. That would be strange, to be honest, and I don't think I would like it. He's just thinking about the project and the fact that he needs it on his desk in the morning. I'm not sure he knows how long it takes me to complete a set of tasks like this, but I'm certain he doesn't care. It's all about the outcome."

A frown had appeared on Ben's forehead. "I don't really know him, but wow. That sounds like a pretty crappy boss. All the more reason not to let him be the boss of your personal life, too." He held out a hand for Melody. "Come on, let's get out of here. You need to eat something. Stretch your legs. Leave work for work."

Melody hesitated. "He...he's not a crappy boss. He might be doing things a little differently than his mom did, but he cares about the mission. Like I do. Like we all do."

Ben nodded. "Alright, then. If you're convinced he's not a terrible boss, then want to prove it to me by coming out for a movie and living a little? Come on, Mel, you're right. We do all care about the mission. It's why we got into this line of work in the first place. But sitting there at your desk for another four hours is not the way to support the mission. For one thing, your brain needs a break if it's going to keep producing any kind of quality output." He crossed his arms over his chest. "And for another thing, if you sacrifice your health for the mission, then I suspect the mission is flawed. Sure, it may support a lot of important efforts all over the world, but if it does that at the expense of your health, then it needs reevaluation." He looked pointedly at her chair, nodding at it. "Haven't you heard that sitting is the new smoking?"

Melody was torn. Ben made some good points, and she knew she would be fresher to do some more work later if she took a break now. But she also felt a pang that he might be right, that there was a deeper problem afoot than whether she was able to watch a movie on a weeknight. She shook her head, getting to her feet as she simultaneously closed her laptop and shoved it into her bag. "You're right." She smiled at him. "Let's go watch the movie."

Ben was staring at her bag, where her laptop had so recently disappeared from sight. "Are you taking that home so you can work on this later? After you get home from the movie?"

Melody shook her head at him. "You're unstoppable, Ben. You're probably going to tell me I shouldn't do that either."

"I mean..." He held his arms out in an exaggerated shrug. "In an ideal world, I'd love it if you went home after the movie and went straight to bed, or at least relaxed. But at least if you're going to do it this way, you still get a break. And I get to spend some time with you."

Melody lifted her bag to her shoulder. "And don't forget about the purse snacks. The best sustenance comes out of a big purse and is eaten in a dark movie theater. Everyone knows this." She patted her bag. "Speaking of which, let's fill this bad boy up!"

Things were going well with Ben, and Melody was happy. Happier than she was used to feeling, which meant a part of her was the opposite of happy. That is, if anxious was the opposite of happy, and she was pretty sure it wasn't. Anxiety and happiness could coexist, even if one of them tended to dull the edges of the other.

A few weeks in, Chloe called to check on her, and Melody practically lit up from within at the sight of her friend's name on her phone screen.

"Chloe!" she answered, a grin encompassing her face. "How are you? How's London?"

"It's awesome," Chloe's voice was tinny as it came down the line, a brief twinge reminding Melody of just how far away her dear friend was. "Sorry for not calling you sooner, except I'm not sorry. The phone works both ways, gorgeous, and if you'll notice, you weren't exactly itching to get in touch with me, either."

"You're right." Melody bit her lower lip. "It's been busy here, actually. It's not that I haven't missed you…"

"I know." Chloe sighed. "And no surprise it's been busy, of course. Mr. Richards would work you into the ground—and you would *let* him—any day of the year, so why should this be different?" A brief pause. "Actually, the only thing that's different is that *I'm* not there to pull you away from your work occasionally and remind you to have a life. Dear God, Mel! Without me there, have you even left your desk once? When was the last time you ate?"

That got a chuckle out of Melody. "Very funny, Chloe. But if you must know, there actually *is* someone taking up that noble mantle and making me leave work at a reasonable time and even go out and do some fun things."

Chloe gasped. "Who is she? My replacement? You traded me in for a younger model?"

"Um, well…not exactly. For starters, it's not a 'she.'" She heard Chloe's shock at that revelation like it was another person on the phone line. "His name is Ben, and we've just been…well, having a lot of fun together."

"Ugh, you are infuriating! You have news *this* monumental to share and you wait for me to pick up the phone to share it? Not cool, Mel! Not cool at all." There was the briefest of pauses. "But I'm happy for you. I mean, I *think* I am. He's a good guy?"

Melody nodded as she spoke. "The best, actually. He's attentive, caring, funny. He cares about the work that we do, so I know he's compassionate and conscientious. But he also cares about me not burning myself out at work, so he's better than me in that way."

"How do you mean?" Chloe sounded like she was scowling. "Who could be better than you?"

Melody sighed. "I just meant he's like you. He's got boundaries around work, I guess, in the same way you do. You know how you can leave at the end of the day and not spend your whole evening thinking about work and then come back to it on the next work day? Ben is like that, too."

Chloe's chuckle—it sounded more like a strong exhale—was humorless. "That's true of a lot of people, Melody. It doesn't make any of them better than you."

"Maybe not. But it's a skill I definitely don't have, and it's one I'm not sure I even care to develop, to be honest."

"Really? Okay, now that's concerning. You don't think there's a problem there? That it would be good for you to have a break every now and then or maybe even a hobby?"

"It's just..." Melody paused. "I get that work-life balance is a thing and we're supposed to be able to leave work at work. I definitely get that for most people, like...I don't know...people who work at banks or in regular businesses."

Chloe's sigh was exasperated. "But?"

"But it's not the same for us. The work we're doing matters. It isn't just about making rich people richer, it's actually making the world a better place. If I slack off and don't do my job, the consequences...I can't even let myself think about it. If I'm not giving my best all the time, then there are women around the globe who will feel those consequences. Who will miss out because of me. And I just can't live with that."

"I get what you're saying, I really do. But if I may remind you...you're not a surgeon, Mel. You aren't getting called in to the hospital in the middle of the night to perform an emergency, life-saving surgery. You're a vital part of EduPowerment's mission, sure. But even important work like ours shouldn't require you to sacrifice your health or your personal life to get it done."

"Maybe." Melody spoke through gritted teeth. "But maybe you and I are just different. Maybe you're more efficient and get all your work done in the office and I, I just need more time."

"That's nonsense and you know it. No one works harder than you in the office, and I know for a fact that none of them work harder than you do at home."

"And that's why Mr. Richards brings his extra projects to me. Because he knows I'll prioritize them."

Chloe scoffed. "That's a nice way of saying that you don't have boundaries and can't say no to him, but yeah. He knows you'll prioritize them."

Melody had heard enough. She and Chloe just saw the world—and particularly the world of work—differently. But if she didn't force her way of working on Chloe, then Chloe shouldn't do the same to her.

So she told her that. "Let's stop talking about me," said Melody. "You didn't call to lecture me, and if you did, then I'm sorry I answered. We're not going to see this the same way, and that's okay. I can't convince you to have my work ethic and you can't convince me to slack off more."

"I didn't say 'slack off,' geez—"

"No," Melody interrupted. "No more about me, no more about work. Tell me about London. How are things going there?"

Chloe's sigh was dramatic. "It's amazing, Melody. I love it here so much. I wish I could stay forever, and if it's possible I just might."

"Really? Like...leave EduPowerment and get a job for UK Hope instead?"

"I mean, I haven't thought about the logistics yet. Like...how it would actually work. I'm sure there are visa things and legal questions and all that." Melody could practically hear Chloe shrugging. "But I'm not you, and I don't tend to think like that, now do I?"

Melody chuckled. "Indeed you do not. So...what? Are you just going to figure those things out when the time comes? You're not researching it now?"

"Nah. I'm just trying to enjoy myself here, Mel. If I get too hung up on the future and stress myself out about it, I'm not likely to have that much fun here, am I? And if I do that, I probably won't end up wanting to stay, anyway. This way, I give London a real college try. If at the end of the year I still want to stay, then it's time to start thinking about how I can do that. Otherwise, I'll be on my way back home, ready to share the cubicle next to yours."

The thought of her cubicle was—unsurprisingly—not comforting and homey to Melody. Would *she* want to be in it next year? Was her happily ever after with EduPowerment, and did it include those same four low cubicle walls?

She shuddered to herself, forcing herself back to the moment and back to Chloe's words. "I don't know how you can do that," she admitted. "The thought of not worrying about future possibilities sounds...well, great. But I'm also not convinced that's a part of myself I can just switch off. Or that I would even want to. Isn't thinking about the future what keeps me safe and happy and with a roof over my head and with money still in the bank when I'm waiting for my next paycheck?"

"Maybe," said Chloe. "But it's probably also what causes a lot of your stress and anxious feelings, too. I mean...do you *only* worry about things that actually end up happening, or do you worry about possibilities that never see the light of day?"

A laugh barked out of Melody's throat. "Oh, I am exceptionally gifted in this regard, and I can actually do *both*." She paused a beat to consider. "Though most of the ones that really haunt my mind are things that never end up happening. Like...I worry a *lot* about locking myself out of my apartment. And yet, it has never once happened to me."

"Right. Because every time you even approach the door to your apartment, you literally have your keys in your hand and are talking about how you don't want to lock yourself out."

"*Every* time?"

"Every time that I've been with you, yeah."

Melody sniffed. "Well, that's probably why it's never happened then. So, I guess that proves your point wrong, despite your best attempts to prove it right. Sorry, friend. You can't win this one."

"You're ridiculous. I hope you know that."

"And I love you, too."

A few days after her conversation with Chloe, Melody was enjoying a brief respite at work—even if it *was* making her feel guilty. Mr. Richards had taken the day off to meet with a few large donors out of town, and though the work to prepare the materials he needed for the meetings had been formidable, now that he was away from all lines of communication, Melody's work felt quiet.

She spent the morning fine tuning the ad copy for an upcoming social media campaign, creating versions to split test to find the most compelling tactic. When she had tweaked and tugged on the copy and the creative material until it felt like there was nothing else she could do—but that *had* to be wrong; there was *always* more she could do—she let herself slip into research mode, opening up a few high-ranking articles about current marketing trends in different tabs and settling in to read them all.

A throat cleared behind her. "I hope I'm not interrupting something important."

Melody swiveled in her seat to face Ben, a smile spreading across her face at the sight of him. "Not at all. It's nice to see you."

"Yeah, I didn't *really* think I was interrupting." He nodded towards her computer monitor, full with a full-screen image of an advertisement for a standing desk with a pool instead of a treadmill. He gave her a reproachful glance. "Looks like you took all my encouragement to have some fun and chill out a little bit about work a little too seriously, Melody." He made a *tsk*ing sound. "What would Mr. Richards say?"

"I'll have you know that this is research, Ben." Melody felt her cheeks heating, despite the fact that Ben was smiling at her, a playful glimmer in his eye. "I wouldn't dream of wasting the organization's money by screwing around on company time."

"I know." He put a light hand on her shoulder. "Believe it or not, I was teasing you. And I'm already endlessly fascinated to hear how you're going to relate this—" He gestured to the pool desk on the screen. "—to what we do here." His lips twisted in a crooked smile. "In fact, I'd love to hear about it after work today."

"Oh yeah? What did you have in mind?"

"Well, even before the pool desk, I was heading over here to see if you'd like to join me for some Turkish coffee this evening. At my place. I mean...it's not about coming over to my place, though I realize you haven't been there yet. It's more about the fact that, at least the last time it came up in conversation, you'd never had Turkish coffee and so it's high time we remedied that..."

Wow. Ben is cute *when he's all flustered and pink-cheeked,* Melody thought. And all the cuter to think that she was the one who was having that effect on him. As much as she was enjoying the show, she needed to put him out of his misery.

"I would love that," she said. "It won't keep me up all night, will it?"

At her question, his cheeks turned impossibly redder, crossing the border to full-on maroon territory.

"The coffee, I mean," she hurried to add. "I'm not...I mean. I don't want to imply anything else." Now she was the one feeling heat flushing her face. It was just coffee. That was all he had invited her over for, right? Coffee wasn't *code* for something else, was it? And if it was, was that "something else" something she wanted right now?

Too many questions. Too many things that she should probably talk to Ben about, but right here in her cubicle hardly seemed like the place to do it.

Ben's smile was reassuring, as if her nerves had calmed his and now he needed to return the favor. "Most people drink Turkish coffee in the evening and have no trouble falling asleep with it. It's like Italians and their espresso. And I won't give it to you on an empty stomach, so that should help, too."

"Oh? Are you...*making* me dinner? I mean, it's fine if you want to get takeout or something, too. I'm up for whatever."

"You'll just have to wait and see." And with one more smile and the quickest wink she'd ever seen, he was gone.

To continue the story, turn to **page 8**

75

"I'm sure it's not for me, Chloe." Melody forced the corners of her mouth higher. "Now's not the time. Maybe next year," she promised, knowing full well that next year would bring its own reasons to stay put. Responsibilities couldn't be shirked just because there was an alluring new possibility on the horizon.

"If you're sure," said Chloe, shaking her head. "It's your decision, after all. But I'm *not* missing this chance." She sat back down at her desk, reading the email again from the beginning. "I'm going to make a list of all the programs that sound good to me. Did any of them catch your eye?"

"Definitely." Melody nodded, her smile finally genuine as she thought of the locations that had created a stirring in her chest. Though they were cities she'd never been to, in countries she'd never even visited, her pulse had quickened despite her best efforts to stay even-keeled and not get too excited about something that couldn't be.

"Well?" Chloe was looking at her expectantly. "Which ones were they? I've already jotted down Tom Conley's office in Ireland. Did you see his TED Talk?"

Melody nodded. "It was great. He would definitely be an inspiring person to meet, though I guess he's not in Ireland much these days, is he? I thought I'd heard he was primarily working out of Chicago." Off a shrug from Chloe, she continued. "The ones that caught my attention, here...scroll back up? There." She pointed at the screen. "Izmir." And then again, she gestured. "Dresden. If I were going to apply for this program, those would be my top two choices."

Chloe wrinkled her brow at Melody. "And the fact that you aren't applying astounds me. But...why those two? Izmir, that's...in Turkey, right? And Dresden sounds familiar. Probably from a band or a book or something."

"It's in Germany."

"Any particular reason those are the two that made the cut?" Chloe scribbled a note on her pad and then kept scrolling. "I didn't know you to be a Germanophile or whatever they call people who love all things Turkish."

Melody shrugged. "I couldn't say, honestly. They just...caught my attention. Something twinkly and magical about them that leaped off the screen, I guess," she joked.

"Couldn't have been the job description," said Chloe, nose wrinkling. "A university? No thank you, just got out of one of those. No plans to go back anytime soon."

Melody chuckled. "I'm not saying that just because something sounded good to me, it's going to be a perfect fit for you. After all, it's clearly not a perfect fit for me either, or I'd be applying to go there, wouldn't I?"

Chloe nodded slowly. "You definitely would." She squinted at Melody, as if by peering into her brain she could understand her friend's decision. "Are you sure you're not going to consider it at all?"

"I'm sure." This time, Melody's smile had some strength behind it. "The more I think about it, the more it sounds like…too much. Too much effort to find the perfect position, then to make myself a competitive candidate. Loose ends to tie up here, the lease for my apartment, my family…to say nothing of the fact that I've never moved out of Michigan, let alone out of the United States." She shook her head, confidence building with every word she spoke. "No, this is the right decision for me. I'm sure of it."

"Well, I can definitely respect your decision," Chloe admitted, "but don't think you're going to be talking me out of taking this chance. Just because *you* don't want to have an international adventure doesn't mean *I* shouldn't get one."

"Of course not." Melody smiled and patted Chloe on the arm. "I'm going to want to hear all about it. And if there's anything I can do to help you, I'm all yours."

"Thanks, Mel. You're a good friend."

Melody went back to her cubicle, her computer finally ready to tackle the work of the day. It might not feel like it—because *of course* there was a part of her that had ached to answer the call to adventure—but she knew she was making the right decision. Nothing was more important than furthering the mission of EduPowerment, and she never would have been able to enjoy an opportunity that was more motivated by her own selfish desires than by the meaningful impact that it could have on the people who needed it most.

The days passed at EduPowerment in much the same way that they had been unfolding since Melody first started there. She came in early—even earlier than normal these days, thanks to that warning she had received from the boss—and left late, and in between she did work that lit her up from within. Every project that she was involved with was a reminder of the work EduPowerment was doing in the world, and even if Melody wasn't the one traveling to far-flung locations and meeting the beneficiaries of their services firsthand and seeing the impact that they were creating...she was still a part of it.

Even if the role she was playing was simply finding the perfect words to describe a new initiative, or the subject line that would get more people to open an email, she knew it all mattered. It all played a role in the bigger picture, and the actions that she was taking in her little cubicle in their modest office in a southeastern corner of Michigan directly translated to funds raised for women all over the globe. And what those women could create with the funds they received...wow. It humbled Melody every time she heard about it.

"Check this out." Melody carried a printout over to Chloe's cubicle. "One of the programs in India...it's a poultry farm, right? With the initial funds, they got some chickens and started selling eggs. But then they wanted to grow it from there, so they let the chickens sit on some of those eggs and now they've got even more chickens and even more eggs to sell. They're even looking at expanding it and selling chicken, too. They already had to expand to a bigger building, which they could easily do with all the profits. It's just amazing, isn't it? Starting with something so small and turning it into..." She looked up finally, noticing that Chloe was craned over her desk, reading something on the computer screen with her eyes just a few inches away. "Chloe! You're not even listening to me, are you? What's so important that you can't even pretend to care about this?"

Chloe waved her away. "Yeah, yeah, it's all great. I'll read it later. Just leave a copy on my desk."

Melody stepped closer. "What is it that you're so tuned into there? Some 'hot goss'?" she asked, using Chloe's favorite expression. With her last step, she could make out the words on her screen easily. "Oh my goodness! That's that Generosity Exchange program you applied for, isn't it?" Chloe nodded. "Well go on, then. Open it! Don't you want to find out if you got accepted or not?"

Chloe shook her head. "I'm not ready to make it real yet, you know? Like...right now, who knows what my future holds? I might be about to jet off to London and I might be staying put in this hellhole for all of eternity. Or both. Like Schrodinger's cat. I think. I never really did understand that." She shrugged. "I just...I don't know if I even know what I want the email to say, you know? So why open it?"

"That makes no sense." Melody gestured for her friend to move aside, then leaned in, blocking Chloe's view of the screen with her body as she clicked the email open. "*Dear Ms. Allen, we regret to inform you that you have not been selected...*"

Chloe groaned. "I knew it! Aw man, that's such a bummer. Wait. Why are you smiling like that? Do you think this is funny?"

"Hilarious, actually." Melody stepped back to let Chloe see that the email open on her screen was, in fact, an acceptance notification. "I just couldn't handle you 'not knowing what you wanted.' Because as it turns out, you *do* know what you want. Aren't you thrilled, now that you know you A) wanted to be accepted and B) were?"

Chloe was staring at Melody with her jaw hanging open. "That was a pretty shady way of finding out what I wanted, friend. Not a fan of your tactics." She moved closer to her computer monitor. "I am, however, a big fan of finding out that I get to go live abroad for a year, so...I guess I'll allow it this time. And also make a mental note never to let you be the one to break me any kind of news in the future."

"That's fair." Melody smiled. She was happy for Chloe. This was an amazing opportunity, and the fact that she was going to get to experience that excitement and growth vicariously through one of her favorite people was thrilling. No, she didn't regret that she hadn't applied—this was exciting enough. She barely managed to restrain herself from asking Chloe how she was going to manage all the logistics and emotions of this big journey, all the very things Melody would have been concerned about right now if she were the one reading the acceptance email.

Instead, she asked the next logical question. "So, what does it say? Where are you going?"

Chloe's eyes moved quickly as she scanned the email before they widened, and she turned to Melody with sheer joy on her face. "London! Oh my gosh, I'm so excited! I always wanted to visit London, go see a play in the West End and take a selfie with Big Ben and all that...now I'm going to *live* there! Can you believe it?"

"You know, I really can't." Chloe's joy was contagious, and Melody felt the smile spread across her own face to match her friend's. "I have a feeling you're really going to love it there."

When Melody made the short journey back to her desk, she wondered briefly what it would feel like to be in Chloe's shoes at a time like this. What it might feel like to be about to turn your whole life on its head...and then shook it off and got back to work. That was a question for a more adventurous person, or for someone who was less content than she was. No, she was happy to stay in the city that she loved, in her cozy apartment, working every day at the job that gave her life meaning.

The time between the arrival of Chloe's acceptance email and her departure for jolly old England flew by. Melody was vaguely aware of the orientation meetings Chloe had attended, her concerns about packing, some general preparations she was making...and yet still, her last day of work arrived far more quickly than Melody was prepared for it.

"You won't say no to drinks after work today, right?" Chloe asked that morning, depositing a plant on Melody's desk that would *not* be making the journey to London with her. Though Chloe insisted it was a gift and not an extended plant sitting gig, Melody already knew she would give the plant back to her friend when she returned home. The whole plant exchange and subsequent realization that today was Chloe's last day had left both women emotional and just a bit teary.

"Of course not." Melody sniffled as she brushed some moisture away from her eye. "I can't believe you aren't going to be here tomorrow." She gestured to Chloe's desk, empty of all her personal artifacts, with nothing left on the table but her computer. "What am I going to do without you?"

"You won't be without me, not really." The emotion in Chloe's eyes matched what Melody felt blocking her throat. "Tomorrow I'll be on a plane, so I probably won't be texting you...but as soon as I land, I'll be texting and calling and Skyping with you all the time. It'll be like I never even left. And hey, I'll be back before you know it."

Melody shook her head. "Don't say that. I don't want you to wish away your time in London or even to spend it all chatting with me, as much as I would love that. You have to really *be* there, you know? Do your work and have some fun and make some friends."

"Just don't replace you, right?"

Melody swatted her on the arm. "Of course! Make all the English friends you want, but leave space in your heart for little old me, okay?"

And then they were hugging again. "You know I will," Chloe reassured her. "And I'll find the balance between having fun and making friends there and hanging out at home in my pajamas video chatting with you. I can do both, just you wait and see."

If it were Melody moving to a new city, a new country, she knew which of those options sounded better to her. She'd never been much for adventuring out into a new city—or even a new bar, really—on her own. With a friend meeting her, she could go anywhere—to a party, a restaurant, all the way across town to some place she'd never been before—but on her own, she tended to be a homebody. And she preferred it that way, when she was honest with herself. All the times she'd ventured out to a bar or a club or even a party at the urging of a friend, it had been to appease that friend. To get them to back off and not give her so much grief for preferring her own company and the peace and quiet of her own home.

But that wasn't Chloe. Chloe always wanted to soak up all the flavor and goodness of life, like rubbing a piece of bread over your dinner plate to get every last drop of deliciousness. And so Melody would continue to reassure her that spending her time out and about in London was the best use of her time and that she shouldn't stay at home on a Friday night to chat with Melody. And Melody? She would manage. She probably wouldn't make a new friend—how did people actually do that at her age, anyway? But she could spend more time visiting her family...and maybe even get a pet. A cat would be nice...

Chloe was saying something; Melody must have zoned out because she nearly missed it. "...hottie cubicle neighbor," were her last words, combined with some scandalously wiggling eyebrows.

"Er...what? Could you repeat that?"

A sigh huffed out, blowing Chloe's face-framing layers back with its power. "I knew you weren't listening to me.

Whatever. I was reminding you that you're going to have your own Generosity Exchange participants here in the office and that, with any luck, you'll end up with a new office mate. Preferably an attractive, fun person sitting right there at my own cubicle and making it so that you don't miss me at all. But, uh...I guess I would prefer if it's a romantic distraction this person provides rather than a 'new best friend' kind of distraction. That would make me jealous, and we don't want that, now do we?"

"You're ridiculous." Melody rolled her eyes. "For one thing, I'm not sure dating someone in the office is really a great idea. I seem to remember something in the employee handbook about disclosing relationships to HR or something like that—"

"Too literal! I ask you to imagine a hot guy sitting at my desk and looking at you like you're a divine being and you take it to sitting down with human resources to make sure nothing inappropriate is assumed about your relationship. Don't be so boring! You know I love you, but you've got to turn off your over-attentive chaperone when you engage your imagination. Even for just a minute, Mel."

Melody sighed. "Fair enough. I will be open to the idea of discovering someone to have a workplace crush on...and if that crush turns out to be mutual, then who knows what might happen? After we both sit down with HR, of course." She winked at Chloe, just to annoy her. "I'm still going to miss you, though, even if you try to distract me with hot hypothetical men. You can't change that with some close-up magic sleight-of-hand distraction nonsense."

"And I wouldn't dream of trying. Now get back to work so we can leave right at five for beverages and fun and probably some weepy emotional outbursts, if I know the two of us."

"Oh, there will definitely be tears," Melody agreed. "You can count on that."

At five o'clock on the dot, Chloe was steering Melody out the door, despite her insistence that she could finish everything on her to-do list with just five more minutes of work time.

"No way!" Chloe cried, forcing Melody towards the door bodily. "You can be as much of a workaholic as you want to be once I'm gone, but tonight belongs to *me*, friend."

Finally, Melody stopped resisting. "Fine." She stopped fighting back and needing to be pushed, falling into step next to her friend. "You know I'm just trying to delay the inevitable, right? Like...I don't *actually* want to stay at my desk for hours and hours and work, but I feel like if the work day doesn't end, then you're not really leaving?"

Chloe rolled her eyes. "Nice try. I know you're sad about me leaving, but I also know how often you stay in that cubicle long after everyone else has left, and I'm not buying it."

"It was worth a shot," Melody muttered to herself.

There was a nice bar a short walk up the street, and Melody and Chloe walked there together. They'd both made plans to get home today without driving, making it easier to have a little fun—and an adult beverage or two—without worrying about safety on the road.

As they entered the bar, it became clear they weren't the only EduPowerment employees who'd had the idea to celebrate there that evening. The place was jam-packed with familiar faces, and as far as Melody could tell, every single person who'd been accepted in the Generosity Exchange program was there as well.

"Hang on a second," she said, copping on to a suspicious feeling as she turned towards Chloe's face and saw the guilty expression waiting there. "Is this, like...a *thing*? I mean, is it a going away party? Or an event of some kind that I didn't know about? What happened to the two of us going out for happy hour?"

Chloe held up her hands, palms facing Melody. "Hey now, I don't know that I ever specifically said anything to suggest it would be *just* the two of us. After all, don't you normally beg out of things like this? How am I supposed to celebrate my last evening in Michigan if my wing woman suddenly decides she'd rather stay home and leave me to go out on my own?"

"I wasn't going to do that *tonight*," Melody grumbled under her breath. It wasn't that she had a problem with any of her colleagues from EduPowerment, but Chloe was the only person there that she would really consider a friend. The rest of them seemed nice enough, but Melody hadn't exactly felt a keen sense of loss that her workplace wasn't her dominion of popularity. She saw the cliques forming around her, marketing folks tending to stick together at lunch time while the fundraising crowd did their own thing...and she was happy not to be a part of it.

Or that's what she told herself. Sure, there may have been some part of her, the part that was never invited to the coolest parties in middle school perhaps, who would have liked to join in on some of the fun that the cliques were so obviously having...but she reminded herself regularly that she was at EduPowerment to make a difference in the world, not to win a popularity contest. And in particular, she wasn't interested in being the most popular person amongst a group of people who didn't seem to share her passion for EduPowerment or the work they were doing to make the world a better place. More than once, she had overheard comments form those cliques about "what a drag it was to have to work so much" and "how they definitely deserved to be making more money," and those were, quite simply, statements that didn't sit well with Melody's value system.

And yet here she was tonight with—she scanned the room to confirm—the exact same people she had heard say both of those things. Great. She could comfort herself with the hope that things would be a little better at EduPowerment over the next twelve months, now that so many of the originators of discontent and dissatisfaction were going to be leaving for greener pastures. She could only hope the new team members coming through the Generosity Exchange program would be more enthusiastic workers. More than anything—and certainly more than the *hotness* that mattered so much to Chloe—that was what Melody hoped would be waiting for her at the office the following morning.

Despite her resolve not to, Melody had enjoyed herself at the going away party. Though she had originally intended to leave by seven o'clock and only have one glass of wine, both the hour of her departure and the number of drinks she had consumed had significantly exceeded her expectations.

As she woke up the next morning with a headache, she groaned. "Never again. Good riddance, Chloe. This is all your fault, you know." Of course, Chloe couldn't hear her—she was already at the airport, if not in the air, on her way to London. Or was she already there? A direct flight from Detroit to London couldn't take that long, and Melody was almost convinced her friend hadn't even planned to sleep last night, as excited as she had been to begin her new adventure.

Melody made her way into the kitchen, filling a glass with water from the tap and drinking it down before filling it again. Considering how bad her head felt—and that was *without* going through the pressure changes of takeoff and landing—she sorely hoped Chloe had done a better job hydrating herself rather than just drying up her insides like little raisins and prunes, glass of wine after glass of wine.

Scrolling through the notifications on her phone while she continued to mainline water, Melody had to take a moment to appreciate the fact that, while she was ever-so-slightly hungover, at least she hadn't overslept. One irresponsible decision had not snowballed into two, and she still had every intention of arriving at work on-time, showered, and fresh as a daisy.

Melody fumbled with the coffee maker, setting it up to brew while she made herself presentable with a quick shower. On normal days, her morning efficiency system served her well, but on a morning after wine overindulgence, she could really use a caffeine boost *before* trying to keep herself upright in the shower. She shook her head, chastising herself twice, for both her lack of self-control last night and her lack of inner strength this morning. Not only would she make a point *not* to overdo it with the adult beverages again anytime soon, but in fact, she might also start getting up half an hour earlier and throwing a few more discipline-boosting practices into her morning routine.

Not to torture herself, no. Not because she thought she deserved some punishment first thing in the morning...though it did sometimes feel that way...

No, adding in some meditation and maybe a little exercise...and what if she turned her morning shower into a *cold* shower? That was supposed to be really good for you, wasn't it? All the personal development influencers were talking about the importance of a cold shower for strengthening your willpower and also health benefits or whatever...she was going to try it. Right now. No time like the present.

Melody stood outside the shower, sticking her hand into the cold water streaming inside. How in the world was she going to make herself take the first step inside?

"It's no big deal, Mel. Just some cold water." She gave herself the pep talk out loud, confident her roommate Felicity was sound asleep and unlikely to overhear her. "Think of the women who use EduPowerment's services. Do you know how happy some of them would be for running water? And *clean* running water, too! This water is so clean I could definitely drink it, and it's just flowing freely right out of my shower head. Amazing! Now...if I can just..." She reached one foot into the shower, shrieking as the icy water touched her calf before jerking it back. "Shit! That's cold!" Her hand hovered over the temperature control, debating whether she could cop out and turn it all the way to warm without feeling like she had failed.

"Oh, screw it," she said as she stepped into the shower and directly under the cascading—and very cold—water. "Holy crap!" she cried out before clapping a hand over her mouth. Felicity was sleeping, and she had been at the lab late again last night. She did *not* need to wake up to the sound of her roommate screaming like she was being murdered in the shower, reenacting that terrible scene from *Psycho.* Melody stayed in the shower long enough to make sure the iciness had touched every inch of her body, then slammed the tap shut and bolted out, enveloping herself in her fluffy, clean towel.

Granted, it wasn't a *total* success. She hadn't touched even a square inch of her body with soap or shampoo, making the shower less about getting clean and more about...uh...torturing herself, as it turned out. But as she dried herself off, she had to admit that she did at least feel invigorated. Alive! A little less like death warmed over, and just a tiny bit more ready to face the day ahead.

After choosing her best professional outfit—something that both made her feel like she knew what she was doing and looked good at the same time—and slamming one cup of coffee, she filled her thermos with the rest of the pot and grabbed a granola bar to eat on the walk. It was going to be a good day. It might be her first Chloe-less day, and it had certainly started in a fairly unpleasant way, both with the hangover and with the cold shower...but there was no reason to believe it would continue that way.

As she arrived at work, Melody smiled. Being here always changed things. Whenever she arrived at work, she felt a moment of gratitude that she was getting to live her dream of doing impactful work. Even if she was tired when she pulled in, or if she had received disappointing news from Mr. Richards...there was still something about this place. Something about knowing that every action she took inside those walls, no matter how small or insignificant it seemed, was directly impacting the work EduPowerment was doing for women all over the world. How could she feel anything but gratitude for that?

Of course it would be nice if Mr. Richards hadn't canceled this year's raises, but that didn't say anything about EduPowerment. It was a budgetary decision, she knew, and it wasn't anything personal. Surely, he would make it up to them somehow. And even if he didn't, how could she feel bad about it? She could afford to pay her rent and buy her groceries, and that was more than a lot of women all over the world could say. While other women were staying in unhealthy relationships just because they couldn't afford to leave or struggling to put food on the table for their kids, was she really going to ask for more? For what, so she could take a vacation or buy new shoes that she didn't really need or treat herself to a piece of jewelry that one of those women couldn't even begin to fathom?

It was better this way. It kept her humble. And sure, it was hard to be around her colleagues who didn't feel the same way, who grumbled about how little money they made or openly searched for other jobs during their lunch breaks. She couldn't change them, but she could spend less time around them.

As she entered the building and made her way to her cubicle, the first thing she noticed was a large bulk of man who was clearly lost. Standing over her desk, broad shoulders and towering height, she couldn't help but wonder what this giant being even thought he was doing.

"Excuse me, are you lost?" She directed her voice at his back, as he was standing in the doorway to her cubicle, looking down at her desk and bulletin board. She tried to keep the irritation out of her voice, but she couldn't help but feel violated with him in her personal space like this. That bulletin board was covered in inspirational quotes for her eyes only, thank you very much.

He turned around then, and Melody's stomach dropped. What had appeared to be just a hulking figure, unwelcome and fairly intimidating in its size, revealed itself as something very different when she was facing him head-on.

He was handsome, for starters. No, "handsome" didn't do him justice. He was breathtaking, with deep soulful eyes and a warm, open face that felt like the sun was shining directly on her, so bright she felt like she needed to shade her eyes with her hand or dig her sunglasses out from her purse. Melody wasn't inclined to notice the physical things, or at least that's what she always told Chloe when she'd asked Melody to describe someone.

That, apparently, was inaccurate though, because with this man, she couldn't help but notice his physicality. His height, the broad shoulders that tapered to a narrow waist, the clear outline of arm muscles she could see through the fabric of his shirt. She stopped her eyes from trailing farther south, directing them back up to his face in expectation of some reply to her question.

"Hi," he said, reaching out a hand. "I'm Ben, and it's my first day. I'm just...finding my way around. Is this your cubicle?"

She took his hand in hers and shook it twice before forcing herself to let go. Of course, his grip had been nicely firm and his palm had been warm and ever-so-slightly rough, like he had worked with those hands. Goodness, what was happening to her? And where was Chloe when she needed her? Chloe would know what to do with this man...

"Oh, wait!" Melody slapped her hand to her forehead. "You're here with the Generosity Exchange, right?" She couldn't imagine anyone else would be having their first day today, not with the influx of new team members already coming thanks to the exchange program. "You're probably looking for Chloe's desk then. Let me show you where it is."

"It's not this one?" Ben gestured to Melody's workspace. "I quite like this one."

Her cheeks heated inexplicably. There was no need to take a man's compliment of her bulletin board that personally, it wasn't as if he'd said he quite liked *her*. Although it did feel like her workspace was a part of her, as attached as she was both to her job and to the time and effort that she expended there.

"This one's mine," she said, walking a few steps away to Chloe's abandoned desk. "This is where Chloe usually works, so it will be yours. Let me know if you need any-thing, okay?"

Before Ben could say anything else, Melody slunk back to her cubicle and dropped into her chair. What she wouldn't give for a door on this thing right about now, something she could seal shut to keep attractive men and the unwanted feelings they made her feel securely on the outside. Why couldn't it be a woman sitting at Chloe's desk? For all the time they spent together at the office, for how closely they worked together, it would definitely be easier to work with someone she wasn't attracted to. Maybe she could suggest switching him to another cubi-cle? Surely Chloe's desk was too small to fit his long legs under...they could find some place else where he'd be more comfortable. And preferably farther from her, too.

That wasn't going to happen. It wasn't as if the cubicles here came in different sizes, or first class and coach options. A cubicle was a cubicle, a desk was a desk.

Melody put her head in her hands and stared at her own desk, willing it to give her the answers she so desperate-ly craved. What was she going to do with Ben? Could she handle working this closely with someone like Ben? Should she direct those feelings some place else, like into a rivalry that would surely only make them both better at their jobs? Or should she do the most uncharacteristic thing possible and acknowledge the fact that she felt a connection with him, a spark?

*To acknowledge and act upon her attraction, turn to **page 40***

*To put aside her attraction and focus on befriending Ben, turn to **page 287***

*To channel her attraction into rivalry and competition, turn to **page 128***

96

She shook her head, overwhelmed by all the emotions that were rushing to express themselves. "I...I don't know how any of this is supposed to work, Ben. I don't know how to be in a relationship in the same city, the same office...so how am I going to figure out how to be in a long-distance one?"

His face lit up the slightest bit with her words. "Are you saying that you *want* to be in a long-distance relationship with me?"

She nodded. "I mean...no, I'd rather be in a short-distance relationship with you. A same neighborhood relationship with you. But if the choice is between long-distance or no relationship, then it's an easy choice."

She was in his arms now, and he was pressing kisses all over her face—her cheeks, her temples, her nose, her forehead, and finally, her lips. As his lips merged with hers, her arms wrapped around his back, pulling him closer, closer, yet never close enough. How could she possibly say goodbye to him tomorrow?

When he finally pulled back, his eyes were shining with unshed tears, but there was a smile, too, nearly blinding her with its intensity. "I didn't...I wanted to hope that you would say yes, but I didn't dare. I didn't want to pressure you or decide for you, but...I just couldn't imagine letting you slip out of my life so soon after you came into it."

Her nod was fervent, her eyes searching his. "I know. I couldn't imagine it either. And...and I don't know how we're going to do this, Ben. I'm terrified, if I'm being honest. I don't have the first idea how to be in a long-distance relationship, and I'm so, so scared that the distance, the time apart, is going to be the end of us...but we have to try. We *have* to try, don't we?"

"Of course we do." His relief was evident. "It's not going to be easy, I know. But I really believe we can do it." Now, he was kissing her hands, first across the backs of her knuckles and then her palms, resting them on his cheeks. "I love you. I don't care if it's too soon to say it, because it's true. I've loved you for longer than I'm entirely aware...I think I loved you before I even liked you."

She snorted, unexpected joy in the middle of all the serious, heavy emotions of their impending separation. "First of all, how does that work? And second of all, how *dare* you not like me? I'm delightful!"

"You certainly are." He turned his face into her hand, placing another kiss there. "I just mean that before I knew you well enough to know that I liked you because you were smart or fun or cool...something about you got my attention. Kept tugging it in your direction, in fact. It was like I was being called home." He shrugged. "I don't know how these things work, Melody, but I felt like I was being pulled to you. And before you can get all cynical and say that's just attraction or pheromones or something, don't you dare. It was *you*. It's just that simple."

"Who am I to argue with that?" She pulled his face down to hers, his mouth against hers as she kissed him with everything she had. "And I love you, too. I don't know when it began, either, but I can't imagine my life without loving you."

They stayed there like that, embracing and sniffling and smiling and murmuring to each other, for far longer than was appropriate for the setting. There was plenty of work waiting for them on the other side of this moment, suitcases to be packed and long discussions to be had about how their relationship was going to work. But in that moment, wrapped around Ben and soaking in the warmth of his presence, Melody couldn't imagine breaking the spell and taking even a single step from that spot on the sidewalk. Tomorrow might bring a whole fleet of new concerns, but for tonight, she had Ben Kaya in her arms and all was right in the world.

It had been a late night, to no one's surprise. Between moments of packing up suitcases and setting aside items to be left behind, Melody took every moment to steal an embrace, a kiss, or a sweet nothing from Ben.

And there had been no sleep—how could she be expected to waste any of their precious time together on being unconscious, even if she got to spend those hours wrapped up in his arms? There would be time to sleep later, after the next day that would be full for both of them—full of travel or full of going through the motions in the office, mourning the new distance between them all the while.

Among the kisses and embraces, there were promises. Promises to text, to call, to video chat, and to save all their best stories to share with each other. There were plans for virtual dates and calendars compared to find the days where they could make arrangements to be together. It wasn't as if they could just meet in the middle, but Christmas in Dresden? A beach getaway in Turkey in the summer? A visit from Ben in the spring? All of those possibilities kept Melody's heart uplifted even when all it wanted to do was crack in two at the unfairness of being parted from this man by an entire ocean.

All too soon, the moment of departure was upon them, timed such that leaving for the office and leaving for the airport were happening at the same time. Whether that was a small mercy or a cruelty that prevented them from sharing a romantic moment of bidding each other farewell at the airport, Melody wasn't sure.

"I'll see you soon," he said, kissing her through her tears on the sidewalk yet again. "I promise."

"You'd better," she responded. "Don't you dare forget about me."

"How could I?" His eyes studied hers, bouncing back and forth between them. "That's impossible. I'll be thinking about you all day, counting down the minutes until we can talk on the phone."

"Me, too."

The waiting taxi driver glanced at his watch, reminding the lovebirds of the time.

"I love you," said Ben.

"I love you, too."

"We're going to figure this out. I promise."

"I know." One last kiss. "And I can't wait until that happens."

He kissed her knuckles one final time before stepping away. "You and me both. Just hold on to that belief. It'll be sooner than you think. Or that's what I'm holding onto, anyway."

When he was gone from sight, she sniffled once more and wiped her eyes. It was already harder to believe that things were going to work out in their favor without him there to remind her, but for him—for Ben, good man that he was—she would do her best.

On Monday morning, things were back to normal—or at least back to the normal that had existed pre-Generosity Exchange and pre-Ben coming into her life. It was a normal that had worked just fine for Melody for years, but which now she could barely stand.

She had woken up in her bed, in the tiny apartment she shared with Felicity, made herself breakfast, gotten dressed for the day, and made her way to the office, all of it happening like she was running on autopilot. Like no time had passed, nothing had changed, and Ben had never existed.

Only, he was on her mind the entire time. She wished he were there for all of it. Waking up with her, eating breakfast in silence with her while she waited for her caffeine to kick in and turn on her charm, walking hand-in-hand with her to the office.

That he, in contrast, wasn't there for any of it felt wrong. It was like a cruel joke of the universe, dangling what she really wanted—the partner she hadn't even known she'd been missing—in front of her and then ripping it away, putting a whole ocean of distance in between them for good measure.

The bright light—the *only* bright light—of the day was that Chloe was back, too, and she and Melody were about to be reunited. Even as frustrating and meddlesome as she could be, Melody had missed her friend, and the thought of seeing her face, of getting to hug her and gossip with her and work alongside her was a great consolation prize. If she couldn't have Ben in her life, at least she could have Chloe.

When Chloe arrived at the office a few moments after Melody, there was a chill in the air, a distance in her demeanor that took Melody aback. "Chloe!" she cried, throwing herself at her friend. "Oh my gosh, I'm so glad you're here."

Chloe stepped back, extricating herself from Melody's arms. "Yeah? You have a weird way of showing it."

"What do you mean?" Melody shook her head. "Did something change while you were in London and now you're no longer a fan of workplace PDA? You're anti hugs now?"

Chloe huffed and puffed as she made her way to her desk and took a seat. "Sure, that's it."

"No, seriously. What's going on?" Melody came closer, perching on the edge of Chloe's desk. "Talk to me."

"Oh, now you want to talk? It's convenient for you to talk to me now?"

"What do you—"

"I've been trying to talk to you all weekend. Hell, I figured I'd see you this weekend, you know, since we were both in the same city and all that. But no, you go totally radio silent and now you show up here like nothing is wrong and we're just two colleagues who have fun together in the office but never even check in with each other outside of it?"

Melody hung her head. "I'm sorry, Chloe. I just...I've been processing life without Ben, you know? It's not easy...it was hard to say goodbye to him, and now I'm just...trying to figure out how it all works, I guess."

Chloe was switching on her computer, setting up her workplace for her first day back in three months, all the while nodding sarcastically. "Well, that all sounds very challenging for you. Believe it or not, though, I wasn't trying desperately to get in touch with you this weekend because I was just *dying* to know how you were doing without your brand new boyfriend."

"I...I didn't think that." Melody recoiled. "I like to think I'm not the most self-centered person in the world, thinking a thing like that."

"No? Well, you certainly haven't gone out of your way to ask me how *I'm* doing with all of this. Ever since I told you about the program being canceled, every thought you've had, every word you've said to me, has been about how it impacts you and Ben. And that's it. The two people

Melody Critchfield cares about." Chloe gave her head a disappointed shake. "Did you ever even stop to wonder how *I* was doing with it? How it felt for me to pack up my whole life again and give up on a dream of my own?"

Melody was quiet, her mouth agape. Was that how she came across to Chloe, of all people? She racked her brain, trying to remember every interaction they'd had in the past week...even in the past three months...and she came up empty. She could remember pouring her heart out to Chloe, sure. But had that favor ever been returned? Had *she* ever been the listening ear on the phone while Chloe worked through something that was weighing on her mind, her heart?

"Chloe, I...I'm so sorry." Melody tried to move closer, to put her hand on her shoulder, but Chloe shrugged her away.

"Let's not do this right now. I'm glad you're aware." She gave a sneering smile. "They always say awareness is the first step, don't they?" The smile evaporated. "But it's going to take a little more than that before we're 'cool' again. I've got feelings of my own that need to be worked through, so I'm sure you can understand if I'm not really in the mood to hear right now about how sad you are that the guy who was technically your boyfriend for a day is on the other side of the world."

Melody felt her hackles rise at Chloe's words, her tone. "You *know* it was more than that. Don't be mean, Chloe."

But Chloe just scoffed. "Okay, then. If you suddenly care more about a man than you do about your job, it will truly be a sign of the impending apocalypse. So..."

She made a shooing motion in the direction of Melody's cubicle. "Back to work with you, then."

Melody walked in a daze the few steps back to her cubicle, sitting down to stare at the screen. What sort of bizarro reality was she in now, if Chloe wasn't even by her side?

But as the last weeks once again flew past in her mind's eye, her most egregious mistakes played on rapid repeat, making her wince each time. There had been hints there—there *must* have been—that Chloe felt dejected. A tone that implied she was growing weary of listening and not being heard, a sigh as she settled in to play armchair therapist. The dynamic between them had been off for quite some time, with one of them talking and one of them listening, and Melody was cringing at which side of that divide she fell on.

She was a bad friend. Maybe she'd always been a bad friend. Maybe that was why Chloe was—or at least had been until recently—her only real friend. Maybe that was why she and Felicity had never moved past the roommate stage into anything resembling friendship.

An old instinct kicked in, the same one that had kept her texting or calling Chloe every time she got frustrated or felt an unwanted emotion, only this time it was directed towards Ben. Should she tell him what was going on? Get his advice?

She shook her head at herself. What was the difference between treating Chloe like her own personal unpaid therapist and treating Ben that way? No, this seemed like something that she was going to need to unpack on her own...as soon as she had the time to do so.

Because just then, as if on cue, Mr. Richards materialized in the entrance to her cubicle. "Melody," he said with a curt nod. "Come with me."

As he turned on his heel and stalked back to his office, she gulped and got to her feet, hurrying along behind him. Whatever Mr. Richards had to say to her could usually be communicated in an email, so the fact that he was summoning her to his office couldn't be good, could it?

"Right," he said, as soon as she closed the office door behind her. "We need a plan for cleaning up this whole Handout Exchange debacle." He shuddered as if the program were a particularly frightening film. "We can't afford to have something like that come up again. Just a colossal waste of time and money."

"Really?" Melody asked, her pen poised over her pad to jot down some notes. "I was under the impression from the information Madeline Andrews shared previously that it was known to boost productivity and outcomes for all the participating organizations." If that was not, in fact, the case, then she was sure the other partners would need to know. These were non-profits and universities, after all, and they couldn't afford to be spending money they didn't have on programs that didn't make a difference.

"Yeah, yeah." Mr. Richards waved a dismissive hand. "That may be true for some of them, but I don't particularly care, now do I? No, I care about the fact that if we're going to make moves, if we're going to be taken seriously for what we do...we can't be aligning ourselves with those bleeding hearts and tree huggers." He shuddered again. "No, I've put in my time in this whole 'non-profit' space and I think I've had just about enough." He gestured towards her notebook and pen. "I don't know how this works, but I want you to find out for me. How can we move into the for-profit space? Get ourselves out of this hippie dippie network of freaks and get me invited to some networking events with the CEOs who are *actually* power players and not just wannabes?"

Melody's mouth was hanging open, her pen still poised over the paper. "You want me to do what?"

His gesture was a cross between requesting the bill in a restaurant, summoning a child, and waving goodbye, but it seemed to imply that with a few strokes of her pen she could capture every word he'd said *and* make it make sense. Find a solution to this seemingly unsolvable problem of his. "You heard me," he said finally. "Just...figure it out." With a pointed nod towards the door, he turned back to his desk, and Melody took the cue and left.

"What the..." When she arrived back at her cubicle, she dropped into her chair, head in her hands. She didn't have the first clue where to begin on a task like this, nor did she particularly care to start. After all, she had come to EduPowerment for its mission, for the role that it played in creating educational opportunities around the world, and in no small part because it was a non-profit. It wasn't that there hadn't been businesses with missions she'd believed in...there certainly had been. But EduPowerment had been special, thanks in no part to Mr. Richards and entirely to the legacy of his mother. It had been a special place with an exemplary mission, *in spite of* the fact that Mr. Richards was now at the helm.

Melody sat at her desk until lunchtime, going through the motions of a normal work day, yet refusing to touch the latest task that Mr. Richards had given her. There were other marketing campaigns to check in with, to tweak the copy on, and she kept herself busy doing that. All the while, her mind was racing a mile a minute with the revelation Mr. Richards had dropped on her that morning and its implications.

Did she want to keep working for him after he had single-handedly been responsible for the Generosity Exchange program falling apart? Even worse, did she want to keep working for him after he turned EduPowerment into some kind of for-profit nightmare that was all about padding his salary while the existing programs' beneficiaries were treated as afterthoughts?

The more she thought, the clearer it all became. This place no longer aligned with her values. And it stung to realize that. She had given so much of herself—*of my youth,* she thought, before reminding herself that she was too young to use that phrase unironically—to an organization that would give her nothing in return. Certainly, there was the satisfaction of the part she had played in furthering EduPowerment's programs, all of which she still believed in.

But had it been worth the sacrifice of her free time, her health, and her personal life? She wasn't sure any longer that had ever been the case.

And that realization felt like the ground had dropped out from underneath her. If it hadn't been worth it, then what was? If she couldn't wrap up her life in meaning thanks to her job, then where could she find that meaning?

Ben. Her first thought was him, but she immediately wrinkled her nose at the thought. Ben was a good man—the best, actually. But asking that of him was a sure-fire recipe for the demise of their relationship. Not only was it not fair to expect someone else to give her life meaning, but it was also unfair to that person to expect them to be in love with someone who existed only to please them. A shell of a person, dancing around him like a satellite when he deserved to be with a whole, complicated being with her own world of likes, dislikes, interests, dreams, passions...

It's not just him that deserves that from me. I deserve it, too. She needed to go back to basics. Figure out for herself why she was here on this planet and what was going to give meaning to her lifetime.

"Right then, so...that sounds easy," she muttered under her breath. "No big deal at all."

Talking this through with Chloe would be helpful, but clearly wasn't an option. That reminder crested over Melody's consciousness like a rogue wave of guilt. Not only did she not know what her purpose in life was, which, to be fair, was a massive, monumental question...but she also didn't even know the simple truths like how to be a good friend. All of it left her feeling like a colossal failure, counting down the minutes until the day was over and she could retreat home, bury herself in her blankets, and settle in for a good wallow.

And that is precisely what she did. The moment the clock struck five, Melody was out the door, letting nothing come between her and the cocoon that was her bed. She resisted the temptation to try to talk to Chloe, which was easy enough to do, considering that she seemed to be avoiding Melody. She didn't even check her messages from

Ben or send him one to let him know she was heading home. If she had, he would have suggested a video chat, and she was too embarrassed and too much of a mess to face him right now.

When he had been with her, even in the last moments before they had parted, she had been someone different: Melody Critchfield, who loved her job, was a competent colleague, good friend, and delightful girlfriend. Now, she wasn't sure how many of those things she still had going for her. Loved her job? That didn't seem to be the case anymore. Good friend? Chloe would disagree with that. And delightful girlfriend? She felt more like an empty shell, a human imposter.

And that was the part that scared her the most.

Alone in her room, Melody buried herself in her blankets and stared at the ceiling as if she might find the answers to all of it there. What a horrible cliché it was to learn—or perhaps remember—that her worth wasn't inherently tied to her job. But it had given young Melody, fresh out of college, such comfort to find a job doing something she believed in. Idealist that she was, she had struggled to find places to even apply to, always asking herself if she believed in the mission of the company, if she supported their ethics, if she was comfortable with where her salary would be coming from.

And people had applauded her for it, even if some of them had raised their eyebrows at her apparent aversion to finding a job that actually paid well. She heard, "You're a better person than I am," enough times that she took it on as an identity, and it wasn't long before the connection was formed in her brain: her worth as a person was irreversibly tied to her selfless career decisions and nothing else.

For the first time since she had started working at EduPowerment, a cynical thought crossed her mind. What if people like Mr. Richards didn't pay their employees such low salaries because that was what the organization could afford but because they knew that young idealists would consider it noble to scrape by doing too much work and barely making enough money to pay their bills? That thought wouldn't have found a foothold a few days before, but now? With Mr. Richards talking about changing the very structure under which EduPowerment operated? Well, now *anything* was possible.

"If the meaning of life isn't my job, then…what if it's actually about everything I've been neglecting? Taking care of my health and sleeping properly and having a hobby and…" She sighed. "Taking the time to be a good friend. Just enjoying being with someone because it's fun and it feels light and we laugh when we're together."

And that sealed it. Her first order of business was to make things right with Chloe. After that—and *only* after that—it was time to make some serious decisions about her future and her career.

The next morning, Melody got to work early for a different reason, busying herself to arrange things before Chloe arrived for the day.

She was still in Chloe's cubicle thirty minutes later when she entered, her eyes immediately widening at the sight awaiting her. Melody had arranged a vase full of flowers—yellow roses because they were the symbol of friendship and tiger lilies because Chloe loved them—along with the cookies she had spent the previous evening baking. She had restrained herself from writing her apology in a card, opting to save it for the face-to-face conversation that was about to happen.

"What is all this?" Chloe asked as she set down her bag and slowly took her seat.

"Grand gesture?" Melody said, holding out her hands to encompass the contents of the table before she turned to Chloe, meeting her gaze. "I'm so sorry, Chloe. I've taken you for granted, and I haven't been the friend you deserve. Not while you've been in London, and not for a long time before that, either. But I want to be better, and I'm going to work on it."

"Yeah?" Chloe's face had lit up, aglow with a childlike hope. "I think I'd really like that. I could use a friend, you know."

"And I'm so sorry that you didn't have one these last three months." Her eyes searched Chloe's. "But if it's possible to make up for lost time, I'd like to try to do that now. I want to hear all about London, all about your experience and what you liked and what it felt like leaving and what you think you want to do now. Can we do that?"

Chloe was already nodding. "I would love that." She looked around her at the office surrounding them. "Now's not really the time, though. Don't you have, like, a ton of work to do, as always?"

Melody waved that thought away with her hand. "You're more important. Why don't we have lunch together, somewhere that's not the office or the kitchen—"

"Or sitting at our desks eating while we keep working? Who would do such a thing?" Chloe quirked an eyebrow at her.

"Not me. Not anymore. What do you think...lunch?"

"Lunch." Chloe nodded. "It can't come soon enough. And thanks for the cookies, the flowers...the whole grand gesture. I have to say, a gal could get used to this."

Melody nodded. "As she well should. If you don't get a grand gesture every now and then, then what's the point of any of this?"

When lunchtime came, the friends found themselves a bench at the park across the street to eat the meals they had brought from home. As Melody listened, Chloe told her about London and the adventures she had enjoyed there. Melody laughed at the antics of Chloe's coworkers, feeling the tiniest twinge of envy at the fun she had so evidently filled the last three months with.

And when Chloe came to the part of the story where it was time for her to leave London, her voice and her eyes had filled with emotion. She hadn't been ready to go, not by a long shot, and she likely wouldn't have been even at the end of the full year. Her heart was still in London, much like Melody's heart was still with Ben.

"What are you going to do?" Melody asked. "You shouldn't stay here if it's making you miserable."

Chloe leveled a look back at her that gave Melody goosebumps. "I could say the same to you, you know."

"Sure, but we're not talking about me." Melody dismissed the barb, fully intending to revisit it on her own later.

Chloe's nod was thoughtful. "I'll go back there somehow, I'm sure. I haven't figured it out yet, but..." She shrugged. "Well, they say where there's a will, there's a way and I'm counting on that being true."

"So you're going to leave EduPowerment?"

Chloe winced. "I mean...yeah. I think my time here is up." Her eyes darted between Melody's. "Are you mad? I'm not doing this to try to hurt you or get back at you for feeling frustrated at you."

Melody's eyes widened at that. "I didn't think you were. I just figured you were doing what was best for you." She reached over and placed her hand on one of Chloe's. "And I want you to be happy. I want that even more than I want you to be near me."

"I want you to be happy, too." The smile Chloe returned to her was warm, sincere. "For a long time I thought working together and complaining about work with each other was what made us both happy. But I think we are both capable of *far* more happiness than that."

"You're right." Realization dawned on Melody, a knowing so deep and so sure that it was laughable that she'd ever thought differently. It was the kind of *knowing* that changed everything.

Chloe nodded, oblivious to the change that was happening inside Melody before her very eyes. "I am. So think about it, okay? Before you end up staying at EduPowerment until Mr. Richards leeches every last ounce of life and goodness and joy right out of you?"

Melody shook her head. "That won't happen. It has to change. *Now.* I can't do this anymore." She met Chloe's eyes, hers widening with what she was about to admit. "I have to quit, Chloe."

With a resolve that surprised her in its intensity, Melody made her way to Mr. Richards's office and knocked on the door, waiting to hear his grunt of acknowledgement before she opened it and entered.

"Well?" he said, without looking up. "How's the progress on our little project? Did you figure it out yet?"

She shook her head but didn't speak yet, forcing him to look up at her.

When he did, his annoyance was evident in his sneer. "Come on, now. It's not that hard. Do I have to do everything around here myself?"

That got a laugh out of Melody. "Do everything yourself? In what reality is that even remotely the truth?" She shook her head. "If you didn't have me here, nothing would get done."

His face turned beet red, bordering on purple. "You have a lot of nerve—"

"I don't, actually. Or at least I haven't, not until now." She crossed her arms over her chest. "But you've gone too far, and I guess enough is enough, even for me. So I came here to tell you that I'm leaving. I can't work for you anymore."

"Absolutely not. This isn't how it's done. There's a right way to do things, and this—" He gestured vaguely in her direction. "This isn't it."

"With all due respect, sir, I believe we have crossed the line of the right way to do things some time ago. It probably began when you first started assigning me tasks that weren't within the scope of my job, and I played a role in that, too, by not objecting at the time. I accept my responsibility for that. But now...well, now it *has* gone too far. I am not your Girl Friday, nor am I your personal assistant. And it is time for me to find a new position where my talents will be utilized and where I can have some semblance of work-life balance."

Mr. Richards scoffed. "Well, good luck with that, dearie. And don't come crawling back to me when you realize just how good you had things here."

"I'm sure I won't be doing that, sir."

He waved towards the door. "If that's all, then you're free to leave."

She was surprised that it was that easy, that he had accepted her resignation without a fight.

He leveled one final barb in her direction before she walked out of his life—and out of EduPowerment for the last time. "This is what I get for hiring a fresh graduate, isn't it? Remind me to do things differently next time."

Without looking back, she spoke through gritted teeth. "It is no longer my job to do that. Goodbye."

Home again at the end of the day, Melody flopped onto her bed again, all the heaviness she had felt the day before replaced by lightness and possibility. The hope of change.

She pulled out her phone and opened Ben's messages, smiling as she caught up on the play-by-play of his day. She had written to him yesterday only to say it had been a long day and wish him a good night, promising they would talk more today.

And now, well, now it was time to catch him up on all of it.

She dialed his number, and he answered on the first ring. "Hello there," his gorgeous voice crooned across the line. "How's my favorite person?"

She sat up. "Better than she's been in a long time. I quit my job, Ben. I just...I want to be happy. And it needed to go. And as I'm saying all of that aloud, I realize it might sound a little, well...impulsive? But I don't care. I don't know what I'm going to do next, but I know I'm going to prioritize being happy."

To carry Ben and Melody through to their happily ever after, turn to **page 311**

But there was a crack in her resolve, something she became aware of only as a dramatic sigh escaped through her lips.

"I *am* thinking about it, Chloe. How could I not? Doesn't it just sound like the most exciting, most wonderful opportunity? The professional challenges alone would be amazing. Just think of all the new situations we'd have to navigate, the cross-cultural competence required...don't roll your eyes at me, Chloe. You might be thinking about this like a year-long spring break trip, but let's not forget that it's a *work*-sponsored experience."

"A work-sponsored spring break, sure." Chloe stuck out her tongue at Melody, then rolled her eyes when Melody's expression didn't crack. "Fine, yes, I'm sure it would be a great professional experience and look really awesome on our resumes."

"I'm not talking about resumes! I'm talking about real-world experience. The mission of EduPowerment. The missions of all these partner institutions. Seeing real impact on real lives through the work we all do. If that doesn't light a fire under your butt to do the work we do here, then what will?"

"Touché," said Chloe with a nod. "It's definitely not our paychecks lighting that fire. Mine is good for about the spark you'd get from using a box of matches that fell into the toilet. Yours probably isn't much better than that, huh?"

Melody bristled at her friend's words. "It's enough for me, Chloe. I've gotten a raise since I started, and even without that, I'm still doing just fine. We may not be rich by American standards, but when we look at global wealth distribution—"

"I know." Chloe cut her off. "I know how lucky we all are just to have roofs over our heads and three meals a day. How could I not know that? I work *here*. I'm *your* friend. I'm reminded how lucky I am all the damn time, and in particular every time I have something to complain about." She looked down, shaking her head. "God, Mel, it's exhausting. Sometimes I just want you to listen, you know? I'm not always looking for a perspective check."

Melody winced. "I'm sorry, Chloe. I guess I just talk to you the same way I talk to myself. I never considered that it might actually be super annoying. I'll try to do better." She gave her friend a tentative smile. "Which of the positions are you excited about?"

"Oh, we'll get to that. Don't think I didn't notice your attempt to distract me from the fact that you, apparently, guilt and shame yourself for feeling something even remotely resembling ungratefulness. We're going to be talking about that at some point." For how sweet-looking and practically pocket-sized Chloe was, she sure could level Melody with a look.

"Duly noted," said Melody with a pained smile.

"Good, glad we got that out of the way. Now back to that fun and exciting question you asked me..." Her eyes were practically twinkling, something Melody was sure she'd never seen an eye do prior to that moment. "I've got Ireland on my list. London, too...got to at least consider all the English-speaking countries considering my foreign language skills or lack thereof, unless high school Spanish counts. Oh!" Her eyes brightened even further, lit from within by the idea that had seemingly just occurred to her. "This could be a great opportunity to brush up on my Spanish! Let's see what partners there are in South America or...ooh! Dominican Republic! Guatemala! Mexico! Or what if I could learn French? My God, Melody, the possibilities are seriously endless!"

Chloe's excitement was so effervescent, so contagious, that Melody couldn't resist getting pulled into its vortex. She leaned over her friend's shoulder, reading the postings together while the thrill of possibility seeped into her bones.

She had thought she could resist the pull, that she'd be able to tamp down that initial thrill she'd felt and resume her business as usual with no possibility of—or need for—an international move on the horizon. But as she looked at this list with fresh eyes—with Chloe's eyes—she was struck by a new and completely enticing idea.

Every single city listed on this document, every single partner institution...each one was its own universe. Each one came with colleagues and cafes and museums and paths to walk and people to bump into that were completely unknown to her. If she chose one of these positions and packed up her life here to immerse herself in that world, she'd be gaining more than just a new professional experience. She might meet a new dear friend, discover her new favorite dessert, or…well, there was always *that* possibility. Meeting someone. The "one," if such a thing existed. She shook her head to dislodge that thought from her brain. What a strange turn this morning had taken, from being berated by Mr. Richards for her tardiness to wondering if soulmates existed.

But it did add another layer of pressure to the decision, didn't it? In one of these cities, Melody might find the great love of her life. In another, she might find nothing more than heartbreak and disappointment. It was almost enough to make her choose *not* to choose. To stay put where everything was safe and predictable and familiar. Better that than the wrong choice.

"What's that look on your face about?" Chloe's suspicious eyebrow quirk interrupted her thoughts. "What are you thinking right now?"

"Well, I…" Melody paused, surprised by the words she knew she was about to speak. "I caught myself thinking about this all like it was a foregone conclusion. Like I was already in the process of picking the best option from the list and then I started to talk myself out of it again. But I realized with that thought that apparently I had already decided that this whole thing was, in fact, for me."

"I knew it!" Chloe squealed, clapping her hands. "This is so exciting! But wait…why are you already trying to talk yourself out of it again?"

"It's silly." Melody waved her hand dismissively. "I was just getting philosophical, I guess. We don't have to get into it."

"You, philosophical? I'm shocked. *Shocked*, I tell you!" Chloe dipped her head with one aggressive nod. "Spill!"

"It's just that…when you make a choice…*any* choice, but especially a big choice like this one, there's the possibility of making the *wrong* choice, isn't there? As much as this could be exciting and wonderful and life-changing and life mission-defining…the opposite could be true, too. What if you choose a place and it ends up being the place where you have a car crash or meet the person who breaks your heart or, I don't know, there's a massive, scary earthquake?"

Chloe blew out a sigh. "Those are some real possibilities, Mel. But isn't life full of risk? Couldn't you have a car crash right here in Michigan? Or have your heart broken by a seemingly nice guy you meet on one of the apps? It's true that an earthquake is unlikely, but there are certainly other natural disasters, don't you worry. How about a tornado? Or even a particularly nasty case of food poisoning? They say if you don't want to take a risk, don't leave your house, but even that isn't exactly true, is it? You could slip and fall in the shower, or forget how electricity works and stick a knife in the toaster to retrieve a burned piece of bread and end up regretting it for the rest of your very short life."

Melody scoffed. "So you don't think this choice matters then? You think, what, things are going to work out just the way they're *supposed* to, whether that's good things or terrible things happening?"

Chloe shrugged. "I don't know, Melody. You're the philosopher, not me. I just think asking questions like this might be the perfect excuse to justify acting on your fears. Not taking a chance that you *know* you need to take. Reminding yourself—by reminding me yet again—why you stay committed to a job where you're overworked and underappreciated by waxing on and on about right and wrong choices."

That blunt honesty left Melody gasping like a goldfish, unable to find her next words. "Do you really think that's what I'm doing?"

Chloe paused, thinking through her next words. "Maybe not intentionally. I mean, let's face it. You *do* talk about the mission of this place more than any other person that works here. Probably even more than Mr. Richards at the annual board meeting. I know it matters a lot to you, what we do here. But that truly doesn't mean you need to sacrifice everything else in your life just to further the admittedly important work we're doing at EduPowerment."

Melody shook her head, blowing out a sigh. "This is...a *lot* for a Tuesday morning, Chloe. If I promise to be a very good girl and think my way through this...um...some *other* time, then can we move on?"

Chloe looked skeptical. "I know you're trying to appease me, but I also know there's no chance you're going to keep talking about this and letting me make you this level of uncomfortable." A hint of a smirk appeared at the corner of her mouth. "Want to know how you *could* get me to drop it?"

"More than anything."

Chloe tapped on the top right corner of her monitor. "Tell me your first choice. And then get your butt back in your cubicle and apply for it."

Why was it easier to act on what she wanted when she was doing it "for" her friend? A lightness appeared in Melody's stomach, replacing the lead weight that had settled there while she'd been hemming and hawing over the merits of right and wrong choices. Having the decision of whether to apply or not—just *apply*, not even actually commit to going—taken out of her hands, the conclusion reached by her dear friend...it was a relief. Her FOMO was at bay, vanquished by the steel will of one Chloe Allen, and now all Melody had to think about was which of the partner institutions was at the top of her list.

She smiled at Chloe, thanking her with the warmth in her gaze even if she wasn't able to bring herself to say the words. "That's easy enough. It's this one..."

To choose Izmir as Melody's top choice, turn to **page 158**

To choose Dresden as Melody's top choice, turn to **page 222**

124

She steeled herself and nodded. It wasn't just about what was best for her and her career. It was about what was best for Ben, too. And he had things of his own that needed to be dealt with, a whole life to get back to that didn't include her.

"It's for the best," she said. "I can't move across the world to be with you, and you can't move across the world to be with me. We both know that would be ridiculous." She shook her head. "And I don't think a long distance relationship when you've only been out once is a great idea either, do you? Let's face it, we would just be making things harder for ourselves."

"No, it's not that simple." Ben's eyes were desperate, his hands coming to her cheeks to hold her gaze to his own. "I don't want to throw this away, and I know you don't want to either. Do you? Do you really? Can you look me in the eye and tell me you want to walk away from me and forget I ever existed? That we ever meant anything to each other?"

The backs of her eyes were burning, tears threatening to spill over the longer she held his gaze. She pushed back with all her strength, breaking free from his grasp and from his gaze. "We're at work, Ben. We can't behave like this with each other here." She took another step back, moving towards her own cubicle. "We'll talk later."

Melody went to her desk and busied herself with the fallout from the dissolution of the Generosity Exchange program. It wasn't as if she didn't have plenty that needed to be done. From the sounds of it Mr. Richards was going to be expecting things to be back to business as usual within the next couple of days and today was the only time that was really allotted for all the program participants to tie up their loose ends and make arrangements to get back to their homes.

She kept her hands busy, sending off emails and tidying up her workspace, but even though her hands were occupied, her mind was with Ben.

Of course she didn't want things to be finished between them, not before they even had a chance to begin. But what choice did she really have? She couldn't ask him to change his life for her. Neither one of them could uproot their life to be closer to the other one. And she didn't want to be the one to hold him back from realizing his full potential, nor did she want to be held back from fulfilling her own. She knew she was good at her job, and that job had kept her warm through a few years now as a single person, so there was no reason to believe that it couldn't continue to do so.

No, her mind was made up. Even if it made her sad, this was the way things had to be.

At the end of the day, when Ben approached her, his face fell at whatever he saw in her expression. "So that's how it's going to be, then?" he asked. "I don't get to have a say in whether we try to make this work? You've already decided, haven't you?"

"You can say your piece," she said. "I can't promise it will change my mind, but it wouldn't be fair to make you leave things unspoken between us."

He gestured with the tip of his head towards the door and she followed him outside, away from the office where they could have some privacy for their conversation. They stopped in the shade of a tree and Ben turned to her, taking both of her hands in his own.

"You know, Melody, that I really believe we could be something great. That you don't find a connection like this every day. And that connection, the possibility of true love...well, that's worth sacrifice. Isn't it?"

She sighed, her head tipping to the side as her reaction to his words fought to break free.

"Don't say anything, please," he said. "I mean, if you're going to disagree, change your mind, tell me we're meant to be...then sure. Go ahead and say it. But if you're holding on to the idea that this is going to be over..." He exhaled deeply. "I just don't think I can hear it. I mean, I accept it...I respect your wishes. But if you say something right now that spells it all out like that, I think those words will haunt me forever."

He lifted one hand to her cheek, his thumb stroking gently across it. "So? Is there anything you want to say?"

To tell Ben that it's for the best to end things, turn to **page 266**

To tell him that you don't want it to be over, turn to **page 96**

128

With the realization that she and Ben were going to be working in close proximity, it was clear to Melody that there was only one way to proceed: clear boundaries.

She didn't need him and his obnoxiously handsome face distracting her from her important work, and she couldn't avoid him entirely either. They *did* have to work together, after all.

"This is *so* inconvenient," she grumbled under her breath. "The worst luck, really." Why couldn't she be working alongside someone who *didn't* complicate things with their excessive friendliness, distracting face, and unceasing smile? She already had one work friend, after all. It wasn't like she needed another one.

I miss Chloe, she thought. *This was all so much easier with her and I can't believe now I have to work side-by-side with a boy. Yes, that's right. He hasn't even earned the title of "man."*

But was this really about Chloe and nothing to do with the fact that Ben was a dangerous combination of attractive and friendly that made Melody want to hide under her desk until the coast was clear? Request a transfer to a department far, far away from him? As far as she was willing to admit out loud, sure. That was absolutely and undeniably the reason for her distaste for Ben.

But if she were writing in a secret diary, spilling her heart and soul onto the page before she burned the evidence so that no earthly eyes would discover it...she might just admit that Ben felt like the kind of person who could break her heart before lunch time. His charisma and warmth could make her feel special, pull her right in to feeling like she mattered to him, like she was someone he uniquely cared about. And then as soon as she discovered—as was sure to be the case with someone like Ben, she could tell it just by looking at him—that his warmth had nothing to do with her but was, in fact, just who he was as a person...she was likely to be crushed.

On a normal day, Melody Critchfield didn't need to feel special. She had a job that she cared about that let her make a positive impact on the world, and that gave her more meaning and purpose than any man ever could.

But if she dared to let a man make her feel like she was special, then how silly and foolish and utterly stupid would she feel to discover that none of it was real. She couldn't risk that. Heartbreak like that was sure to set her back at least a week, to leave her reeling and broken and sad when she had so many more worthy and important ways to be spending her time.

Like her work, which was certainly what she should be doing right now.

And with that thought, Melody straightened her posture, switched on her computer, and lost herself in the world waiting for her inside her email inbox.

By the time she resurfaced for lunch, Melody had nearly forgotten about Ben. It was only when she saw his large frame hunched over his own desk that felt a pang at the absence of Chloe in the station next to hers. She even missed her friend's well-intentioned teasing, reminding Melody to get up to eat or stretch her legs.

Before she could stop herself, a loud sigh escaped her lips. Ben wheeled around, concern on his face. "Are you okay?" he asked. "You sounded so dejected, like you just got some terrible news or something."

Melody steeled herself against his charms. "Just disappointed. Missing my old office bestie, who's in the Generosity Exchange program. It feels like this year can't go by fast enough." Yes, it felt unnecessarily harsh to remind Ben that he wasn't her favorite cubicle neighbor, but if it helped her establish the space between them that she needed in order to preserve her sanity, then so be it.

His face fell ever so slightly. "I'm sure you miss your friend, but I hope I can help fill that void while she's gone. If there's anything you would have gone to Chloe for, then feel free to come to me instead. I can be your surrogate Chloe." He flashed her that winning smile, and her fortress against him and his charms nearly crumbled.

She clenched her hands into fists behind her back, digging her finger nails into her palms until she felt a pinch of pain, anchoring her back to the present moment. "I appreciate the offer, but it's impossible to replace a friend like Chloe."

Melody made her way to the kitchen to retrieve her lunch from the refrigerator. She felt a twinge of discomfort as the image of Ben's downward-turned lips flashed in her mind. It didn't feel right to be cold, clipped like that, and she was tempted to turn around and offer him some kindness instead. Maybe a genuine offer of help would get things off on the right foot.

She turned on her heel and nearly slammed right into a solid wall of chest. As she stepped back and looked up, her eyes met the same lips that had just been haunting her mind, though they were now turned up rather than down at the corners.

"Whoa there," Ben smiled at her. "Don't you know you have to use your turn signal if you're going to make a U-turn like that?"

And just like that, whatever desire she had felt to play nice with him vanished without a trace. Maybe it was that cocky smile or the way his eyes felt like they looked a little *too* intently at her, but there was something about this guy that definitely made her uncomfortable. Like she couldn't help but be mean to him, even if the better part of her had wanted to be nice.

Something twinged on the periphery of her consciousness. Wasn't that how she had behaved around the boys she had had crushes on in high school? Middle school even? It had all been so uncomfortable, that cocktail of hormones, puberty, and crushes, that she had literally *never* known how to interact with a boy she liked. All of her attempts at being clever and cute had manifested themselves as nothing more than poorly executed jokes and teasing that had seemed more like unkindness.

That had been the case in the past, sure. But it was decidedly *not* the case with this Ben character now. No, the iciness she was directing his way wasn't any kind of attempt at flirting with him. If anything, these were *boundaries* she was establishing.

Yes, that's it, she told herself. *Boundaries are so important, aren't they? And I'm setting* boundaries *with the hot new guy at work. Look at me go, learning about boundaries like all the other adults—apparently—are.*

Melody made a mental note to report back her success with boundaries to Chloe later. She had heard that word too many times from her friend—granted, it was usually in the context of setting boundaries with Mr. Richards and work in general, but still—not to take it to heart, it seemed.

Melody huffed an approximation of a laugh at Ben's joke, nearly too late for him to realize it was a response to his comment, and then spun around again, once again headed to the kitchen. She would just grab her lunch and then take it back to her desk, eating in blissful silence there while getting some more work done.

Ben fell into step next to her. "I, er…where are you going so fast?" He put his hands up when she shot a glare in his direction. "Sorry, I'm sure that's not my business. There's just a group lunch thing going on today, and I was wondering if you were going to join us. I didn't know if you knew, since you seemed to have your head down working all day…" Ben trailed off once he seemingly realized he wasn't getting a reaction out of Melody.

It felt wrong not to at least say *something* to him, though. Her parents hadn't raised her to be outright rude to people, even if she didn't like them.

"No, thanks." She gave him a tight-lipped smile, once again *nailing* her professional boundaries, she reminded herself. "I've got a lot of work to do today, and I don't really have time to hang around and chat with everyone, though I'm sure you'll all have a nice time."

Ben's expression closed up as her words landed, almost as if he had seen the door to their potential for friendship slamming in his face. "Okay, then. Didn't want you to miss out, but I see that you can take care of yourself. Have a good lunch, then."

Melody had arrived in front of the refrigerator by then, opening it quickly to grab her salad and retreat back to her desk. The sounds of the luncheon reached the edge of her awareness, but she snuffed out any desire to socialize before it could begin. "Not what you're here for," she muttered to herself as she once again spun on her heel, this time making her final retreat back to the haven of her desk.

Ben returned to his desk half an hour later, as much as Melody tried not to notice. The way her desk was positioned, it was impossible to miss his movements around the office. While that might not be a problem if it were, say, Chloe's comings and goings she was monitoring, she would prefer to have as little awareness of Ben as possible.

On that note, maybe it was time to rearrange things a bit, she thought as she got to her feet. *These desks weren't bolted down, were they?* If she could create just a little physical space between them, that might help represent the much greater emotional space in between them, the divide that she had no intention of bridging.

Ten minutes later, she was grunting and groaning while trying to shove her desk—it was much heavier than it looked—as far from Ben's as she could get it when a voice sounded behind her.

"Need some help?"

Melody managed to keep herself from letting another groan out—the first one had been decidedly unladylike and she'd regretted it as soon as it had squeaked out—before turning around to give Ben a tight-lipped smile.

"I've just about got it, I think. Thanks, though."

"Oh, come on. Let me help." He rolled up his sleeves as he stepped closer, and she did her best not to eyeball his forearms. It was true what they said, that men's forearms were like catnip. Irresistible. *Did they really say that?* Melody wondered. *Or was it just Chloe who said that?*

With Ben at one end of the desk, pushing, and Melody at the other end, pulling and positioning, they made quick work of the reconfiguration of her office. While her end of the desk had felt shockingly light and nearly made her feel like her efforts had been unnecessary, she still wouldn't give him the satisfaction of thinking his male muscles had been an indispensable help. She could have done it herself, and she would have, too...if he hadn't butted in and come to show off.

"That's good like that. Thanks." She wiped her hands off on her thighs and gave Ben her most dismissive, our-work-here-is-done smile and began to reposition the items on top of her desk.

But when she looked back, Ben was still standing there, studying the layout of her new workspace. It was true that it was a bit unusual, especially compared with the setup most of their colleagues enjoyed. But she couldn't back down now.

"Are you sure you like it like this?" Ben asked. "It feels a bit awkward, with your back to the door like that."

Melody nodded. "It's more for me, my focus. It was distracting the other way, and I need to focus on my work."

"Ah." Ben bit his lip, thinking. "So...am I right in thinking this change might have something to do with me?"

Melody could play along. "I don't know what you mean."

"I think you do, and I'm trying to decide if I should take it personally." He looked concerned, and she almost felt a flash of remorse—*almost*. "Did I do something to offend you?"

"How could that be the case? We've barely interacted. It's not about you. I just don't like being distracted at work."

Ben didn't look convinced. "If you insist, then I won't push the matter." He started to move away from her, back towards his own desk. "I do hope we can be friendly, though, Melody. We will be working alongside each other for the next year, and it would be nice to have a friend, you know."

Melody grumbled under her breath. "I think you'll be just fine in the friend department." Who wouldn't want to be friends with Ben, a friendly coworker who made sure everyone was invited to special lunches?

"What was that?" Ben leaned back towards her, as if he hadn't heard what she'd said. His face, however, gave him away, and that was what gave her the courage to say what she had said louder. "Do you have something against friends?"

Melody sniffed. "Of course not. If anything, it's the lack of focused work time that any of us are getting today that is causing me stress. You know, we do have important work to do here, and it seems as if everyone has decided it should just be social hour all day long."

Ben laughed, and she couldn't help but feel that it was directed *at* her. "Would you begrudge people having a bit of fun from time to time? Truly? How do you expect a team to stay motivated without that?"

"I'm not a human resources expert, Ben. I just know that the *mission* of what we do here is the most important thing. More important than my friendship with you or your friendship with everyone else in the office. Anyway." She turned away from him, back to the pile of work waiting for her on her desk. "If we're done here, then I've got a lot of work to do. I'm sure you do, too."

And even though her attention was focused intently on the desk in front of her, Melody could feel that Ben was still standing there, mouth open like a goldfish.

Not that she cared. She couldn't afford the time to care, even if she'd wanted to—she hadn't been kidding about the work that needed her attention. Mr. Richards had already emailed her about three different projects he wanted her to "have a look over" since lunchtime.

And even if it kept her busy, even if she didn't quite know how she would manage adding these new "top priority tasks" onto her to-do list that was already full of high priority items, she was happy to do it. Spending time and energy on meaningful work that had a tangible impact on lives all over the world? Yes, please. Spending time and energy on the handsome yet obnoxious stranger the next desk over who wanted to be her friend? Not a chance.

In the evening, Melody worked from the living room couch, rubbing her eyes with tiredness from entirely too much screen time in one day. But she couldn't stop working on this project—not when she still hadn't come up with the right hook for Mr. Richards's latest pet project.

A ringing cut through her thoughts, jolting her back to the moment as she checked the time on the corner of her computer screen. It was nearly ten o'clock, and two thoughts occurred simultaneously: when was the last time her phone had actually rung, and who in the world was calling her this late? Or even calling her at all, rather than simply sending a text?

A quick glance at her phone answered that question and brought a smile to her face.

"Chloe!" she exclaimed as she answered the phone. "How are you? I miss you already!"

"I'm good! Tired, though." Chloe's voice sounded tinny and far away, though it was possible that was just Melody's imagination working overtime.

"Of course you are. It's no joke adjusting to a new time zone."

Chloe snorted. "You're not kidding. Jet lag has me all messed up. I know I should be tired, but I'm just not. Maybe you can tell me about work and that will lull me right to sleep, since nothing else seems to be working."

Melody chuckled at the thought. "Further proof that you and I are, in fact, total opposites." She sighed. "Alright, then. I'll give you your bedtime story, but know that this is coming at great personal cost to me, since the same story that's going to put you to sleep is going to keep me up through half the night."

"Ooh." Chloe's tone conveyed textbook sarcasm. "Let me guess. Mr. Richards has twelve *exciting new projects* for you, and they're all priority number one?"

"You are actually wrong," said Melody, "Though your attitude has been noted for future reference." She sighed. "Actually, if you want to hear something *interesting* about work, how about the fact that I think I have an enemy? My first one ever, if you can believe it."

"Oh, I can believe that Little Miss Pleasant to a Fault never made an enemy before. But I am shocked—*shocked*, I tell you—to hear that you have one now. Spill!"

"Okay, so." Melody settled deeper into the couch, getting comfortable to tell the story. "His name is Ben, and I can't really explain it, but there's just something about him that gets under my skin, I guess. And even worse, I think he knows it and he's actively making it worse. Of course, we have to work in close proximity, too, which just makes everything like an actual nightmare. I'm trying to figure out how to make work more tolerable when he's right there in my face all the time, but it's proving rather difficult."

"Ben…" Chloe sounded like she was chewing on the name, trying to uncover its true flavor. "He sounds hot. Is he hot?"

Melody let out an exasperated sigh. "Honestly, Chloe, it's like you're not even listening to me at this point. And how the hell can someone *sound* hot?"

"Well, it's a good name, for starters. And then there's the fact that he apparently 'gets under your skin,' which sounds like sexual tension if I've ever heard of such a thing. Honestly, I don't know. It's not an exact science, is it? Figuring out if people are hot when you've only heard, like, three sentences about them? It's more of an art. A psychic art, actually. But it's worth pointing out that you didn't actually answer the question. So?"

"So what?"

"Gah, Melody! Is Ben freaking hot or not?"

Melody took a deep breath. "I'll address the question. But first you should know that you sound like a parent telling their young daughter that the boy at school is mean to her because he likes her, and we both know that's utter bullshit."

"Whoa, whoa, whoa…is he *mean* to you? Because that would change things. I would come there and hand his ass right to him if he's being mean to my best friend."

That got a chuckle out of Melody. "Easy, killer. No, he's not mean to me, actually. He's more like infuriatingly nice, as if he's trying to be my friend. But I don't need another friend. I've got you."

"I mean, right now you don't exactly 'got' me, Mel. It wouldn't hurt to have another friendly face at work. Especially a hot one. Because he's a total hottie, isn't he?

That's why you're not answering the question, and that's why you didn't shoot it down immediately. I love it when I'm right."

Melody sighed with exasperation. "Okay, so...objectively, I suppose you are correct. I mean, I'm sure people who appreciate conventional handsomeness would consider Ben hot. Unfortunately for me, though, I have the burden of knowing his personality and that eclipses his physical appearance."

A cheer came across the line from Chloe. "Called it! And I think you can ease up on poor Ben just a bit, Mel. Pretend he's me and try being just a tiny bit nice to him. See what happens. I'm not saying you should marry him or anything like that, but it wouldn't hurt to have a cup of coffee together or something."

Melody groaned. "I'm not making any promises."

"But you'll at least think about it?"

Melody hesitated for a beat. "Fine. I'll think about it."

Over the following weeks, it became clear that Chloe hadn't been wrong when she'd teased Melody about Mr. Richards's dozen top priority tasks, but at least she didn't know that. If she'd been clued in to the reality currently facing Melody inside her email inbox, she would never let her live it down.

As a new message popped up, yet again flagged with Mr. Richards's shorthand to convey that it required immediate attention and action, Melody barely suppressed a groan.

"You've got to be kidding me," she muttered under her breath.

She heard a scuffling sound behind her that nearly had her jump out of her skin before she remembered that Mr. Richards couldn't possibly be standing behind her if he had been emailing her mere seconds before. Turning, she found Ben hovering at the entrance to her cubicle, raising his hand in preparation to knock on the low wall.

Melody frowned. "Yes? Something I can help you with?"

"I just...uh." Ben shuffled, looking down as he placed his hands in his pockets. "Well, a few of us were going to order lunch, and I wanted to see if you wanted to join us."

"Oh, uh...thanks. It looks like I'll be eating at my desk again today, lots of work to do." She lifted her lunch bag from the table and gave it a sheepish smile. "At least I brought my own sustenance, though, right?"

Ben frowned at the bag. "You know you should really take a break. Step away from the computer, at least. You don't even have to sit with us in the kitchen, but at least, I don't know...stretch your legs, go outside for a minute or two? It's not good to spend so much time looking at a screen, or sitting, for that matter."

Melody's sigh was exasperated. "Believe it or not, I've heard all of that before." She nodded pointedly at her computer monitor. "But it doesn't change the fact that I've got a lot of work to do and none of it will get done if I 'step away from the computer.'" She said the last part like she was mocking the dumbest idea she'd ever heard, barely restraining herself from using air quotes in the process.

As Ben looked down and nodded, Melody felt a pang of guilt. What was it about him that had her this irritable? And not only irritable, but outwardly expressing that frustration to him? It wasn't like her and she was inclined to let herself feel terrible and apologize profusely...until he spoke.

"Suit yourself, then," he said. "Just know that, on some level, at least, you're choosing to accept this treatment from him. Judging by the way you interact with me, you are perfectly capable of standing up for yourself, and why you don't do that with him is a mystery I will probably never understand."

Her jaw fell open in shock as Ben gave a slight wave and left, no doubt to continue collecting lunch orders for the kitchen social hour she would decidedly not be a part of.

How dare he? she thought, fuming, as she aggressively typed an appeasing response to Mr. Richards's email. *But also...is he right about me? Of all the people to be a pushover to, clearly Mr. Richards is one of the worst to choose.* She looked at the email draft open in front of her, waiting for her to click "send" and let her boss know that she would have no problem completing all the tasks he had given her. *Should I delete it all and tell him that his timeline is unrealistic? That I need at least a few more days?*

Even the thought made Melody laugh mirthlessly. While there *may* be the slightest bit of truth to Ben's protestations—and Chloe's too, if you wanted to get technical about it—how was she supposed to pull a 180 degree change and become some opposite day bizarro version of herself? If she told Mr. Richards that she needed more time or bothered to imply the need for boundaries and work-life balance, there was no telling how he'd react. There simply wasn't a precedent for such a thing. Sure, other employees had probably done it in the past, but Melody didn't know any of them personally. After all, the people who were really good at setting boundaries like that—*the ones who don't care about the work as much as I do*, she reminded herself—usually didn't stay at EduPowerment long, or at least not in Mr. Richards's chain of command.

Melody dismissed her moment of doubt as nothing more than temporary insanity, firing off the email to Mr. Richards with resolute assuredness that all of his new projects would be completed in a timely manner, and that none of the existing projects would suffer as a result, either. If she knew herself at all, there was nothing like the sheer panic of letting down her boss to motivate her to do her best work—and quickly.

A couple hours later, after Melody had finished the sandwich she had packed from home and eaten an apple that ended up forgotten and browning on the corner of her desk while she lost herself in the flow of a really great idea, a knock came from behind her.

She turned to find Ben, holding out a paper towel with a couple of cookies on it. "Yes?" she asked him, immediately chilly as she recalled their previous interaction.

"I came to share this with you," he said, placing the paper towel on her desk. "I did some baking last night, and I didn't think you should miss out just because you're a workaholic." He held up his hands in a placating gesture before she could even respond. "I also wanted to apologize for perhaps offering a little too much input into how you should live your life. If what you're doing with Mr.

Richards is working for you, then who am I to tell you to live your life differently? It's possible I was also feeling a little—as they say—*hangry* and projecting that onto you."

"I appreciate that," Melody said, picking up the cookie to give it a sniff, eager to take a bite and yet not wanting to have her mouth full while she talked to Ben. "I get a little sensitive about the topic—clearly. It's just...well, do you think there's a difference between workaholism and just really genuinely believing in the mission and wanting to make a positive impact on the world?" The question slipped out before she could question why she had asked him.

Ben pursed his lips, looking thoughtful. "Not really, no. I think the 'typical' picture of a workaholic, the CEO taking calls on vacation or the lawyer working 80 hours a week...well, I think they believe in what they're doing too, even if only in terms of how much money it can make them. And unfortunately, I think that managers and leaders can exploit people with good hearts like yours, the people who want to make a difference, and use that to breed workaholics of their own who serve their mission."

Melody recoiled, shocked by just how jaded his response was. "That seems like a messed up way of looking at it. Don't you care about the mission? Isn't that why you do nonprofit work?"

Ben blinked slowly. "Of course I do. But, if you'll come up from your desk long enough to notice, it's not my entire life. I don't take it home with me, I certainly don't spend my weekends thinking about it, and I don't even take it to lunch with me. Life is too short and too precious to be spent solely on work. The mission is important—*al-*

ways—but it can be shared among many of us. It doesn't have to cost me my life. Or cost you yours."

"What life?" A humorless laugh barked out from between Melody's lips.

But Ben didn't laugh. Instead, he nodded towards her computer screen. "Is there something I can help you with? A project I can take off your plate?"

Melody shook her head. "You don't have to do that. I'm sure you have work of your own, and I couldn't ask you—"

"You didn't ask me. I'm offering. And it's the perfect illustration of what I just told you. The mission can be a burden if it's just placed on one person's shoulders, but when we share it amongst ourselves, it's quite easy to carry it."

"It's okay, really."

Ben crossed his arms over his chest. "Melody, I'm not leaving until you give me something to do." He looked pointedly at the cookie on her desk. "And judging by the way you keep glancing at that cookie there, you're waiting for me to leave before you take a bite." He leaned back against the cubicle wall. "And I have nowhere else to be, my friend. What's it going to be? Hmm?"

Melody threw her hands in the air, exasperation playing against something lighter, a feeling she couldn't quite put her finger on, but that felt playful, almost fun even. "Fine! You win. Let me just see..." She scrolled through her inbox, searching for one of Mr. Richards's requests she hadn't delved into yet. "I'll send it in a minute...just go. Are you happy now?"

Ben smiled, stepping away from the wall and preparing to leave. "Oh, I will be. Overjoyed, actually. Feeling victorious and, honestly, a bit excited to see what sort of project is waiting for me."

"Thank you," she said. "And thank you for the cookie, too. It does look delicious, and I'm eager to find out how your baking skills measure up to your negotiation tactics."

"*Guten Apetit*," he said with a nod. "Enjoy it. There are more in the kitchen if it passes the test."

When he was gone, Melody took a nibble from the corner of the cookie and barely stopped herself from moaning out loud. It was buttery and delicious, not too sweet, and there were fruity and spicy flavors playing against each other that she couldn't identify. She would have to ask Ben what was in it later, aware for the first time that the idea of talking to him didn't bring an automatic sneer to her face at the thought.

She opened her email inbox, scrolling through to find the most innocuous project to pass along to Ben. He might think he wanted to help, but there was no need to give him something really tricky, was there? She hesitated, finger hovering over the mouse. Why was she going easy on him? If he wanted to help—and if she wanted him to take seriously the fact that her job required hard work from her—then he needed to see what kind of work Mr. Richards was asking of her. She smirked as she backed out of the current email, a fairly straightforward request, and scrolled down until she found something a little more appropriate for the new goal she had in mind. She clicked "forward" and sat back, waiting for Ben's reaction.

It was nearly immediate. "What the hell is this?" Ben was back in her cubicle in a flash, and one of Melody's hands moved automatically to cover the cookie so he wouldn't get any satisfaction from seeing how much of it she had devoured in the minute that he had been gone. "Is this the kind of project he normally sends you?"

Melody nodded. "It sure is. Why? What's wrong?"

Benn shook his head, looking vaguely disgusted. "How are you supposed to do your job when this is the kind of instruction he gives you? 'New approach needed for social media marketing. Something I would like.' Unless you have a sixth sense and are uniquely gifted with being able to read your boss's mind. Can you?"

"Unfortunately, I cannot." Melody shook her head. "And that is precisely why I spend as much time on his projects as I do. I generally come up with about six different ideas and then weigh all of them against each other until I find the one most likely to win his approval." She shrugged. "I get it right more often than not."

"But...but..." Ben was sputtering, unable to form a full sentence. "But that's not how it should be! It's not fair to you, and frankly, it's just using your talent and your desire to please him to cover the fact that he's a bad manager. An effective manager would know how to communicate his wishes." He sighed, no doubt reacting to something he read in Melody's expression. "Look, if you don't care about saving yourself some time and stress, then at least think about the next person who's going to work for Mr. Richards after you. Is this fair to them? Who else is going to go above and beyond like you do? No one! And then they're going to get criticized or...I don't know, maybe fired? And it will all be because your boss thinks they're incompetent when *he*, in fact, is the one—"

"You've made your point," Melody interjected, holding up a hand to stop Ben. "And how do you know there's going to be someone after me? I like working at EduPowerment, and Mr. Richards is a good boss." She sighed, shaking her head. "Don't give me that look. He *is*. You just can't see it. We're doing great work together and really making a difference in the world. That matters more to me than any work-life balance mumbo jumbo does."

"Fine." Ben took a step back. "I'll help you with this project, but I'm not going to do his thinking for him. If I come up with six ideas, he's getting all of them, and *he* can decide for himself."

Melody sighed, exasperated. "Just send them to me, okay? I'll figure out what to share with him. Don't mess with the system, Ben. It works for us, and I don't need you coming in here and telling me how to do my job."

"Alright, then. Good talk."

Once he was gone, Melody stared at her desk, shaking her head at herself as her hand automatically lifted the remainder of the cookie to her mouth and polished it off in one bite. It was nice of Ben to want to help her, she could admit that much. And he *was* a decent baker. So why couldn't he just help her without trying to teach her some bogus life lesson in the process? Why did he have to make her feel bad about the extra effort she put into doing a good job? And since when was that a bad thing?

When the last morsel of cookie was gone, Melody looked at the paper towel on her desk longingly. If only there were about six more of them, everything would be perfect. She crumpled it up and tossed it in the garbage can under her desk and then set to work on the remaining tasks from Mr. Richards.

The afternoon flew by, and Melody found herself in an unusually good mood and productive energy level, knocking out task after task with a speed and ease that was impressive even for her.

She supposed she had Ben to thank for that. Whether it was the sugar from his baking that was giving her the necessary energy burst or the frustration he had triggered, her fingers were flying over the keys and her chin was jutted out in defiance. She would prove Ben wrong. There was nothing wrong with the way she and Mr. Richards worked together, and she was efficient and good at her job, not hemming and hawing over how best to read her boss's mind. He would see.

Just before five o'clock, a new email appeared in her inbox, announcing its presence with a chime. It was from Ben, a reply to the message she had forwarded him.

She opened the message, a strange anxious feeling fluttering in her belly in the second it took to load.

> *Dear Melody,*
>
> *Attached please find a few different ideas to share with Mr. Richards.*
>
> *Best,*
> *Ben*

Well, that was anticlimactic, she thought. But what had she been expecting? An apology for their earlier interactions? An admission that she had been right about everything? While both of those were welcome options, she doubted Ben would want to leave a written record of either one.

Opening the attachment to his message, Melody was greeted by five different social media strategy proposals, complete with mock-up images and the copy to go along with them. And, as much as she hated to admit it, they were...good. The hooks were enticing, the justifications were compelling, and she could envision any one of these generating ample funds for future projects.

"Dang it," she muttered under her breath. She was going to have to tell Ben he had done a good job, wasn't she? She got to her feet, eyes landing on his workspace, only to find it abandoned. His computer was off, chair pushed in, and there was no sign of him in the area.

She shouldn't feel disappointed not to find Ben at work. She knew that. So why did she? What was the big deal if she couldn't talk to him until tomorrow? Why was any part of her even wondering where he was right now when that was so clearly none of her business? And where was he emailing her from if not the workspace next to hers?

Sitting back down, she fired off a reply to Ben's message. She refrained from asking where he was and kept it simple, thanking him for his help. And then, against every natural inclination of hers, she forwarded his original message to Mr. Richards.

Dear Mr. Richards,

One of my colleagues, Ben Kaya, graciously offered to help with one of your projects, and I am forwarding his work to you. I think you'll agree that all the proposals are excellent and will understand why I wanted to share all of them with you for you to decide on the winning one at your discretion.

Best,
Melody

Melody remained at her desk, working for a couple more hours. It felt like she was waiting for something, either for Mr. Richards to respond and praise the work she and Ben had done or for Ben to come back, to respond to her email, to just be there.

She had sent an email back to him immediately after forwarding his work to Mr. Richards, thanking him profusely and with more kindness and gratitude than she had certainly ever directed his way.

In fact, that was a theme of the thoughts that were plaguing her those two remaining hours that she sat at her desk. It was hard to focus on work when she kept thinking about how kind Ben had been to her today and how undeserved that kindness had been. There was guilt gnawing at her, creating a pit in her lower belly.

The way she had responded to them from the beginning, the coldness, the way she closed herself off, the biting humor that she directed only at him. Where had it all come from? That wasn't like her. She didn't make jokes like that with her friends, or even with people she didn't like. Actually, it was rare that Melody let herself not like someone, so she didn't really know how she treated the people she didn't like. She always found something positive, and she was a master at deluding herself into thinking that everybody had some redeeming qualities.

But with Ben, for some reason, she poked and she prodded like she was trying to get a reaction. But was she? And if she was, what reaction would she want to get from him?

And then it clicked. It clicked uncomfortably into place, the realization that she wanted his attention. She was like a naughty kid or a mischievous kitten doing what they're not supposed to do because even negative attention was better than no attention.

That's why it felt so awful when he wasn't even there that afternoon. When she couldn't even see his face.

She didn't know what it meant to want a man's attention. Well, she had a feeling of what it could mean. But she shook her head, dismissing it and shoving it back down to the depths of her psyche. There was no chance that she had any romantic interest in Ben.

Even if such a thing were possible—and she knew it wasn't, couldn't even imagine it—it would be so unprofessional and such a major distraction from the work that she was here to do.

When Melody finally returned home, a restless evening faced her. All the thoughts and feelings that had come up that day thanks to the help she had received from Ben and the feelings it made her aware of were all creating a mess of confusion. It was confusion not just about what she wanted as it came to things like relationships and partnership, but a larger confusion about her work, about the direction she was headed, about all of it. It had become clear that completing Mr. Richards's tasks on her own was unsustainable, unrealistic. If it hadn't been for Ben's help that day, there was no way she would have been able to finish it all, and perhaps it was that thought that was the most frustrating to her. Because she was good at her job, dammit. And she was a capable, empowered woman who didn't need a man to save her, to rescue her, or even to help her. *So why had it felt so good?*

It had felt good not only to receive the help, but to have someone—especially someone who clearly wasn't speaking out of his overwhelming affection for her—acknowledge that her job was hard, that the tasks on her plate were unreasonable and unrealistic, and that the responsibilities given to her were more than any one person should be tackling on their own.

It was with that thought that Melody let herself be lulled into sleep, a more shallow sleep than normal but sleep nonetheless, comforted by the fact that she wasn't imagining the difficulty of reporting to Mr. Richards. That someone else could see it too.

The next morning she was happy to find Ben at his desk when she returned from the kitchen after refilling her cup of coffee.

"Hi," she greeted him. "Thanks for your help yesterday. I couldn't have done it without you."

He nodded back at her. "Not at all," he said. "I was glad to be of some use. I take it there were no problems with what I sent you?"

Melody shook her head. "No, it was great. Really. I mean, there was nothing I would have changed. I forwarded it on to Mr. Richards as it was, with compliments to you."

Ben's eyes widened. "You didn't have to do that, you know. You could have claimed it as your own and I certainly wouldn't have held it against you." A shadow of concern crossed his face. "He's not going to think less of you for getting some extra help, is he? I certainly don't want to cause you any trouble like that."

Melody shook her head. "Honestly, I have my doubts that he'll even notice. Sure, I told him in the email and I forwarded it directly from you, so your name is attached to it, but…" She shrugged. "He doesn't always pay attention to things like that. I'm sure he will be looking at it simply in terms of the ideas communicated and whether he can work with them or not."

Ben's nod was thoughtful, his gaze directed at the distant corner of his desk. "So that's how it feels then? Being you in this scenario?"

"Sorry?" she asked.

"I just mean the potential for something that you worked on, for hours, even to be dismissed on the same whim with which it originated."

She nodded, catching his meaning. "Yeah, pretty much." She shrugged. "It's just part of the job, you know?

Plenty of my work does make it to the final round. And lots of it that ends up on the cutting room floor or in Mr. Richards's, recycling bin...well, it's probably for the best."

"So you trust his judgment then?" Ben asked.

Melody licked her lower lip, weighing the question. It wasn't something she had considered before. Not something she had let herself consider, in fact. "I do..." She paused. "I think I have to. If I don't trust his judgment, then...well, then it would really be awful, wouldn't it? I mean, believing that perfectly good ideas and copy were being dismissed on the whims of his mood or whether he'd eaten recently?" She shook her head. "No, it's too much. I can't go there. Keep plowing ahead, working on the next thing. Whatever comes my way, whatever ends up on my desk or in my inbox...that's what's got my attention now."

"I see," said Ben. "Well..." He paused, hesitating though there was clearly something he wanted to say.

"What is it?" she asked. "Go ahead. I know things have been a bit...weird between us, but...well, I owe you one, so whatever you want to say, I can take it. Just spit it out."

Ben's eyebrows wrinkled in concern. "I'm not going to say something harsh or cruel to you. Why would you think that?"

Melody shrugged. "It's just that we're not really friends, you know? We didn't exactly get started on the right foot and...I don't know. Until yesterday, I didn't think you liked me much."

Ben shook his head. "I...was just giving you space because it seemed pretty clear that you were not looking for a new friend."

Melody nodded. "Uh, yeah. I mean...I guess I've been a bit wary and cautious and that might be a little off-putting?"

Ben chuckled. "A little. Sometimes maybe more than a little."

Melody felt her face heat with embarrassment. "Ahh...yeah. Sorry about that."

Ben's head shake was dismissive. "No need to be sorry, there was no harm done. And it seems like things are changing now. I mean, we're working together, at least, right?"

Melody nodded. "We are. Does that make us friends?"

Ben seem to be weighing her question, considering it very seriously before he answered. "Not quite yet," he finally said. "But we're on the way. Which brings me to my original question."

"Right. Go ahead."

"Well, I was just curious if you had ever had Turkish coffee and if you were interested in me making a cup for you some time."

There were no words. That was the last thing Melody had expected him to ask, and it was hard to know what her response should be. This sounded like he was inviting her to his home, which would be taking their friendship—no, it wasn't a friendship; acquaintanceship—to the next level. It wasn't that she didn't feel safe with him or trust him...she just barely knew him.

And yet, as she looked into his eyes, which were searching hers, waiting for her response, she found herself nodding. "I think I'd like that," she said, his face immediately, broadening with a toothy grin.

"Excellent," he said back. "How's today?"

*To continue the story, turn to **page 8***

“Izmir. No doubt about it.”

Chloe clapped her hands, squealing with joy. “I knew it!” Then she bodily removed Melody from her cubicle, demonstrating far greater strength than her demure frame had alluded to, as she shoved her back towards her own desk. “Fill out the form. Don’t talk to me until you do.”

Melody smiled to herself as she logged into her work email, saving the message about the Generosity Exchange for last. She was good for her promise to Chloe, but that didn’t mean she would take more precious work time to move that particular dream forward. The application could wait until her lunch break.

Of course, Melody’s lunch break ended up being, as was increasingly typical for her, eaten over her desk, typing with one hand while she shoveled the salad she’d brought from home into her mouth with the other.

“Melody!” Her relaxing meal was interrupted by Mr. Richards’s booming voice. “Are you here?” She scrambled to swallow the bite she had just put in her mouth, embarrassed to be caught doing something as humiliating as feeding her weak human body by her seemingly invincible boss.

He materialized in front of her before she could swallow the lettuce that had nearly gotten stuck in her throat, let alone check her teeth for stranded vegetables. "Good! There you are. I was looking for someone to take over this project—the marketing copy for the new microlending campaign is all wrong." He looked over at the surrounding cubicles, a lord surveying his domain. "It looks like everyone else is taking a long lunch today." He dropped a stack of papers on Melody's desk. "Can I leave these with you?"

It's not like I have a surplus of free time on my hands. I already can't take a lunch break with all the projects I'm juggling...but what's one more? Especially if it gets me back in Mr. Richards's good graces. She scolded herself mentally for thinking that way. *Especially if it furthers the mission of EduPowerment. Even if I'm tired, even if I have to stay later than planned today...somewhere in the world, the work I'm doing here is making a difference.*

"Of course!" Melody smiled at Mr. Richards brightly. "I can get this done for you by the end of the workday today."

"Good." He checked his watch. "I'm leaving now for one of Gilbert's piano performances at school. I'll work from my home office afterwards, so just leave it on my desk. I'll expect to find it there first thing in the morning."

"You've got it." Mr. Richards dismissed himself with a thumbs-up gesture and was gone as quickly as he had come.

Alone again, Melody eyed her abandoned salad before tossing the rest of the lettuce in the garbage can underneath her desk.

She lost herself in the magic of breathing life into the microlending project. Whoever had developed the old marketing campaign had gotten it all wrong. This project was about getting women set up to run their own business, starting with something accessible, like an egg business or sewing dresses, depending on the resources available in their community. EduPowerment had seen great success with the graduates of this program, with the vast majority continuing to turn a profit in their business—and often in an increasingly complex and higher revenue-generating venture—every year afterwards.

The problem was that the marketing copy Mr. Richards had left on Melody's desk focused on the project in terms of the "help" that the donors would be giving to these "less fortunate" souls. She couldn't quite put her finger on it, but something about the marketing language left her feeling like she needed to take a shower. Like the donors were needed to swoop in and rescue these women who wouldn't even know the importance of money or education or food if it weren't for their benevolent saviors.

"We need a different approach, clearly," Melody said to herself. "What about talking about an *investment*? The contribution that the donor makes is like being an angel investor in a business...quite similar, in fact, except for the scale of the investment. Now, unlike an angel investor they're not going to be getting their money back—that's not how this works—but they are going to see it have a far greater impact than it would otherwise..." She trailed off as her fingers began to fly on the keyboard, bringing the campaign to life with updated donor-facing website copy and social media blurbs, and even a good old-fashioned brochure to send along with the next newsletter, too.

"Are you going home or what?" Chloe interrupted Melody's reverie, making her sit up straight for the first time in...a while, judging by the crick in her neck and the dull ache in her upper back.

Melody stretched, a yawn escaping her lips as she wiggled her ankles to get the blood flowing in her legs again. "What time is it?"

Chloe rolled her eyes. "If I'm leaving to go home, what time do you think it is? I'm not like you, Mel. I don't get excited about staying at work after hours to earn extra credit." She picked up Melody's abandoned thermos from the corner of the desk, using it to gesture towards the exit of her cubicle. "Come on then, let's get moving! I'm not leaving you here to work all night. You've got an application to fill out, missy. Don't think I didn't notice that you haven't gotten around to it yet."

"I'm right behind you, Chloe," Melody promised. "Seriously, go home. I just have a few things to finish up here, but I promise I'll go home at a reasonable time."

"And?"

Melody rolled her eyes. "And I'll look at the Generosity Exchange application again. Happy?"

"The happiest." Chloe bent down to drop a tight-lipped peck on the top of Melody's head. "Who's a good girl?"

Melody groaned. "If you could *not* talk to me like I'm a dog, that would be just great." She smiled up at her friend then. "Seriously, get out of here. I'll talk to you tomorrow."

"Make me proud, girlfriend," Chloe called over her shoulder as she stepped further from the cubicle. "Surprise me with your wacky, wild, adventurous ways."

Alone again, Melody returned to her work, though the refrain of Chloe's words continued to play in her mind. While she wasn't going to do anything *rash*—she certainly couldn't leave work before she'd finished all she'd promised Mr. Richards...and left the documents he'd requested exactly where he wanted them—it might be nice to at least fill out the application for the exchange program without waiting for Chloe to pester and remind her twelve more times.

"Yeah," she whispered to herself. "It can't hurt anything to just fill it out. What are the odds they'll accept me, anyway? No, I can just fill out the form and then put the whole thing out of my mind. More likely than not, I'll never hear another peep about it. Maybe a nice rejection email in a few weeks. But at least Chloe will be off my back and I won't wonder what would have happened if I'd just gotten over myself and filled out the dang thing."

A little more than an hour later, Melody was leaving the office. She had finished everything on her to-do list for the day—apart from a few more brainstorming tasks that she couldn't help but take home with her; she couldn't help it if she got her best ideas right when she was trying to fall asleep—and double-checked that Mr. Richards had everything he needed from her, waiting right where he'd requested on the corner of his desk.

Thirty minutes later, she arrived home at the (mostly) student-occupied apartment building that she still lived in. With her salary at EduPowerment, it had been easier to renew this lease year after year rather than search for a new apartment that would qualify her application based on her monthly income. And so what if Melody was a few years older than most of her neighbors? Apart from a few noisy parties after final exams, she had no complaints.

Well, except the fact that she now lived with Felicity, who she barely got along with. When Luisa, Melody's roommate for all four years of college, had graduated and landed a job in Chicago, Melody had been happy for her. Until the reality hit in that she wasn't going to be following in her friend's footsteps, landing a great job out-of-state, moving away from her hometown...or being able to afford to rent their apartment on her own.

A well-placed ad in the local paper had brought Melody and Felicity together, in part because they may have been the only two people on campus who picked up that particular issue of The Gazette. They'd never really spent enough time together to warm up to each other, both busy with their respective obsessions—Felicity in the chemistry laboratory during every possible waking hour, while Melody was eating, sleeping, and breathing EduPowerment.

Melody let herself in the door, finding the apartment dark and empty. Felicity often stayed late in the lab, and today seemed to be no exception. She pulled a dish of leftover roasted broccoli out of the refrigerator, aware for the first time since her lunch interruption of the hollow feeling in her stomach. Skipping the need for a plate, she took the large Pyrex container and a fork to the couch, slipping her laptop out of her bag before digging in.

While Melody ate, she stared at the photographs that came up when she did an image search for "izmir turkey." There were plenty of city skyline photos, which were never the ones that called to Melody's soul...but the photos of the coastline, the palm trees, and the ancient historical sites from the surrounding areas...those did the trick.

"Wow," she murmured, so awed by a photo of the ancient library of Ephesus that she nearly dropped a broccoli floret on her keyboard. "Okay, let's do this. Chloe will give me a ton of grief tomorrow if I don't at least fill out the application tonight."

By the time Melody snuggled under her covers that evening, she could almost admit to herself that she *really* wanted this opportunity to move to Izmir to come to fruition. But only *almost*. She still told herself that the reason she couldn't sleep, the reason her heart was pounding so fast, must have something to do with having too much caffeine. She *had* eaten a small piece of dark chocolate Chloe had given her this afternoon, after all. That must be the reason she couldn't calm her mind and drift into peaceful sleep the way she normally did so easily.

When her eyes finally blinked closed for the night, images of ancient ruins and the Aegean sea swam through her brain, coloring her dreams. She would wake up the next morning feeling like she'd traveled for the first time in ages.

One week later, the Generosity Exchange was nearly forgotten. Even Chloe rarely brought it up any more, so discouraged was she that her application to go "anywhere but here but especially London" hadn't been received with an immediate acceptance. The first few days after they had turned in their applications, Melody had heard regular dramatic sighs coming from Chloe's office, which she had taken as an indicator that her friend had—yet again—checked her email to find no response from the Generosity Exchange acceptance committee.

On the other hand, Melody had been stricter than ever with her email-checking regimen. She allowed herself to check it once first thing in the work day and then again at around four o'clock. The remainder of her day was spent on the many projects that needed her attention, but checking at those two times to see if there was anything else she needed to add to her to-do list served her well. Kept her from wasting time refreshing her inbox that she knew would be better spent making progress on an important task.

And of course, there were many tasks that required her attention—always, in fact. While at one point in time Melody's responsibilities had been clearly under the umbrella of the marketing department, at times it felt like she was Mr. Richards's personal assistant.

Not that Melody minded. She loved being involved in so many of the projects that EduPowerment was launching into the world, and she loved to be a needed member of the team. Sure, she did find herself getting increasingly exhausted as the workweek went on...and she barely managed to cook a nourishing meal more than once a week...and she couldn't remember the last time she read a book for fun. But those were all normal parts of being an adult, she was pretty sure. Things were bound to quiet down at some point, and when that happened she would probably miss all the fun and excitement and sleepless nights of her twenties. Or at least that was what she was telling herself.

"Oh. My. Freaking. Goodness!" Chloe's voice had increased in volume with every word, her head popping up over the cubicle wall at the end of her exclamation. "Check your email, Mel! Check it now!"

Melody raised an eyebrow at Chloe but kept her fingers flying on the keyboard. She was in the flow of a great idea, and if she stopped mid-sentence, there was a good chance she wouldn't be able to find the rest of the thought when she came back to it. "What is it?" she asked, when she had reached the end of the paragraph.

Chloe's eyes were twinkling, her eyebrows practically dancing with excitement. "It's good news for me. I can tell you that much! But you should really check your own email first, so you can either join in my celebration or I can stop rubbing it in your face and go be happy someplace else."

Melody shook her head as she broke her own rule, logging back into her email. But her expression changed at the words in bold that greeted her there, her mouth falling open in disbelief.

> *"Congratulations, You've been accepted to Generosity Exchange: University of the Aegean."*

And that was just the subject of the email. She had to give it to the Generosity Exchange people; they sure didn't bury the lead by making you read half a paragraph before finding out that you'd been accepted. Still, it was hard to believe this was really happening, and she clicked the email open to confirm it.

Melody Critchfield,

We have reviewed your application for the fall cohort of Generosity Exchange, and are pleased to inform you that you have been assigned to the University of the Aegean. We received a considerable number of applications, and yours stood out. We are confident that the University of the Aegean will benefit from your experience and skill, and that you will simultaneously learn from the experience and skill of your colleagues in the program.

Attached is all the information you should need at this point. Due to the personal preferences of each candidate, we have decided to leave flight booking to the discretion of each participant. As soon as you have booked your one-way ticket to Izmir, please forward it to us and reimbursement will be arranged.

Congratulations again. Please don't hesitate to reach out with any questions.

> *Sincerely,*
> *Madeline Andrews*

"Holy..." Melody's exclamation trailed off as she scrolled back up to the top of the email, sure it had been sent to her by mistake. There must be another Melody Critchfield at EduPowerment who was about to embark on an exciting adventure. It couldn't be *her*.

"I know, right?" Chloe was in her cubicle now, her jaw clenched and eyes huge and round. "It's really happening!" She was squealing, but at a moderate decibel level, which Melody appreciated, and jumping up and down, but bent over at the waist, so it was unlikely anyone in a neighboring cubicle saw more than the occasional glimpse of her blonde ponytail peeking over the top.

"Is this...? Are you...?"

"It is, and I am! London, baby!" Chloe pumped her arm. "What about you? Turkey, right?"

Melody nodded, her mouth suddenly dry. "Yes, Izmir. Holy crap. This is..."

"So freaking exciting? The best thing that's happened to you since you met me? You're darn right it is!"

"I was going to say it's surreal," said Melody. "As in, I can't believe it's actually happening. I'm pretty sure any moment now I'm going to wake up and find out I dreamed it all. No, don't get me wrong. I'm sure it's real for *you*...I just think it might be some colossal mistake for me. That's all."

Chloe's jaw dropped as she shook her head. "You are a piece of work, you know that? Why can't something cool and exciting and fun happen to you, too?"

"It's not about fun, Chloe. I didn't see anything in that email about all the *fun* we're supposed to have in this program. I *did* see a few mentions of experience and skill sharing and learning from each other and collaboration..."

"Yeah, yeah, spare me." Chloe waved her concerns away. "This is your thing to work through, Mel. On your own time or with a therapist or whatever. Life is short, but if you don't learn how to have a little fun every now and then, it's going to feel intolerably long. Don't say I didn't warn you."

Melody bit her lip, forcing herself to stay silent and not push this argument about the merits of fun and the precise proportions at which it should be deployed in one's life. Chloe was entitled to her beliefs about how much Melody needed to relax and let loose and not take on unnecessary responsibilities...just like Melody was entitled to her beliefs about the merits of discipline and commitment and loyalty. Did she hope Chloe would come around to her way of thinking? Of course! But did she push it on her? Well, not intentionally, at least. But she couldn't help it if she got a little excited and soapbox-y every once in a while.

"So what's next, then?" Melody asked Chloe. "Assuming you're right and this is actually real and not an elaborate prank."

"You didn't see the invitation?" Chloe *tsk*ed at Melody. "You've got to work on your reading comprehension skills, love. It was right there at the bottom of the email, an invitation to an orientation meeting on Friday. Bring all your questions, and no doubt they'll answer them all! Except, maybe don't ask if this is an elaborate prank. They might not like that one."

"Thanks." Melody's smile to Chloe was tight-lipped as she dove back into her work. No need to waste any more time on daydreaming about the future, especially not when all the answers she was so desperately craving were waiting to be delivered to her in a few short days.

When Friday afternoon rolled around, Melody had to temper her excitement in order to avoid being the first person in the conference room. True, she was *usually* the first person in any conference room and the last to leave...but she didn't think that would be a good look for a meeting of this nature, and she didn't want to give anyone the wrong impression.

After all, it wasn't excitement about the international opportunity ahead of her that was prompting Melody to set up shop outside of the meeting room like she was a Swiftie camping out online for tour tickets. Naturally, it was the excitement of anything to do with EduPower-ment, to do with marketing a cause she believed in, to do with doing her little part to make the world a better, more compassionate place.

Yikes, she thought. *That's a little intense, even for my own inner monologue. It's a good thing I didn't say that out loud to Chloe, or I would never hear the end of it. Maybe it's time to find some new talking points. But what* do *adults*

*talk about if not their love for non-profit work? The weather?
Sports? There's got to be something better than that.*

Melody walked back to the breakroom to refill her water
bottle, despite the fact that she'd only had a few sips since
the last time she filled it. No one else knew that, so if they
saw her filling her bottle, they'd just think she was well-hy-
drated. Maybe even be inspired to drink a little more water
themselves. It was a nice service she was providing them,
when you looked at it like that. Plus, okay, maybe it had
the added bonus of giving her something to do with herself
while she waited for the clock to tick over to four o'clock.
Meeting time.

At five minutes before meeting time, she couldn't wait
any longer and let herself into the conference room. A
few of her colleagues were already there, but the majority
of them came flying in at four on the dot, most of them
looking harried and stressed.

Chloe entered with a smile on her face and a pep in her
step that was beyond Melody's comprehension. Sliding
into the seat next to her, Chloe grinned at her and held out
a plastic sandwich bag. "Cookie?" she offered.

Melody shook her head and shot Chloe her best disap-
proving stare. A sugar rush and the corresponding crash
wasn't the way anyone needed to spend their afternoon.
To say nothing of the fact that greeting the leader of
the Generosity Exchange with a mouth full of chocolate
crumbs might not make the best first impression.

"Suit yourself," said Chloe, shoving another cookie in
her mouth before tucking the plastic bag into her purse
and hanging it from the back of her chair. "More for me,
then."

At that moment, a presence swept into the room. Not a ghostly presence or anything like that, but a commanding one. An impossible to miss one.

"Good afternoon, everyone," said a statuesque woman with the poise of a dancer and the wisdom of a librarian. "I am Madeline Andrews, the director of the Generosity Exchange." She smiled out at them then, looking in turn around the conference room table. "You are all so welcome here today, and I am looking forward to getting to know each and every one of you. You have been selected for this program because you are truly the best of what EduPowerment has to offer, and also because the selection committee and I saw a special spark in each one of you. We believe you have what it takes to help both our partner institutions and EduPowerment move to the next level in our impact, both out in the world and within our institutions and teams." Her smile took on a mischievous edge for the barest flash of a second. "Of course, we also hope this experience will be rewarding for you *outside* of your career and the time you spend at the office. After all, what is work-life balance without a life?"

"See?" Chloe leaned over to mutter in Melody's ear, elbowing her in the ribs at the same time. "Was I right, or was I right?"

Melody lifted a finger to her lips and gave Chloe the stink eye before returning her undivided attention to Madeline. Looking at her, at the way she carried herself and the appearance of confidence, balance, grace...for the first time in her adult life, Melody knew what she wanted to be when she grew up.

Barring the fact that she couldn't actually *be* someone who already existed, she hoped to at least get on Madeline's good side, learn as much as she possibly could from her...and maybe pick up some tips for being much cooler and more self-composed than she already was.

Madeline gestured to her assistant, a younger woman who Melody instantly wished she could bodyswitch places with, who began dispersing a stack of folders amongst the people assembled in the room.

"While I realize the typical way of conducting a meeting like this would have been to send you all the information beforehand," Madeline said, a slight smile playing at the edge of her lips, "what can I say? I'm old school. Back in the day, when I was an overseas volunteer, I communicated with my loved ones back home by letter. Not even a phone call, so certainly no internet. And the anticipation of waiting for those letters, well...sometimes it was even better than the letter itself." She chuckled at the memory. "All that to say, if I'd sent you a PDF with all the information about your Generosity Exchange year ahead of time, you would have digested the whole thing in twenty minutes and showed up here with nothing but questions and concerns." She nodded her head toward the blue folders that had been placed on the table in front of each of them. "Instead, now we get to discover everything together. Keep a sense of the excitement and magic of it all."

Chloe raised her eyebrows at Melody. "Are you hearing this?" she whispered. "Excitement and magic...next thing you know, she's going to start talking about all the *fun* we're going to have."

"Believe it or not, I'm hearing all the same things you're hearing," Melody hissed back. Chloe was right, though, to comment on what Madeline was saying. With every word Melody had heard so far, she'd felt her pulse pick up, her palms start to get sweaty. Classic signs of stress and anxiety, she knew, especially as they were paired with thoughts of doubt and uncertainty. What if this program wasn't, in fact, for her? It sounded more and more like Study Abroad for Grown-Ups, when what Melody was looking for—what she thought she had applied to, actually—was something more like Very Serious and Professional Experiences for Very Serious and Professional People on a Mission to Save the World.

In hindsight, that might have been a lot to expect of a program tailored to the young and inexperienced end of the workforce. Melody had been told she was an "old soul" ever since she was a young girl, and her inability to relate to the needs and wants of people her age had created no small amount of awkward situations from preschool through the present day.

If that turned out to be the case, if the Generosity Exchange ended up being more like spring break in Florida with a side of non-profit work, then she would bow out. Gracefully excuse herself. Today, in fact. She stared at the cover of the folder in front of her, willing its contents to answer her existential questions and give her a definitive answer about whether or not this was the right opportunity for her.

Madeline smiled and cleared her throat, calling their attention away from the colorful papers in front of them and back up to the front of the conference room. "Naturally, the packets in front of you contain mostly general information about the Generosity Exchange, things you will likely already know if you've been doing your due diligence and researching us online in your free time." Melody smiled a secret smile to herself, as she acknowledged that she had, in fact, been doing exactly what the teacher...er, director...had expected. Star student, yet again. "We will be connecting each of you with your counterparts in country, introducing you via email in the coming days. This is where the real important information will come from. Not only will they be able to answer your questions about packing—appropriate cultural attire, weather, things you could easily look up online again...but they will also be informing you about the project you'll be working on." She looked over the top of her glasses at the faces crowded around the conference table. "As much as we are aware this will be a fun and exciting experience for you, there *are* also important projects that we're assigning each of you. Please, make us proud with the effort and professionalism you bring to the tasks assigned to you. No one is asking you to work 80-hour weeks or give up the idea of having a social life in country...but we *are* asking that you arrive with a basic sense of your responsibilities and some ideas to contribute."

That was it? It sounded like the bare minimum, and Melody already knew she would show them just how helpful a Generosity Exchange partner could be. As soon as she knew what her project was, she would get to work on it. Set some goals, break them down into projects, assign tasks to each of the projects...

She was nearly lost in a daydream, so focused on the work she was going to get to do in Turkey that she almost missed Madeline's next words.

"...the end of the month, at the latest."

"What's happening at the end of the month?" Melody hissed to Chloe, feeling no small amount of panic rise up in her throat. It wasn't like her to zone out for important information. The meeting thus far had been a lot of excitement and very little substance—not that she was complaining, Madeline could do no wrong in her eyes—but how could she have missed something important in just a few moments of planning and scheming?

Chloe's eyes were big, her eyebrows sky high. "Was *someone* not paying attention?" She was loving this, and Melody had to put a stop to it.

She shushed her friend. "Tease me later if you have to, just tell me what I missed!"

"It's about our departure dates," Chloe explained. "We can start booking our flights soon and then submit the receipts for reimbursement. They want us to plan to arrive in country by the end of the month at the latest."

Melody checked the date on her watch, though she already knew what she would find there. It was the 15th already, which left just over two weeks before her new life in Turkey was going to begin. Two weeks to pack up and move there, not to mention two weeks to figure out what to do about her apartment, to make sure she wasn't leaving any loose ends behind.

True, it wasn't as if she had a lot of close friends in Michigan. Chloe would, after all, also be living on the other side of the Atlantic Ocean. Her parents were going to be thrilled that she was stretching her wings, trying something different. They had always been much more free-spirited than her, often wondering out loud how they had gotten a daughter who was quite as stuck in her ways as Melody was. Not that it bothered her. She knew they loved her just as she was...they just might understand her better if she let loose and had a little more fun once in a while.

There were no pets she would need to worry about finding a long-term pet sitter for, and not even any plants that would need to be watered while she was gone. Certainly no boyfriend to figure out a long distance relationship with, she lamented to herself before shaking it off. It was better not to have someone else who would be impacted by her decision at that level, even if it meant her evenings in her apartment *had* been lonelier than she might have preferred.

In theory, there was no reason why Melody couldn't be ready to leave within two weeks...so why did it feel like this was all happening too fast? Like she had made a huge mistake?

Sitting across the table in the café, Chloe sipped her cappuccino, her eyebrows climbing sky high. "Is that all?" she asked, in response to Melody's word vomit about all the reasons why the Generosity Exchange was no longer the right choice for her.

"Yeah, well…no. I mean…" Melody sighed. Chloe was being entirely too chill about all the *very valid* reasons Melody had given her why she needed to stay put. Why wasn't she reacting? Why hadn't she agreed with Melody that *of course* she was making the right decision. "I just have too many things keeping me here. It's not the right time now. It's too soon, too short notice." Then, to throw Chloe a tiny glimmer of hope: "I can try again next year."

Chloe hooted with laughter. She actually hooted. "No way, missy. If you give up on this, I can guarantee you that you won't be putting yourself through this process again next year." She shook her head. "No, you've given some great reasons why you should give in to your fears and stay put. It *does* sound scary to move to a new country and start over there. Even with a whole program in place, so you're not actually going it alone. A built in job and support network." She pointed to herself. "Your best friend going through the exact same experience just a short flight away and ready and willing to talk through all the tricky emotions coming up."

"Tricky emotions?" Melody scoffed. "That's not what this is. This is just me being responsible."

"Maybe." Chloe nodded. "I'm just telling you that I'm feeling some tricky emotions, so it would be perfectly natural if you were, too."

"You are?" Melody was incredulous. Chloe had been the one pushing this all along. She practically had a paper chain countdown to her London departure date streaming across her cubicle. "I thought you were just feeling pure excitement."

"Oh, there's that. For sure." Chloe ran her finger around the rim of her mug. "But it's not just that. I'm imagining it being this wonderful adventure, sure...but there are still a lot of unknowns about it. Am I going to feel homesick? Are people going to like me or just think I'm a weird American? And what if I can't find any good peanut butter? I've always heard that's a thing in other countries...like, peanut butter does exist, but it's never the right kind. It's too sweet, or it's too oily...it's never just a jar of Jif, you know?"

"Huh." Melody was quiet. She hadn't expected *that* from Chloe. "I had no idea you were feeling like that. Not about the peanut butter, I mean. All the rest of it. I thought I was the only one who wasn't totally and completely on board and excited."

"Don't get me wrong, I'm thrilled...overall. And the fears aren't enough to keep me from going or anything, but they do take up a lot of real estate in my mind." Chloe shrugged then. "I'm just trusting they'll go away with time. That I'll figure out how to manage things when they come up." She sipped her drink again. "It sure would be easier to work my way through all these feelings if I were talking them through with *someone* in the same boat." She coughed, which sounded distinctly like the word "you," while glaring at Melody. "No pressure, though. I'll understand—eventually—if you need to chicken out on this one."

"It's not chickening out! It's thinking through a big decision rather than leaping impulsively into it, Chloe. You should know me well enough by now to know that. I'm going to...think it through, I guess. What's best for me, what's best for my career, and most importantly what's best for EduPowerment. If I'm going to go, it has to be a win-win for everyone. Whatever challenges would come up for me in Turkey, cultural differences and homesickness, and whatever else...I can handle any of that if I know it's the best thing for EduPowerment."

Chloe rolled her eyes sky high. "Please. Mr. Richards isn't here, so you can cut out the 'EduPowerment is my life' bullshit." Then, reacting to what she saw on Melody's face, she gasped. "You're not serious...you *actually* care more about what's good for the blasted non-profit that employs you and—okay, let's be honest—takes advantage of you than you do about your own happiness and well-being? I knew you were a *bit* of a martyr, Mel, but I had no idea you took it that far."

"It's not like I'd be able to relax and have fun there if I knew that the Generosity Exchange program was actually creating a financial burden that was impacting the communities we serve. I could never enjoy it."

"Okay..." Chloe bugged her eyes out at Melody. "But EduPowerment willingly partners with the Generosity Exchange, which would suggest that it is beneficial for them to do so. As much as people think 'non-profit' means there's no money involved, there's actually a *ton* of money in non-profits. Trust me. There's no way this program is doing more harm than good for EduPowerment. It's good publicity, good training for their employees, and let's not forget that they get to bring in talent from the partner organizations as well. They'll probably get someone even better than you to do your job while you're gone." She gave a nonplussed shrug at that, waiting for Melody to take the next move in their verbal chess match.

"Dang you." Melody groaned. "You can't just let me cop out on this one and then wimp out and stay home? Flake out? Flip out?"

Chloe tipped her head to the side in thought. "Well, you *did* already flip out, so good job there. But no, no need to do any more *anything* out-ing. I'm just here to offer some much-needed perspective and make sure you don't throw something amazing away. And you *know* this is an amazing opportunity. Not something to pass up, and certainly not something to push off until next year, when your resistance to change will be even stronger than it already is."

"Ugh." Melody put her head in her hands. "You know me too well. Not that I'm actually complaining about that. It *is* great to have a friend. Just...maybe not at a time like this, when it would be so much nicer to have someone who just agrees with me."

"You mean enables you?"

"Potato, po-tah-to." Melody shrugged. "I really don't see the problem, as long as I get to do what I want."

"You're a monster," said Chloe. "You know that, right?"

"It takes one to know one, I guess." Melody paused, a thought occurring to her that she wasn't quite sure how to verbalize. "Thank you, though. I mean, I'm thanking you on behalf of my future self, who *definitely* does want to go to Izmir and is so grateful to be there. It's just my present self who's not exactly crazy about you right now."

Chloe shrugged. "You're welcome, then, I guess. I'm more interested in Future Melody's happiness than Present Melody's comfort zone, anyway. And I can handle a little attitude from Present Melody if it gets Future Melody where she wants to be."

The next two weeks flew by, just like Melody had known they would. Actually, they'd passed even more quickly than she had expected, and she subsequently found herself saying goodbye to her parents outside the airport, tears streaming down all of their faces. She hadn't had time to say goodbye the way she wanted to, to get herself to a point where this airport farewell would be joyous rather than emotional.

She had wanted to spend more time with her mom and with her dad, in the hope that their "daughter love cups" would be full to overflowing and they would be able to say goodbye to her easily, with a minimum of emotion.

And maybe it would have been easier for her, too, in that ideal vision she had.

With one last hug for each of them, she waved a final farewell and began to make her way to the terminal. Chloe was supposed to meet her inside, having opted to show up an extra hour early for her flight just to be a good friend to Melody and keep her company at a time when she had—correctly—expected that she might need it.

"There you are!" A blur of activity to Melody's right as a figure slammed into her from the side.

"Oof!" She nearly lost control of her suitcase as she stepped back to keep from being toppled out of balance. "Chloe! Are you seriously trying to maim me before I can even go on this trip that *you* insisted I take in the first place?" She reached up to wipe the tears that had escaped her eyes off her cheeks, hoping Chloe wouldn't notice them.

"Whoa, whoa, whoa, what's going on there?" Chloe caught Melody's wrist gently, eyeing her face with concern. "What's got you so torn up, friend? You're going on an amazing adventure today, and that's definitely not something to feel sad about!"

"It's not about that," Melody said with a sniffle. "It's just…saying goodbye to my parents. I can't help but feel like I failed these last few weeks. If I had just spent more time with them, we wouldn't all have been so emotional today. And now it's going to be such a long time before we see each other again and I just hate the thought that they're going to be sad and miserable without me!"

Chloe's expression was incredulous. "You really think that if you had just spent, I don't know, a few extra hours with your mom that she wouldn't be sad about sending her baby to another country? Friend, I don't know if you know this about your mom, but she loves you. A lot. And she was *always* going to be emotional to say goodbye to you, but that was *never* going to mean that you shouldn't go or that you did something wrong. If you had spent every waking moment with your parents for the past two weeks, do you think…what, they would have gotten sick and tired of you? Be ready to kick you out of the house? No! They would miss you no matter what, and they would *still* be the ones to drive you to the airport and support your dreams."

"So you're saying this misery we're all feeling is un-avoidable? Dang. Life sucks sometimes." Melody knew she was wallowing in self-pity, and she knew she was being ridiculous. Yet, she couldn't help it. Pulling herself out of it, getting herself excited about the adventure ahead, just didn't feel like what she wanted to do right now. Wallowing was comfortable, like snuggling under the covers on a cold winter day, and changing that would feel like ripping the covers off and feeling the cold air hit her face. No, thank you.

"I'm saying..." Chloe wrapped an arm around Melody's shoulders, tugging her closer with every other word. "...that your parents existed without you before you were born, that they managed to be happy together when you went off to college, and that, even now, they have things in common *besides* just being your parents. They are going to be fine. It's good that they're a little sad right now, because it means that they actually like you...but I bet they'll have a nice meal tonight, some good comfort food, and they'll watch a movie that makes them laugh, and they'll be okay. More than okay."

Melody sniffed. "That's good. Yeah, it did feel a little egotistical to think that my presence alone could make or break their happiness. It's possible I'm being a *tiny* bit dramatic right now."

"Just a tiny bit." Chloe poked her in the ribs, steering her towards the Turkish Airlines counter to check in for her flight. "And you know you're going to be just fine too, right? You've got me for now, and as soon as we get checked in and through security, we're going to find a nice glass of wine and some overpriced potatoes. Fries, maybe?"

They had arrived at the end of the check-in line and came to a stop behind a family with two small children. "On the plane, they'll feed you well," Chloe continued. "We'll still pick up some snacks, just in case. Maybe a book or a magazine, too, though they usually have a great selection of movies on long flights like this."

"Your flight is way shorter than mine, isn't it? I'm jealous that you're going to be in London, like, five hours after we leave, and I'll barely be halfway to my destination."

Chloe shrugged. "And *I'm* jealous that you'll have time to watch at least twice as many movies as me. Long flights were always my favorite time for a veg out movie marathon, and I haven't had one of those since spring break last year." She waved a dismissive hand. "You'll be fine. I know you won't be able to do your favorite thing—*work*—but you'll manage. You might even enjoy yourself..."

After completing check-in for both Melody's flight and Chloe's, they made their way through security. The time they had together—the last time Melody was going to be spending with a familiar face for quite a while—was passing so quickly, and she wished she could grab hold of it. Savor it a bit before she found herself alone with only her thoughts and worries for company.

Even the security process was quick and smooth. If there was ever a time she wished for a delay, she wished for it now. A long line, a bag that needs to be rechecked a time or two, a "random selection" for being patted down.

None of it happened, though, and they were on the other side of security, with only their gates to find before the inevitable departure arrived.

Too soon, Chloe was hugging Melody goodbye at the gate, grabbing her upper arms firmly to reassure her, yet again, that she *could* do this, she *wasn't* making a terrible mistake, and everything was going to work out just fine.

A drop of emotion escaped from Melody's eye, and she hastily wiped it away. "And what about you?" she asked Chloe with a sniffle. "Are you good? I wish I could stay with you until your flight leaves..."

Chloe rolled her eyes. "But that would defeat the whole purpose of me seeing you off. Seriously, everything is fine. I'm going to go zone out at my gate until it's time to leave, and *you* are going to get on that plane and stop delaying your adventure." She gave Melody one last hug before pushing her away, a little more forcefully than necessary, if you asked Melody. "Now get out of here. I'm proud of you for doing this, and I love you dearly. And I can't *wait* to meet up with you in Izmir. And London. And who even knows where else?"

Melody barely managed to stop herself from responding that while Chloe was welcome to visit Izmir, Melody had no plans to travel anywhere else. As soon as she arrived in Turkey, her first order of business was to figure out her new role at the University of the Aegean and then dive into it headlong. She highly doubted there would be time to travel, but she could at least take Chloe out for dinner when she came to visit.

Instead, she simply smiled at her friend. "See you on the other side, then." Then she gave a little salute—which she *instantly* regretted because who did that?—and then took her place in the line to board. When she glanced back,

Chloe was waving her arms in a silent celebration of glee. She blew a kiss at Melody then left for her own gate.

Chloe had been right about the flight. It had been a long time since Melody had taken a longer flight than just the few hours to visit her aunt and uncle in St. Louis, and her last international flight—that ill-fated spring break trip to Cozumel that she tried to forget ever happened—had definitely not been on a luxurious airline.

But the journey from New York to Istanbul was a treat—between the tasty food and the large selection of movies, she almost could have wished the journey were longer. That might, in part, have been because she was nervous about what was waiting for her on the other side of the ocean, but she was happy to pretend it was about continuing her movie marathon just a bit longer.

When the plane landed in Istanbul and it was time to depart, the steady drip of anxiety Melody had been feeling crescendoed into a full-on downpour. In all the preparation she had done to get ready for this big move, she hadn't focused too much on the basic logistics, she now realized. She had three hours before her next flight—the one that would take her to Izmir—departed, and she had no idea what awaited her between deplaning and that next, shorter journey. Was she going to need to collect her bag, go through customs, and recheck it? And if that was the case, were three hours going to be long enough?

She remembered seeing something about customs on the screen of the entertainment system, but she had ignored it in favor of searching out her next movie. Now, while she was waiting for her turn to exit the plane—why *did* people stand up and wait in the aisle when there were still rows and rows of people in front of them waiting to leave?—she clicked over to the information screen about customs...

...and immediately let out a sigh of relief. Right there, on the screen, was a notice that passengers transiting through Istanbul to a selection of other airports in Turkey would not have to go through customs in Istanbul and would instead do so in their final destination. Izmir was right there on the list, and Melody was relieved to know there was one less thing on her to-do list for the next three hours.

Once off the plane, she followed the signs for transit passengers and passport control, all of which were taking her in the same direction. Passport control, it seemed, was one thing that would *not* be waiting for her final destination. She found a spot in line and dug out her passport and the printed visa that was stashed in her purse.

Because of the relatively short passage of time between selection for the Generosity Exchange and departures to their respective countries, most of the participants were entering their host countries on tourist visas, Madeline had explained. Procedures were in place to turn those tourist visas into longer-term visas or residence permits, depending on the country, but they had all been assured that everything was above board; nothing to be concerned about, especially given that Generosity Exchange participants were still on the payroll of their home employers.

No money would be paid by the foreign institutions, who would be paying their own employees who had been sent abroad, just like EduPowerment was doing for people like Melody.

It was all very complicated, Melody thought, and it did nothing to reassure her that she actually wasn't doing anything illegal by entering the country on a tourist visa despite having plans to stay longer. She reminded herself of that fact like it was a mantra, while she waited for her turn to speak to the passport control officer.

When it was finally her turn, a serious-looking officer beckoned Melody forward with a single wave of her hand. Melody stepped forward with a smile and a tentative "*Merhaba*"—one Turkish word that she hoped she'd actually managed to learn to pronounce. It was generally a good idea to know how to say hello to people, even if the officer didn't acknowledge her. Of course, it was possible that in her uncertainty of how to pronounce the greeting, Melody had actually said it so softly that the woman hadn't even heard her say it.

Melody handed over her passport and visa, prepared to answer any additional questions, and almost dismayed when she was directed to look at a camera and then handed back her stamped passport with nary a comment. That was it? Really?

"Excuse me, don't you want to know more about my stay in Turkey?" Melody asked, desperately hoping the officer spoke English. "I am coming on a tourist visa, but I'm going to be helping out at a university in Izmir. They will go through the procedures there to help me get a residence permit for the year..."

The officer tilted her head up sharply. "No," was all she said, as she directed Melody towards the passageway through to the other side of passport control.

"I'm sorry, I can't?" Melody felt a bubble of panic rise up. "I can't stay longer?"

The officer just smiled. "Welcome to Türkiye. Step through, please."

Melody took a single step closer, still not comprehending. "I'm afraid I don't understand."

"Lady, come through." The officer's tone was more serious now. "Whatever you do with the university in Izmir is between you and them. Nothing to do with me. Now, please—" She gave one last—clearly intended to be *final*—gesture to the exit, and Melody took the cue.

Finding her way to the connecting flight wasn't as challenging as Melody had feared. Sure enough, all the signs in the airport had been in both Turkish and English, and now that she thought about it, it made the utmost sense for airports to be clear and self-explanatory. No international airport anywhere in the world would benefit from unclear signage resulting in stressed out travelers needed constant assistance. She would try to remember that the next time she was flying, but she already knew that if she was in an airport again, there was a good chance she'd be feeling just as anxious as she was in this moment.

Melody's contact at the University of the Aegean was someone named Zeynep Öz, and Melody pulled out her phone to connect to the airport Wi-Fi and send off an update. Zeynep had informed her a few days ago that she would be the one picking up Melody from the airport. Nothing sounded worse than arriving in a new city and not having a clue where to go next, so a check-in just might go a long way to ease Melody's nerves about that particular worst-case scenario.

Once she was secure in the knowledge that her airport pickup had been arranged, Melody parked herself in a hard chair at the gate where her flight to Izmir was scheduled to depart in just a couple hours. Only then did she let the fact that she was in Turkey sink in—and sink in, it did, with the vaguest hint of something bordering on panic.

She looked around, taking in the unfamiliar sights. While many of the shops and restaurants were not that different from what she had seen at the Detroit airport, the words written on the signs and the language used in the announcements being broadcast every few minutes were far from familiar.

Of course she had known, intellectually, that this would be the case, but it didn't change the shock of being confronted with the reality. The temptation to feel that she had gotten herself in over her head and that she should look for the next flight back home threatened to bubble up, but she shoved it back down. Now was not the time to panic. It was somehow both too late and too early to do that, and she resolved to keep herself distracted until she was alone for the evening, wherever that might be.

Right, she reminded herself, *because I don't actually know where I'm going to be spending the night.* That was decidedly *not* the kind of thought that helped to reduce one's anxiety levels, but it was the truth.

Zeynep had assured Melody that she would be dropping her off at her accommodation for the night, but there hadn't been enough time to clarify where that would be. A hotel room? An apartment? Someone's guest bedroom? Melody was prepared—well, as prepared as she could be—for all of those options.

A rumbling in her stomach provided the perfect opportunity to seek out a distraction. She was hungry, and it probably wouldn't hurt to find a bit of caffeine, too, to keep her moving forward on this seemingly endless day.

Getting to her feet again and slinging her bag back over her shoulder, Melody was aware for the first time of just how physical the exhaustion of traveling could be. She'd thought she was tired from being awake for so many hours straight, but as she shuffled through the airport, following her nose in the direction of something that smelled a bit like heaven, she could feel it in her bones. Her feet, her lower back, her shoulders...from head to toe she felt like she'd been run over with a giant cosmic rolling pin. Stretching out on a bed was going to feel so good whenever it finally happened.

The nutty, warm smell beckoned Melody closer, her mouth watering at something that called to mind baked goods both sweet and savory. She approached a small café kiosk, the glass case of pastries glowing warm under fluorescent lights.

The one that caught her attention was shaped like a football, gleaming like it had been brushed with an egg wash before being baked at a high temperature, and dotted with small black seeds that looked like burned sesame seeds. She pointed to it, hoping the woman working behind the counter spoke English. "Sorry, what is that?" she asked.

"*Zeytinli poğaça*," the woman answered without hesitation. "Olive pastry. Would you like one?"

After the briefest hesitation—after all, who had ever *heard* of olives in a pastry?—Melody nodded. "Yes, please. And a cup of coffee."

After paying, Melody made her way to a small table, sighing with relief as she placed her heavy bag on the empty seat next to hers. She took a sip of coffee and then slid the pastry out of its paper bag, closing her eyes as she smelled its warm buttery, savory smell again.

She ripped it in half, surprised to see both slices of black olives and steam coming from the center. She took a tentative bite, unsure if she should expect the olives to taste and feel like they had come out of a can, but smiling automatically as she realized they were pungent, salty, and so flavorful that it was clear they came in small slices only so that they wouldn't overpower the warm dough that surrounded them. Even the black seeds on top of the pastry contributed to the flavor, rounding it out with an absolutely delightful nuttiness.

When Melody was revived from her snack and caffeine, she returned to the gate, pleased to see it had filled out a bit more, with a few folks waiting for the flight to Izmir. Before she knew it, they'd be in the air again.

The flight to Izmir was blissfully short and uneventful, and almost as quickly as the plane leveled out at altitude, it was descending again to arrive at the airport. After landing,

Melody collected her bag, breezed through customs, and was making her way outside to meet Zeynep far sooner than she had expected.

But if she had worried that Zeynep wouldn't be there waiting for her, her worries had been needless. Sure enough, there was a woman with long black hair and a toothy grin holding a sign that read MELODY CRITCH-FIELD who started waving as soon as Melody's eyes landed on her sign and she gave the smallest wave of acknowledgment.

"Hello!" Zeynep cried, taking Melody's bag from her and leaning in for a hug and quick double kiss on each cheek. "It's so nice to meet you, Melody. I'm Zeynep, but I think you already knew that."

Melody smiled back at her. "I did, just like you already knew my name, but it's still better to meet you in person. Thank you for coming to pick me up."

Zeynep gave her a dismissive wave. "Of course! How could I not? You traveled all this way to work with us, the least I can do is welcome you with some Turkish hospitality." She clapped her hands together. "Now, what are your needs? Food? Water? Or straight to the apartment to sleep off the day's journey? Whatever you need to do, that's our priority."

Melody balked. While it wasn't entirely out of the question to defer to the needs of the traveler, the fact that Zeynep, her future—or rather *current*, considering that she was in Turkey now—supervisor was prepared to follow Melody's lead rather than take her straight to the office to get to work was unfamiliar territory. "Er...well, I'm up for whatever. If we need to do some work today, that's fine, too."

"Absolutely not." Zeynep shook her head, decisive and final in her conviction. "Not only is the work day nearly over, but what would even be the point of that? You are exhausted, and you probably want nothing more than a shower, a meal, and a good long sleep. No, we don't even have you scheduled to socialize with the rest of the staff for another couple days. Tomorrow you're off, and I'll send someone to help you settle in, make sure you know where everything is and how it all works. I don't want to overwhelm you with the details now, but just know that you won't have to worry about anything with the apartment or utilities. That's all handled by the university, but you should still know how it all works and who to go to for any technical issues that may come up. I'll send Ben to you tomorrow morning—not too early, since I don't know how long you'll need to sleep..."

Zeynep continued talking, listing all the things that Melody would be sorting out the following day, but Melody was hung up on one particular detail. When she had a chance to get a word in, she asked her question. "Sorry, did you say Ben? Is...is that another American?"

Zeynep shook her head, a warm smile spreading across her face. "No, he's Turkish. Well, a German Turk, I should say. Born and raised in Germany with Turkish parents, but we're lucky enough to have him here with us for a while to help out." She frowned, a quizzical expression on her face. "Is that alright? I didn't think to ask, but if you're not comfortable with a strange man coming to your apartment, I can make different arrangements. Come myself, if you'd like."

"Oh no, that's not necessary." Melody waved a hand in protest. Zeynep was really bending over backwards and Melody didn't know what to do with that. "It's totally fine, of course. I was just surprised by the name, is all. It sounded like you were sending an American with me and that wasn't what I expected. Is...is there a big team of us here, actually?"

"No," Zeynep said. "From the Generosity Exchange, it's just you. And then Ben is here from Germany, of course. The rest of our staff is quite established. It wouldn't work that well for the department or our students if we had a complete staff turnover."

"Of course." Melody gulped, the anxiety of taking on an unprecedented challenge—getting out from behind the computer and into the classroom? What was she thinking?—catching up with her.

Zeynep placed a reassuring hand on her forearm. "Don't be nervous. I am well acquainted with how the Generosity Exchange program works, and I can assure you that you were hand picked. Just because you haven't spent time teaching before doesn't mean you aren't exactly the right choice for our program or that you aren't *very* good at what you do. You won't be alone in the classroom, but you *will* be bringing valuable knowledge and experience that our students couldn't get anywhere else. It's going to be a great experience."

Feeling better, Melody smiled. "That helps, thank you. Even though this is a very new experience, I'm really excited about it. I think it's going to be great."

"It's a new experience for us, too. You're the first Generosity Exchange participant we've received, though it's only our second year entering the program."

"Really? I'm surprised. Izmir is so beautiful, I can't imagine why you aren't overrun with applicants."

Zeynep shrugged. "Different things appeal to different people. I know our counterparts in English-speaking countries typically get the most applicants. And I don't blame them, moving to a new country is a big enough change without having to worry about learning a new language."

"Right." Melody gulped. "Speaking of which, I've been trying to learn a little Turkish, but I have to say...it's really hard. The new letters, the pronunciations...I mean, a 'c' sounds like a 'j,' and I keep forgetting that. I'm going to do my best, but I can't make any promises."

That got a laugh out of Zeynep. "Oh, trust me. It only gets harder. Wait until you learn about all the suffixes and vowel harmony...oh, and the cases, for sure." She shook her head. "Luckily for you, our university is conducted in English. We have international students who don't speak Turkish, and we want *all* of our students to be able to compete and excel on the global stage. Your lack of Turkish won't be a problem there. But in terms of getting the best deals at the bazaar, you should probably at least learn your fruits, vegetables, and numbers."

"I think I can handle that. And thank you for the reassurance. It hasn't been that long since I first learned about the program, even, and I'm very glad you didn't expect me to become fluent in Turkish in six weeks."

Zeynep laughed again—her hearty laughs were so joyful and contagious that Melody wondered if she would become addicted to them, to making Zeynep laugh. "If you could do that, you would be some kind of prodigy. But really, it was a quick change for us, too. We'd already established the teaching schedule for the fall and then we found out that you were going to be joining us. That's why I called in a favor to get Ben here. The two of you will be working in very close proximity, sharing classes, as I couldn't very well pull any of the other instructors off their course load."

"Ah." Melody nodded. She had been prepared for this Ben person to show her around the neighborhood tomorrow, to show her where the fuse box was and tell her who to call if her internet went out...but sharing classes? Working together day in and day out? Well, that was a whole different kettle of fish and put a lot more pressure on whatever impression the two of them made of each other tomorrow. She stifled a yawn. That was a concern for tomorrow. For now, she just needed to do exactly what Zeynep had suggested and get herself settled with food, a shower, and a bed as soon as possible.

Zeynep drove them past unfamiliar sights—first the open fields immediately surrounding the airport, and then towards increasingly urban buildings. At the end of their journey, the coast came into view, and Melody fell silent as the views she had missed from the plane—the one negative of claiming an aisle seat—materialized before her eyes. The water was turquoise dotted with white, thanks to the wind that was bending the branches of the palm trees dotting the shore. "Wow," Melody breathed, barely audible. "It's gorgeous."

Zeynep murmured in agreement. "It's good that you arrived in time to enjoy it. Soon, it will be too cold to swim." She chuckled then. "Though you might disagree about that. The tourists who come from colder countries have no problem swimming even in October, so maybe that will be the same for you."

As tired as she was, Melody still ached to dip her toes into the water, to feel the sun on her face. "It looks perfect."

Zeynep brought her car to a stop on a narrow street bordered very closely by apartment buildings and small shops, pulling the parking brake before exiting the car to retrieve Melody's suitcase from the trunk. "It's this one here," she said, gesturing to a building tucked between a bakery and a convenience store.

Melody followed her inside and up the stairs, stopping on the second floor for her new boss to unlock the door with a key she dug out of her purse. "Here it is!" Zeynep crowed, flinging open the door. "Home sweet home!"

The room awaiting Melody was nothing like she had expected—if she had, in fact, had an image in mind of what her new home would look like. The living room that they walked in to was cozy and yet classy, with wood floors, floor to ceiling windows, and a glass door that led out onto a small balcony overlooking the street. There were couches and a coffee table, and the room led right into the kitchen and dining space. It was all a marked improvement from her old apartment back home and Melody felt a pang at the thought of leaving *this* to return to the tiny space she shared with Felicity.

"Do you like it?" Zeynep asked, chewing her lower lip. "Let me show you the rest of it. If you don't like the apartment, we can find something that will work better."

Melody shook her head. "No, I love it. I mean, yeah. I'd like to see the rest of it." She chuckled. "But I can't imagine seeing anything that would make me not love it. It's beautiful."

Zeynep exhaled a sigh of relief. "Oh, I'm so glad. If you'd said it was terrible, we would have looked, but I'm not sure what we would have found." She gestured over her shoulder, leading Melody away from the living room and its beautiful view back down the hall. "Come on, let me show you this."

Melody followed along behind her, a spring in her step replacing all the tiredness she had been feeling. This place was *hers*. All hers. No roommate to share it with. "I guess people have all different kind of standards for taste," she said, "But it would be really surprising to me if someone said this wasn't suitable."

Zeynep shrugged, gesturing to the bedroom for Melody to step inside. "You never know, I guess. As I said, we've never had a Generosity Exchange volunteer before, so it was hard to know what to expect. And I hope you aren't spoiling us for the future. What if our next volunteers want to be put up in a five-star hotel?" She pulled a face, and Melody laughed.

"I can't imagine there are too many non-profit employ-ees with champagne taste," she said, stepping into the room. It had a large bed, adorned with fluffy pillows that looked entirely too inviting—okay, so maybe her exhaustion wasn't completely gone. There was also a wardrobe and curtains covering... "Another balcony?" she asked, pushing the curtains aside to slide open the door and step out onto it. This one overlooked the apartment building's courtyard, a small green space with a handful of orange trees.

She turned back to Zeynep, eyes wide. "Forget what I said about champagne taste. This place is better than anywhere I've ever lived by far and I'm afraid you all just might be spoiling me. How am I supposed to go back to my balcony-less apartment and long Michigan winters after this?"

That got a laugh out of Zeynep, who placed her hand on her chest and slightly ducked her head. "I'm very happy to hear that, Melody. And who knows, maybe we'll convince you to stay longer and you won't have to think about going back to your chilly apartment." She winked. "Let's just see. A lot can happen in a year."

After Zeynep finished showing Melody around—there were basic groceries in the fridge, new toiletries in the shower, and fresh linens on the bed—she made a gracious exit to allow Melody the time and space to do what she needed, reminding her again that Ben would be by the following morning.

"Are you sure you don't want to stay for a cup of coffee?" Melody asked, stifling a yawn.

Zeynep shook her head. "We will have plenty of time to get to know each other, Melody. For now, the most important thing is just for you to rest. If you feel up for it tomorrow, I will ask Ben to bring you to the university in the afternoon for that cup of coffee and so I can show you around a little." She put a hand on Melody's forearm. "But don't think about that now. Let me just get out of your hair and then you can get settled in. If you need anything, you can call me, text me, email me...but if you just need to shower, eat, and sleep, there's nothing wrong with that at all."

"Thank you." Melody stretched her arms out and embraced Zeynep before she could even think twice. She immediately felt her face heat at the realization of what she had done. *What is happening to me and why am I hugging my boss?* "I'm sorry," she said, pulling back. "I think I'm just so tired I forgot how to be professional for a second there. It won't happen again."

Zeynep laughed. "If you'll notice, I hugged you back. I didn't think anything was strange about it until you mentioned it." She shrugged. "But my students hug me sometimes—they're young, many of them away from home for the first time, so that's to be expected. And I hug teachers, too, when they're having bad days. I don't know, I guess I'm just a hugger. But if you don't want me to be, I won't be."

Melody shook her head. "No, I think it's really nice, actually. Just a bit of a change of pace from my old work place and my boss."

Zeynep frowned. "Mr. Richards, right?"

Melody nodded. "Uh, yeah. You know him?"

"Not well." Zeynep shook her head. "We met on a big video conference for the Generosity Exchange program." She frowned. "He seemed concerned about still being able to contact his employees for projects of his while they were abroad. I hope he's not thinking of doing that to you, since you'll have plenty to do just settling in to the neighborhood, exploring all Izmir has to offer, and getting to know your new job here."

"Well..." Melody bit her lip, fighting the desire to say something unflattering about Mr. Richards, yet knowing that wasn't the right move. "I'm sure if he needs some work from me, I'll be able to manage both. After all, I'm here to work, so it's no problem if I need to spend some out-of-office time working on his projects." She shrugged. "It wouldn't be that different from what I was doing back home."

Zeynep's eyes were wide as she shook her head. "I would never ask you to do that. Part of the point of the program is for you to experience a new city, a new country, a new culture. You can't do that if you're working two full-time jobs."

Melody nodded. "I'm sure it won't be that much." She forced a smile. "Don't worry about a thing, Zeynep. I'll be able to handle it, I promise. And it doesn't feel like work to me. I care a lot about our mission, you know? Both at EduPowerment and also here, teaching more young people how to do what I do." She chuckled softly. "Honestly? I don't even need a hobby. I love what I do that much."

Zeynep blanched, visibly recoiling. "I...I honestly don't know what to say to that. I love what I do, too, but it is *definitely* not a hobby." She pursed her lips in thought. "And if I have my way, we just might have you picking up a hobby or two of your own before your year here is done."

Not likely, Melody thought, *but I don't need to let her know that.* "Maybe," she said with a smile, closing the door behind Zeynep and turning to face her empty apartment.

Melody woke the next morning with a smile on her face, stretching her arms and legs in opposing directions yet still not reaching any corners of the mattress. Sleeping on a giant bed was decidedly *not* one of the overrated pleasures of life, especially not after a transatlantic flight.

She sat up, sliding her feet down to the floor before padding over to the balcony door to slide back the curtain and open the glass, the cool morning air making goosebumps rise all over her skin. The smell was fresh and crisp—*green,* somehow—and she itched to be out on the sidewalk, exploring the streets of her new neighborhood.

Yesterday, she hadn't left the apartment after Zeynep had said goodbye to her. After a large glass of water and munching on a few snacks she had found in the stocked cupboard, she had fully intended to unpack, hanging her clothes up in the wardrobe and arranging her things in the bathroom cupboards. But when she had sat down on the couch to send a few messages—just letting Chloe and her parents know she had arrived safely—all of her motivation had seeped from her body right into the cushions and she had stayed there, eyes glued to her phone for a mindless hour or two.

She had managed to fight the urge to take a nap, knowing it would only make getting over the jet lag harder, opting instead for a nice long, hot shower, cozy and clean pajamas fresh from her suitcase, and a bit of Turkish television with the dinner she pieced together from the things she found in the fridge. The energy that had sustained her enough to shower hadn't translated into energy to cook a meal, but there was nothing wrong with some bread and cheese and a piece of fruit.

Melody checked the time on her phone, noting that she had about an hour until this Ben person arrived to show her around. *Perfect.* She responded to the messages that were waiting for her there, hesitant to text her parents in the hopes that they had silenced their phones considering it was the middle of the night back home. But Chloe, at least, was sure to be awake. After all, she was practically in the same time zone.

Sure enough, Melody's phone lit up with an incoming video call from Chloe, her smiling face filling the screen as soon as Melody answered.

"Hey, you!" Chloe crowed. "God, I'm so happy to see your face. Your very *sleepy* face, if I may say so. No, I mean, you look great." She grimaced at her word choice. "I just mean, uh...you look like you slept really well, and you probably needed it. And also like maybe an eye cream might be a good idea before you face anyone other than me."

Melody laughed despite herself. "Way harsh, Chloe! I'm barely out of bed and you're already roasting me!" She turned the camera to show Chloe the view from her balcony. "I'm still soaking up some morning sun and trying to wrap my head around the fact that I get to live *here* for the next year. Serves me right for answering before I've even had coffee. I should have known you wouldn't appreciate my morning beauty."

"Ack, you're right, I'm a jerk." Chloe tucked her lips into her mouth, nearly managing to look chastised. "How are you feeling, though? Excited? What are you doing today? Knowing you, I'm guessing you're planning to put in a light twelve hour day, right? Maybe check in with Mr. Richards to see if he's got any extra projects for you?"

"Shush. No more teasing until I'm caffeinated, jerk. I can't even think of a good comeback."

"Like you ever could," Chloe muttered, widening her eyes immediately as if she, too, was wondering who had possessed the nerve to say such a thing.

"But since you're so curious," Melody continued, "I actually *explicitly* have the day off today. Zeynep, my new boss, is sending someone named Ben over to show me around today, so I'll just be settling in, no work for me."

"Ben?" Chloe asked, wrinkling her nose. "He sounds hot. Also not particularly Turkish, though I admit I don't know a lot of Turkish names."

Melody shook her head, making her way to the kitchen for her morning caffeine infusion. "You are ridiculous. How can someone sound hot when you've only heard three little letters about them?"

"It's not just the name!" Chloe protested. "I swear, it isn't." She shrugged. "I don't know, it's a gift, I guess. A rare and specific form of psychic ability that allows me to know how attractive I would find someone solely after hearing a vague reference to them and gaining only the most basic facts." She winked at Melody. "Just trust me on this one."

"I guess I'll have to," Melody said with a roll of her eyes. "And I will gladly let you know if and when you turn out to be wrong about this one."

"You do that."

"Okay, you've got to let me go now," said Melody, "Since you've got to leave for work soon, right?"

"Oh shoot, yeah." Chloe got to her feet, moving through her apartment at high speed, no doubt gathering the things she needed to bring with her before she scrambled out the door to make her way to the Tube. "How did you know?"

"Easy." Melody shrugged. "I figured if I was having a nice leisurely morning here after sleeping in, then it must be about that time. Plus, you were clearly distracted by my pillow-marked face, so I felt some responsibility for making sure that you were on your way on time."

"Well done, you." Chloe blew her a kiss. "Call me later, okay? I want to hear all about your date with Ben and get the full tour of your apartment."

"It's a deal."

Melody made her way through her morning preparations, enjoying a cup of coffee out on the balcony just long enough to force her to rush slightly through the rest of her tasks. When she was finally in front of the bathroom mirror, armed with her toiletry kit, she sighed. "Dang it, I hate when Chloe is right," she said out loud, gently nudging the swollen area beneath both eyes. She looked like she had spent the night crying, not sleeping peacefully in her new favorite bed. But, it was nothing that a few splashes of cold water, her trusty caffeinated eye cream, and maybe a little extra concealer couldn't help.

As she was finishing up, a buzzer sounded in the living room. Melody made her way to the box that Zeynep had pointed out to her the day before, pushing a button to unlock the front door and allow Ben to come in and make his way upstairs. Sure enough, a short moment later, there was a knock on the front door, and a smooth deep voice called, "Melody? It's Ben. Zeynep sent me?"

Melody smiled as she unlocked the door and pulled it open, the corners of her lips dropping as she took in the sight waiting for her on the other side. "Damn, Chloe. Right *again*!" she mumbled out loud.

Ben's forehead creased in confusion, and Melody clapped a hand over her mouth, shaking her head. "Sorry about that." She stepped to the side, gesturing towards the open kitchen. "Come on in, please."

Ben stepped through the doorframe with a smile, and Melody sucked in a breath. He moved with a grace that didn't quite compute given his height and the size of his frame, but it was clear that he was confident in his body, in the space that he took up. Plus, it didn't hurt that he smelled *divine*, and Melody caught the faintest whiff of a clean yet spicy smell—it couldn't be aftershave, judging by the neatly kept beard on his face—that was bound to haunt her dreams tonight.

"Welcome to Turkey," Ben said, holding out a bag to her that she hadn't noticed. "And welcome to Izmir, too."

"Thank you," she said, as she accepted the bag. "Um...am I supposed to open this now? I don't know if it would be rude to wait or ruder not to open it, and I'm only now realizing that's a pretty important cultural rule to know."

Ben chuckled. "You're right, that is the key to avoiding misunderstandings, I'd say. And we all want to avoid those as much as possible." He nodded towards the bag. "You can open it. You might even need me to tell you what it is, so...that's what I'm here for. All day, actually, or at least as long as you need me around. Any questions, I'm your guy."

"Thanks." Melody felt her cheeks heat slightly at something he had said or some inaccurate way her brain had interpreted it, so she busied herself opening the gift. Inside, there was a flat rectangular box, which she opened. Inside, there were gelatinous looking squares of different colors covered, some with powdered sugar, some with coconut, and a few with what appeared to be chopped pistachios.

Realization dawned on Melody a moment too slowly. "Oh!" she crowed. "Is *this* what Turkish delight is? I'd only ever tried that weird one that Cadbury makes, but this looks *way* better. I mean, I'm about to start drooling here."

Ben closed his eyes with a smile and silent chuckle, nodding at her question. "It is. I picked out a few different flavors from the bazaar, but I wasn't sure if you had any allergies or anything like that." His expression grew serious. "You can eat coconut, right? And pistachios? I don't want to give you something that's going to make you sick, and it's definitely not on our agenda to go to the emergency room today."

"Relax." Melody shook her head. "As long as none of these are flavored with dog hair—that's the only thing I'm allergic to, by the way—then we should be good." She smiled at him then. "Thank you so much, for all of this. It's very nice. A very warm welcome."

"Well, we're all really glad to have you here. Just trying to convey that."

Melody and Ben locked eyes, both of them smiling and both of them holding the gaze slightly longer than felt normal or appropriate—especially for work colleagues.

Melody was the first to break the gaze, looking back down at the table and replacing the lid on the Turkish delight. "I'll try one of these later. Should we head out now?"

Ben nodded. "Yes, that's a great idea. I'm parked downstairs, but I figured we could walk around first, get the bearing of your neighborhood, before I show you some of the places a bit further away." He looked down at her feet. "Are you wearing okay shoes to walk a bit?"

"These will be just fine," Melody answered, touched that he had thought to ask that question, but then chastising herself for it. *For one, we need to have a higher standard for men than basic human decency. And two, he probably has a girlfriend who likes to wear sexy and impractical shoes when he's showing her off around town, and so he has to ask questions like that.* Melody squeezed her eyes shut, just barely stopping herself from visibly recoiling at her thought. *And three, let's not be too quick to judge women who may or may not exist. Good for her for wearing sexy shoes, and no, she is not an object to be shown off.*

She pasted on a smile, picked up her keys, and started for the door. "Shall we?"

·♥·♥·♥·♥·♥·

Getting to know a new neighborhood in a new city in a new country on the day after she'd traveled across an ocean was—unsurprisingly—exhausting. Melody had pulled out her phone to type a note about something Ben had told her—where the post office was, which soups were made with brain or stomach so she could avoid them—so many times that at some point she ceased putting it back in her purse.

"Any questions so far?" he asked as they waited on a corner for the traffic light to change. "I know it's a lot, and I don't want to overwhelm you, but also...I mean, these are all things you need to know, right? So I can't exactly skip any of it, even if I'm sure we would both like that."

"Uh, let's see." Melody scrolled through the notes she'd taken on her phone with one hand, brushing her hair out of her eyes with the other. "Oh, right! The stove in my apartment is gas, right? So, first of all, is it safe? And second, how do I change the tank if it—"

She was still scrolling, mid-sentence, when Ben's hand encircled her forearm and the two of them were crossing the street. She looked up at him, blinking with something bordering on horror, then back down at his hand.

"Sorry," said Ben, dropping her arm, while gesturing with a tip of his head that they needed to hustle to get across the street. "It's a habit, I think. I'm used to walking around with my younger sister and she's often so lost in her phone that I have to literally hold her hand to get her across the street safely."

"Ah. Well, your concerns for my safety are appreciated but unnecessary. No hand holding necessary at all, in fact."

"Right." Was it her imagination, or had Ben's cheeks turned pink? "Anyway," he continued, "to answer your questions about the propane tank. It's very normal and safe to have one in your house. I mean, sure, accidents happen, but that's true everywhere. They're very rare, and every apartment I know has a propane stove. Still, I can check it for you if you'd feel better."

Melody nodded. "I would. It's all new to me and the last thing I want to do is blow myself up."

"I should hope not. Everyone's really excited to get to know you at the university, and they would all be crushed and heartbroken if you did that."

"That's good to know," said Melody. "It makes me feel so loved, by these new colleagues I don't even know yet."

Ben gave her a funny look. "Wouldn't your coworkers back in the US feel the same way?"

"Oh, I'm sure my boss would miss me. If I weren't there, I highly doubt he'd be able to find anyone else to boss around the same way he does me." She clapped her hand over her mouth as soon as the sentence was finished, eyes widening in horror. "Sorry. Uh, that's the jet lag talking. Mr. Richards is a great boss, and I'm happy to work for him. Lucky to work for him, too, actually. I'm really learning some valuable things, and the work we do together is making a positive impact on the world."

Ben held up a hand to stop her. "You don't have to convince me about your boss if you don't want to." He raised an eyebrow, studying her face a little more closely. "Unless it's actually yourself that you're trying to convince." He shrugged. "But I can't help you there. Anyway, I promise you're going to like working for Zeynep. I admit that I might be a bit biased when it comes to her, but she's actually the best. Fun, yet fair. Hard working, yet compassionate and understanding. From what you're saying about this Mr. Richards, it might be a real change of pace for you."

Melody shook her head. "He's a great boss, really. God, please don't think anything bad of him just because I spoke without thinking."

Ben stopped and turned to her. "You're not going to get in trouble, Melody. We're adults, and that's not really how any of this works. But also, I'm not going to run to your boss and tell him you said something the tiniest bit unflattering about him. We're friends, you and I. Or, at least, we can be, if you'd like a friend."

Melody nodded thoughtfully. "I suppose it's probably a good thing to have a friend in a new city. Though, to be honest, we barely know anything about each other. So how can we even know if we would actually be friends in real life?"

That got a laugh out of Ben. "Is this not real life? Are we living in a simulation? Damn, I wish someone had told me."

His laugh was contagious, and she smiled back at him. "That's not what I mean. Just...well, we're sort of forced into interacting with each other, you know? Forced proximity, I'm pretty sure the trope is called. If we met under different circumstances, would we even be friends? Would we even notice each other?"

"These are all great questions," said Ben, pursing his lips. "And also not exactly things we can know the answer to. All I can say is that I'm quite enjoying this time we're spending together, so if there's a different reality where I don't know you, then I have no interest in experiencing that reality."

Melody's cheeks got warm, and she had to look away from Ben. It was all a little too much, wasn't it? Walking around in the middle of the day with a gorgeous man who was giving her his undivided attention was one thing, and then he had to go and say things like that? If she wasn't careful, she was apt to develop a crush on her new coworker, and nothing could be more embarrassing than that. No, that wasn't even an option.

She tipped her head towards the sidewalk near where they had stopped to talk. "Shall we keep moving? I think we've got a few more stops to make before we go check on that tricky propane tank, right?"

The remainder of their explorations were a little less light-hearted than the first hours had been. Melody was careful not to let things between them veer in any direction even vaguely bordering on flirtation. It wasn't the time or the place and Ben wasn't the person for that to be appropriate. What would Zeynep think?

They walked all the way to the water's edge, and Melody stopped in her tracks as the Aegean Sea came into view. "Wow," she breathed. "This...this is stunning. And definitely an upgrade from the alternative."

A quizzical look on his face, Ben asked, "What do you mean?"

"I mean Michigan is beautiful and the Great Lakes hold a special place in my heart, but...you can't beat the sea, can you?"

"In my incredibly biased opinion, no, you cannot. But whether it's a lake, the sea, or even a particularly beautiful river, it's all good. You, however, are especially fortunate to be living walking distance from the Aegean Sea. And thanks to you, I get to spend the next year much closer to it, as well."

"That's right," said Melody. "Sorry for not asking about that sooner. Where do you normally live? And how exactly is it working that you're here now to be my co-teacher?"

Ben nodded. "Right. That's all a bit unusual, isn't it? I live in Dresden, Germany, normally. But when you accepted the chance to come to Izmir, Zeynep called in a favor to have me come here and help out. The timing of the whole program is a bit unusual for the University of the Aegean. I gather most of the Generosity Exchange partners are non-profits, operating on their own schedules, but those that are educational institutions have their academic calendars to consider as well."

"Gotcha." Melody nodded. "So the university already had its plans made for the new academic year, courses underway, and then Zeynep found out I was going to be here? That sounds like this position is causing more trouble than it's even worth."

Ben gave a slight head shake. "Not at all. It will be valuable for the students to have some international input, and that's what they'll get thanks to us. We'll be co-teaching a seminar—so, a fairly reduced course load—about international non-profit marketing. Last I heard, they filled the enrollment for the course to the max within a day or so of announcing it."

Melody gulped. "Wow. So, uh...no pressure?"

"It will be fine, I promise. You're good at your job, and so am I. That right there practically guarantees we'll have plenty of interesting things to share with the students. And we'll be bringing in interesting case studies, maybe a guest expert or two, leading discussions and getting the students to contribute as much as possible. It's not all going to be on you."

"That's a bit unfamiliar to me," Melody admitted. "I know I'm not supposed to say that out loud, but it almost doesn't sound like this is going to be enough work for it to justify the time and effort and expense of even having me here. I should tell Mr. Richards that I can still help him out with some of his projects. Just if he needs me to, I mean."

Ben pulled back in surprise. "You *could* do that. Or—" He gestured to the sea view they were facing, ships coming in to dock in the port. "—you could enjoy this. Being here. Learning what you can. Enjoying some new foods and the culture and maybe even having some fun."

Melody worried her lower lip in thought. "Maybe." But she already knew that if she spent the next year working significantly less than she had back in Michigan, she'd be consumed by guilt before even a week of it was done. Mr. Richards was paying her salary while she was here, and what would he have to show for it? Sure, EduPowerment had Generosity Exchange participants of its own helping out in the office, but how was he going to manage without her? Who cared about her job like she did?

By the time Ben's tour of Izmir—or a small fraction of it, at least—was done and Melody was reassured that the propane tank in her kitchen wasn't an assassin or a ticking time bomb, they were ready to take the short drive to the

University of the Aegean to get to know the rest of the team.

Melody felt a bubble of nerves in her stomach as she climbed into the passenger seat of Ben's car, which had been parked outside her apartment all day while they explored on foot. Ben had been nice enough, and Zeynep seemed to be just as great as he thought she was...but what about everyone else? Would she fit in with her new colleagues? Or did they all already think she was a burden, a clueless foreigner coming to make even more work for them? Not for the first time, Melody questioned if she had made the right decision coming here.

"You're awfully quiet over there," Ben observed, as he brought the vehicle to a stop at a traffic light. "Are you having some first day of school nerves?"

Melody shrugged. "Maybe. I wouldn't call it that, exactly. I just don't know what to expect, you know? I think it's perfectly normal to feel a little nervous about the unknown."

"Of course it is. If there's anything I can say to reassure you, ask away. All I can tell you is that Zeynep is the best, and you're not going to have any problems working for her. And I say that with absolute confidence, so just know that you've got nothing to worry about in that realm."

Melody gave him a skeptical glance. "That's the second time you've raved about her, so I have to ask. How do you know? What if she's just nice to you, but she's going to hate me?" Even as she said it, she remembered Zeynep's warmth and kindness the previous day, how unusual and nice it had felt to relate to a supervisor like that.

Her question earned her a laugh in response from Ben. "Maybe I'm not supposed to say this, but she's my aunt. So of course I'm a little biased about her." He shrugged. "But I would think she was the best even if she weren't my aunt. She's fair and kind and good at her job. What more could you want in a boss?"

Melody was quiet as she contemplated the question. Those weren't adjectives she would use to describe Mr. Richards, and she had no idea what that meant for the next twelve months. She hoped she wouldn't get so spoiled by working for someone like Zeynep that she would forget how things worked when she went back to EduPowerment. At least she could count on regular work coming her way from Mr. Richards. *That* would keep her grounded.

The tour of the University of the Aegean's campus ended up being a whirlwind, thanks in equal parts to Zeynep's enthusiasm and Melody's jet lag. Soon after their arrival, Ben had left the two women alone while Zeynep showed all the places of interest to Melody—the lecture hall she and Ben would use for their seminars, the workspace the two of them would share, the cafeteria, the copy room, and enough other hallways and rooms that all the wires started to cross in Melody's sleep-addled brain.

"Look at you," Zeynep said, stopping suddenly to place a hand on either side of Melody's face, eyes darting between Melody's pupils. "You must be exhausted! I'll get Ben to take you home."

"No, no. That's okay." Melody smiled. "It's a pretty short walk, right? I'd like to learn my way around so I'm not always depending on him."

Zeynep looked taken aback. "He doesn't mind. That's why he's here!"

But Melody just shook her head. Ben was nice enough, and she had certainly enjoyed spending the day with him, but there was no need for her to get attached to or dependent on a man within a day of her arrival in a new country. Surely, it would be better to keep things simple between them...just friendly coworkers, right? He didn't need to be her chauffeur, her tour guide, her handyman.

Or anything else, right? a voice in the back of her mind chimed in. *Would that really be so bad?*

Rather than nurture that thought any further, Melody smiled at Zeynep, holding up her phone. "I'll use my map app for directions," she said, "So I promise I won't get lost. And I'll use the opposite directions to find my way back here tomorrow morning. Is nine o'clock alright?"

Zeynep was nodding with some hesitation. "Yes, but...you don't need to come until Monday, Melody. Please, rest if you need to rest."

She felt a bit bad about not saying goodbye to Ben, but Zeynep had promised she would let him know that Melody had left as she was directing her to the main gate of the campus. It wasn't as if Ben would care, after all. If anything, he would be free to get back on with his life and his regularly scheduled activities now that he didn't have to drive her all over the city.

As Melody walked, she took in the sights with fresh eyes thanks to the slower pace. There was so much that was new, so much that she couldn't wait to experience. Foods to try, cafes to explore, experiences she couldn't even begin to imagine that awaited her.

The walk home served its intended purpose, simultaneously reviving Melody's energy and ensuring that she would sleep well when an appropriate time to give in to her jet lag arrived. She made herself another meal pulled together from the contents of her refrigerator, along with a promise that she would cook something within the next week, and enjoyed it on the living room couch before a shower and an early bed time.

The next morning found Melody the closest to her pre-jet lag self yet. She jumped out of bed at the first chirp of her alarm clock, and she only just managed to stop herself from leaving for work a full hour earlier than necessary.

By the time she was out on the sidewalk, marketing podcast playing in her earbuds, she was well and truly ready to face the day. To try on this new life as a university instructor, even if there weren't going to be any students for her to teach today.

She nodded and smiled in greeting at the faces she saw upon entering the University of the Aegean campus, most of them unfamiliar. As she opened the door to the office she would share with Ben, though, she stopped in her tracks. He was there already, sitting at his desk, and her stomach did an uncomfortable—even if not entirely un-welcome—flip at the sight of him.

"Good morning," she said with a forced smile, propelling herself past him to her own desk. *This is inconve-*

nient, she thought. *A crush on my co-worker? Not going to happen.*

Ben just smiled back, that easy grin threatening to blind her with its brightness. "Good morning. Glad to see you again, Melody. I missed getting to say goodbye to you yesterday."

"Yeah, sorry about that. I wanted to get my bearings of the neighborhood. And you didn't need to be driving me all over the city any more. You'd already done enough."

"I promise I didn't mind."

Melody smiled and sat down at her desk, busying herself with taking her notebooks and pens out of her bag and arranging them just so. The awareness that had announced itself at the first sight of Ben that morning hadn't subsided and was only growing in intensity. What was she supposed to do with it? Could she ignore it, put her head down, and work side by side with him, letting a friendship blossom between them? Should she act on it, tell him she felt a spark between them, and see where it went? Or would it make the most sense to use these confusing feelings to push herself to be a better employee, maybe even turning it into a "friendly" rivalry that would fuel her productivity?

To acknowledge and act upon her attraction, turn to **page 40**

To put aside her attraction and focus on befriending Ben, turn to **page 287**

To channel her attraction into rivalry and competition, turn to **page 128**

"Dresden. For sure."

Chloe's jaw dropped at Melody's words. "That *confidence*! I've never seen such a thing on you, and I must say I am loving it!" She propped her chin up with her fist, practically batting her lashes at Melody. "So tell me. Why Dresden? What has you so sure about this?"

"I...I don't know, exactly. I mean, it's in Germany and I've always sort of wanted to go there, I guess. And it's not Berlin or Munich...I don't think I would be up for such a big city. There's just something about it. It feels right, I guess." Melody felt the heat rising to her cheeks as she shrugged. She didn't sound so confident now, did she?

Not that it mattered to Chloe, who cut her hands through the air dismissively. "Whatever. It doesn't really matter to me what your reasons are, just that you have them." Her face lit up with a grin. "Which you totally *do*! Oh, Mel, this is just the best. I'm going to read through this whole list and apply to—let's be honest—a whole bunch of these positions. You...you're going to apply for the *one* that strikes your fancy and not even look at the others, like you're marrying it, not just trying out a new city for a while, for crying out loud..." She shook her head. "Anyway. We're both going to do those things...and then let's both visit each other wherever we end up!"

Melody bit her lip. It was too soon to be making promises that she would definitely be spending the next year in Dresden. But even more than that...

"Chloe, it's not vacation. Don't you think we're going to be kept busy with important projects? And that's even *if* we end up getting these positions, so let's not get ahead of ourselves." She shook her head, slightly at first and then with increasing power. "No, if this even happens, we owe it to ourselves and to EduPowerment and to whatever partner we end up working for to take our jobs seriously. Not to treat it like a nice long holiday and an easy chance to explore neighboring cities or countries. We can do that some other time."

Chloe scoffed. "Like you're ever going to take a European vacation, Melody. When was the last time you even spent a whole weekend not thinking about work? Hmm?"

Guilty as charged, Melody thought, but she refused to let her face show it. Steeling her gaze, she stared Chloe down. "I mean it. I'm taking this seriously...if it even ends up happening."

A wicked grin crept across Chloe's face. "Ah, so...glad to hear you feel so strongly about taking this opportunity seriously." She pushed Melody toward her own cubicle. "Now take that energy with you and go fill out the damn application while you're still all fired up about it."

Melody shook her head to herself as she shuffled back to her office. "I'm not...I can't...I'll fill it out later," she sputtered. "This has already taken enough time from the workday. I'll do it on my lunch break."

"You mean you'll do it after work," said Chloe with a wink. "Everyone knows you don't take a lunch break, Mel. I'm going to text you tonight to check up on you, though, so you better have actually done it."

"Yeah, yeah, I will." Melody dismissed her friend with a wave, dropping back into her chair and wiggling her mouse to wake up her computer—which had finally come to life. "How did I get myself into this mess?" she muttered to herself as she opened up her email account. The Generosity Exchange message was right there waiting for her to open it, goading her with its obnoxious, perky subject line.

If she were a different person, someone more enticed by the thrill of adventure, she'd open it, let the words wash over her eyes, scroll through all the possibilities and postings and imagine her life in every one of those far-flung places.

But two things were true about Melody Critchfield. The only thing enticing to her in that email were all the good causes that were being supported. She cared a lot more about making her mark, doing her part to create some good in the world, than she did about snapping selfies in front of famous landmarks or eating delicacies she'd never even imagined.

The other thing that was true about her in that moment was that there was no doubt in her mind that if she applied for this program—and that was technically still an "if"—it would only be for the Dresden position. She couldn't explain it to herself any better than she'd explained it to

Chloe, but she just knew there was something magnetic about that city, that some siren call was beckoning her there.

Hopefully the Dresden-based sirens weren't intending to dash her ship against the rocks and leave her to drown. *Yikes,* Melody thought, *I should have chosen a different metaphor—maybe avoided Greek mythology entirely.*

But what was it about Dresden that had a homebody like Melody wondering where her passport was, itching to get on an airplane for the first time since an ill-fated college spring break trip to Cozumel? Ill-fated because the group of friends she'd joined had turned out to be more a group of mean girls than the kind of chill humans she might have enjoyed relaxing with poolside.

Before she could stop herself—remind herself that she was on company time and this was *definitely* not an appropriate use of her work-issued computer—Melody found herself opening a new browser tab and typing "dresden germany" into the search bar.

Immediately, her screen was flooded with images and Melody's jaw was nearly hitting her chest. She'd expected history, sights...she had a basic understanding of how old most European cities were, after all. But she hadn't expected the level of beauty that lept off the screen, adding an alto harmony to the soprano siren call.

There was the Frauenkirche, an impressive church that had been rebuilt after the firebombing of Dresden. The Semperoper, an opera house that was currently showing *La Bohème*, the only opera Melody knew anything about. Historic building after historic building appeared as she scrolled, interspersed with some delightfully modern and kitschy art in a place called Neustadt.

"Is that...a giraffe?" Melody muttered to herself, leaning closer to her screen to examine the artwork. The impressively tall giraffe had been painted in such a way that it seemed to be nibbling the paint around it right off the wall. "So cool," Melody breathed.

It was, of course, at that moment that a throat cleared far too close for comfort. "Am I interrupting something?" Mr. Richards's voice boomed over Melody's left shoulder.

Most of the blood in Melody's body had rushed to her cheeks at the sound of his voice, and she cursed her ancestors for giving her such pale skin that flushed this easily. She spun in her chair, smiling up at her boss. "Of course not! What can I do for you, sir?"

Mr. Richards looked pointedly over her shoulder at the images on the screen. "Right. Well. If you insist that what you're doing isn't more important than *this.*" He looked pointedly down at a sheaf of papers in his hands.

She couldn't help it—her curiosity was piqued. "What is it? Something I can help with?" She almost lifted her arms to reach for the papers, but managed to stop herself. No need to come across as too desperate. Eager. Like she didn't have anything better to do. It wasn't that, of course. Five minutes ago she had Googled something unrelated to work for the first time in three years of working at EduPowerment. And she was grateful—really, she was—for the reminder that she had lost herself for a moment. The work she was doing was more than enough excitement for her, and she honestly couldn't wait to see what Mr. Richards was going to give her.

"It's the marketing copy for the microlending campaign. It's all wrong, I'm not sure what Dave was thinking, but..." He trailed off, his lip turning up as he dropped the sheaf of papers on the corner of Melody's desk. "I need someone to make this right. I don't know what's wrong with this campaign, but it's complete trash. I'm counting on you to do it again and do it better."

"Of course," said Melody, reaching for the papers. "I'll start working on it right away—"

"Good," said Mr. Richards. "I'll be leaving in the afternoon for my son's piano recital, working from my home office after that. I'll expect to find it on my desk first thing tomorrow morning."

"Okay." Melody forced her eyebrows to stay put and not climb up her forehead in proportion with the relative amount of time she had to work on this project. And it wasn't as if she didn't have other projects demanding her time today...but no, if Mr. Richards wanted this one done, then this needed to be her priority. She'd work through lunch if it helped her get everything done.

Who was she kidding? She'd work through lunch no matter what was on her to-do list.

Melody was deep in the zone when she heard a foot tapping at the entrance to her cubicle. She looked over her shoulder to see Chloe there, eyebrows sky high as she tapped her toe impatiently on the floor.

"Are you going home or what? I know you love this place, but it *is* good to see the world outside your cubicle now and then."

Melody stretched as she leaned forward to check the time on her computer screen. "Wow, five already? The afternoon just flew by. This project Mr. Richards gave me to work on has actually given me quite a challenge for a change of pace."

Chloe rolled her eyes at Melody. "Oh yes, it's such a change of pace for you to be so focused on your work that you forget to stand up for four hours and probably haven't even taken a sip of water since lunch. You *did* eat lunch, right?"

"Oh, hush. You know I did. No need to be so dramatic."

"I'm just trying to give you a little perspective, friend. Maybe help clue you in to the fact that your work habits are...shall we say...unsustainable? You need to eat and drink and stretch your legs and go outside once in a while if you want to be a healthy, happy human." Upon apparently seeing the lack of impact this statement had on Melody, Chloe continued. "Okay, how about this? If you want to be able to keep working, to be as productive as possible, to do your part in making the most impact on the world...you need to eat and sleep and rest and maybe consider having some work-life boundaries. *Maybe.*"

Melody started to pack up the things on her desk to take them home. Better to do a little extra work at home this evening than to put up with the wrath of a Chloe who was on a campaign to change Melody's priorities. As far as her friend needed to know, Melody *was* going home, resting, and putting some boundaries in place, whatever that meant.

Chloe eyed Melody's laptop suspiciously as she slid it into her bag. "You're not just going to keep working when you get home, are you? That's barely any different than staying at the office late, which I *know* you already do all the time, anyway. And don't you dare tell me you're bringing it home to watch Netflix because there's no chance in hell I'm falling for that."

Melody sighed. "Fine, you got me. But I'm just going to do a *little* more work, and I'll wear comfy sweatpants while I do it. Maybe even eat some comfort food. Will that make you happy?"

A mischievous look traveled across Chloe's face, and Melody knew she was in trouble. "That *almost* makes me happy...how about one more thing to sweeten the deal?"

"Depends what it is..."

"Okay, then. You have to apply for the Generosity Exchange program. Tonight." Chloe crossed her arms over her chest, leaning against the cubicle wall like she wouldn't budge until Melody agreed to her conditions.

"I'll look at it, okay?"

Chloe shook her head. "Not good enough. You've got to actually *apply* for it. I'm not saying you definitely have to move to Germany or anything like that. Who knows, maybe they won't even accept you." She shrugged, the look on her face conveying just how unlikely she considered that particular outcome. "But if you don't at least fill out the application, then there's a zero percent chance of this happening, and that just won't do. Apply tonight, and then maybe you can turn it down if they accept you and you decide you don't want to go."

Melody barked out a laugh. "I think we both know there's no way you would let that happen."

Chloe simply shrugged. "We'll cross that bridge when we come to it. Okay friend?"

Melody sighed in exasperation. There was no getting out of this one, was there? "Fine," she agreed reluctantly. "I'll look at it tonight. You are relentless."

Chloe grinned, broader than Melody had seen in quite a while. "I know, and that's why you love me. You'll thank me for this later, just you wait and see."

Melody did, in fact, leave for home then, thanks to her desperate need not to be badgered by Chloe anymore today.

When she got home, she was pleased to be welcomed by an empty apartment. Her roommate Felicity was nice enough, but the two of them had never particularly clicked. It likely didn't help things that Melody's old roommate had been a dear friend. Luisa had been with her all through college, and when she had gotten a job out of state and moved away, it had been a real blow to Melody's self confidence. Felicity had found her through a newspaper ad, and the two of them coexisted peacefully enough, sharing responsibilities for the chores and things like that...they'd just never exactly become friends.

Melody could blame it on the fact that Felicity was rarely around, spending most of her time in the chemistry lab where she was working on finishing up her graduate degree. And it certainly wasn't that Melody didn't appreciate someone having devotion to their job—goodness knew she had that in spades herself—but it was different when it was someone else spending all their time at work and not her. She couldn't understand how someone could spend *that* much time on their work when it wasn't something—not to be rude, but it was the truth—that would make the world a better place, like they were doing at EduPowerment.

Once she was in the door, she made a beeline for the kitchen. Hunger had caught up with her, no doubt in part because of her abandoned lunch, thanks to Mr. Richards's intervention. Not that she minded it—the project had been very interesting, and it had definitely made the afternoon fly by. Still, she was human and needed at least some basic caloric requirements in order to survive. Melody dug through the refrigerator for some leftovers, popping them in the microwave while she went to her room to change into comfy clothes. That was the best difference between working at the office and working at home, she thought—the attire. Not that it wasn't fun to put on professional clothes and make herself presentable...there was just something comforting about sweat pants.

Curled up on the couch with sweatpants, leftover fettuccine alfredo and roasted broccoli, and a laptop, Melody was in her version of heaven. The only thing that would make it better was having a documentary playing in the background about a cool initiative from a nonprofit she'd never heard about. Not that Melody believed in multitasking or trying to watch a documentary while getting her work done. She would never dream of splitting her attention like that while she was trying to tackle an important project for EduPowerment. Still, it was the idea of it, of having everything all at once. That was what sounded appealing to her.

She spent another hour working on her projects before pushing her empty plate aside, taking a quick stretch, and checking over her shoulder like she was in a movie and someone was spying on her. Not only was there no one else in the apartment with her, but there wasn't even a window behind her where a creepy neighbor could be pulling a *Rear Window* and looking at her through a telescope.

Nevertheless, when she was satisfied that no one else could see what she was doing, Melody opened up the email about Generosity Exchange and clicked the link to the application. She took a quick scroll through it, realized the questions asked there were far too straightforward for her to make an excuse about not having time to do it, and then sighed. It was now or never...if she didn't fill out this application tonight, she knew she would chicken out about it forevermore. It was time.

To give herself a little boost of courage, she opened another tab and resumed her earlier search for images of Dresden online. Once again, she found herself in awe of the city, its unique combination of history and cool modernity. It looked like the old part of the city, where the Frauenkirche was, was full of old buildings, churches, the opera house, while the new part of the city, north of the river, was where the hip young vibe was.

"Note to self," she said out loud. "If you end up moving to Dresden, probably don't refer to the cool part of the city as 'hip,' unless it's ironic. That's a guaranteed way to not fit in there among all the cool, *hip* people."

And then she sat back, jaw agape at what she had just said out loud to herself...*if* you end up moving to Dresden. Did that mean that a part of her—even a teeny, tiny part of her—was really considering this? She wasn't just filling out the application to humor Chloe, but it was actually something that she wanted to do?

"Maybe." She admitted it—out loud again—to herself, but her voice was tiny. She wouldn't have even heard it if she hadn't known she had said it. What was it about admitting that she wanted something that was so scary?

"Could be the fact that I just want it for myself," she thought. "That feels icky, somehow. If I wanted it because it was beneficial for someone else, that would be something totally different. But do I even dare to move forward with this? If it's just for me...then I can't do it, can I? Especially not on EduPowerment's dime...that just feels wrong."

She pulled out her phone to text Chloe her thoughts, surprised to find there was already a message from her waiting there for her to read.

"Don't chicken out. Fill out the freaking application or you're going to be in so much trouble tomorrow."

Melody smiled to herself. Chloe knew her too well. Still, she responded with her current worries.

"I'm trying to, but I'm having some doubts. This definitely does not seem like the best use of nonprofit funds, and I'm feeling some major guilt about it."

In response, Chloe sent back a series of emojis rolling their eyes.

"You're hopeless, you know that? Also, you clearly didn't do your homework and read up on the program. It's funded separately…a donation from someone who really believes in nonprofit cooperation. Yes, our bosses still pay our salaries even if we go abroad, but the extra costs are covered by this donation. The money is specifically earmarked for this exchange, so even if you don't do it, it's not like that money is going to be going directly to a service user in one of the countries where we work. It's just going to pay for Becky to go on spring break in Haiti, and I know you don't think that's a better option than you doing all the amazing work you're going to do in Germany."

Whew. That was a wall of text, and once Melody had the time to read it all, she felt adequately chastened.

"You really researched this thing from top to bottom, didn't you?"

"Duh! I had to have a rebuttal in place for any possible excuse you could give me to chicken out, which, let's face it, we all knew you were going to do."

"I'm that predictable?"

"I just know you that well."

"You should have been a lawyer. You know that, right?"

"I'm the lawyer of your heart, friend. My only courtroom is making sure you spend your life getting to have just as much fun as possible, and if I win this one, then I'll be satisfied that I've done my job well. Now…stop texting me and get back to that app. I expect a screenshot that shows you submitted it before you go to bed."

"Which you know is going to be at 10 pm, right?"

"You're nothing if not predictable, my friend."

"I prefer to think of it as dependable. Reliable."

"Okay, then. That, too. Get to work now."

Melody put her phone aside and looked up at the ceiling as if the help she needed, the strength she needed to put up with such a determined friend, could be found there. Then she shook her head and got to work. It wasn't help or strength she needed...nothing but gratitude, in fact. Having a friend like Chloe was a gift, even when it could be frustrating and annoying.

The next morning, Melody woke with a bounce in her step. She couldn't help but feel that it was going to be a good day. It had nothing to do with the fact that she'd submitted her application last night and received an obscene amount of celebratory emojis in response from Chloe. No, it was going to be a good day simply because she got to do good, meaningful work for a cause she believed in. She had put it out into the universe, the idea of joining the Generosity Exchange program, but when she asked herself what she expected for the future, she found she honestly didn't believe they would accept her.

And she was okay with that. More than okay, in fact. Life was good here, and she didn't need an adventure to a foreign locale to appreciate it.

Someone should tell that to Chloe, though. Melody had arrived at work twenty minutes early, humming a catchy tune she'd been listening to on the walk over, ready with a smile for everyone she saw in the office. Chloe, on the other hand, had been grumbling at regular intervals from her cubicle.

Finally, Melody stuck her head over the top. "What is going on over there?"

"Still nothing." Chloe flung her hands in the air, flustered. "Not even a 'we received your application and we're looking over it.' Sure, there was that automatic message saying it had submitted successfully, but...how long is it going to take?"

Melody laughed. "Impatient, much? Chloe, the application process hasn't even closed yet. You've got to be patient. And if you keep checking your email every ten minutes, you're never going to find anything new in there. Try leaving it alone for...I don't know, maybe twenty? Just for kicks?"

A crumpled up ball of paper flew through the air, narrowly missing Melody's head. "Your frustration is duly noted!" she cried, as she ducked back into her cubicle.

It was easy to be amused by Chloe's frustration, Melody realized. It felt so entirely impersonal to her, as if it had nothing to do with her own experience. This was Chloe's thing, after all. She was the one who was excited about it, and Melody had only filled out the application to humor her—or at least that was what she was telling herself. She might not go to Germany even if they accepted her. Not that she needed to remind Chloe of that particular fact.

Not unless she wanted another flying paper ball to sail a little closer to her head this time.

But as it turned out, Chloe's enthusiasm for checking her email paid off...eventually. Melody enjoyed the next few days of working distraction-free, thanks to the noise-canceling earbuds she had started to wear to drown out Chloe's dramatic sighs. She could churn out a lot of marketing copy when she was streaming classical music with an absolute minimum of Chloe-driven interruptions.

The one that finally broke through couldn't have been canceled by *any* noise-canceling technology that currently existed, as it came in the form of a full-on shriek, Chloe's head popping up over the cubicle divider.

Melody ripped out her earbuds, directing her full attention to her friend. "What on earth is wrong?" she wanted to know. "Is it a giant spider or something? Paper cut?"

Chloe looked up at the heavens, shaking her head. "It's so good. *So* good, Mel. Get over here!"

That got Melody's attention. It wasn't like Chloe to be needlessly cryptic or to use only ten words, when thirty would do the trick just as well. She pushed back from her desk and ducked into Chloe's cubicle.

And that's when she saw it there on the screen, the email. Underneath the subject, ***"Congratulations, you have been accepted to Generosity Exchange: UK Hope,"*** the message continued:

Chloe Allen,

We have reviewed your application for the

fall cohort of Generosity Exchange, and are pleased to inform you that you have been assigned to the UK Hope program. We received a considerable number of applications, and yours stood out. We are confident that UK Hope will benefit from your experience and skill, and that you will simultaneously learn from the experience and skill of your colleagues in the program.

Attached is all the information you should need at this point. Due to the personal preferences of each candidate, we have decided to leave flight booking to the discretion of each participant. As soon as you have booked your one-way ticket to London, please forward it to us and reimbursement will be arranged.

Congratulations again. Please don't hesitate to reach out with any questions.

Sincerely,
Madeline Andrews

Melody's hand flew to her mouth. "Oh my goodness," she murmured, feeling her eyes widen with each word. "Chloe, this is amazing! Congratulations!"

Chloe's posture matched Melody's, the shock just as evident on her face as it felt racing through Melody's veins. "I can't even believe it." Chloe shook her head. "I mean,

I *can* believe it. I really wanted it, as you clearly knew, and I couldn't stop daydreaming about it." A smile spread across her face. "But even when I imagined receiving this email, it didn't feel *this* good. I want to...I don't know, run around the office shouting and celebrating and carrying on like the best thing ever just happened because it *totally did*!"

Melody grinned at her friend. She really was so happy for her, so tickled to see her get just what she wanted. It was going to be an amazing experience, and she couldn't wait to hear all about it...

Wait.

What if—?

Before Melody could voice the question that had arisen in her heart, Chloe beat her to it. "What about you? Go check your email, too! Maybe we will *both* be running around the office shouting and celebrating." She nodded in encouragement. "Come on, go! Do it! Don't make me die of impatience and old age over here."

Melody felt glued to the floor. It was just checking her email, she told herself. Something she did all the time. It wasn't like it was going to change *everything*, no matter what was—or *wasn't*—there. If she wasn't accepted, she would be fine. Better than fine. She could go on with her life without anyone—especially Chloe—having the right to pester her for not taking chances, not putting herself out there more.

And if she *was* accepted...well, then she would think about it. About her next steps, and if she was going to take them towards a new adventure in a new country...or right back to her desk. Her comfortable, comforting desk where she created documents and slogans and marketing materials that literally made EduPowerment more effective. Gosh, she loved that desk.

"Earth to Mel," Chloe interrupted her thoughts. "Get your butt over to your desk before I do it for you. It's not like I don't know your passwords."

Melody whirled to her friend. "Seriously? How? I use such random things."

Chloe rolled her eyes. "Not random enough for a best friend. A password that your bestie can't crack—or, ahem, one that you didn't spill to her while you two were out for happy hour, bragging about *how great your password is*, like that's the best thing to be bragging about anyway—is truly an impossible feat."

"I did *not* brag about my uncrackable password..." Melody paused in her righteous indignation, suddenly unsure of herself. "...did I?" When Chloe nodded, she sighed. "Even *I* know how uncool that is. Not just because it's the most boring brag ever, but now I have to change all my passwords. And also wonder what else I may have divulged after a glass and a half of wine."

"Yeah, yeah." Chloe was pushing her towards the cubicle door now. "You can think about all of that later. Right now, you know what you need to do. I don't want to hear a peep out of you until you read that dang email."

Shaking her head the whole way—it was a short walk—back to her desk, Melody grumbled and complained about Chloe's bossiness on the outside, but on the inside she felt the tiniest stirring of something. Curiosity? Excitement? Perhaps even desire? Longing? It seemed as if there was a part of her—a tiny part, she was sure—that actually wanted this to happen. That wanted to open her inbox, see that she had been accepted, and then fling all her cares to the wind as she set sail for Germany and left Michigan behind.

Well, she wouldn't *actually* set sail. She would have to fly there, after all. But even if she had to get on an airplane and travel over the ocean that way, there was still a part of her—okay, it might actually be *slightly* larger than she had originally considered—that wanted to do just that.

She held her breath and said a silent wish, only just stopping herself from crossing her fingers—she wasn't superstitious, after all—as she logged into her email account.

I've got to remember to change that password, she thought to herself as she waited for the screen to load. *And maybe come up with some new conversation starters when I'm tipsy.*

But before she could start brainstorming the right combination of letters, symbols, and numbers, it was there. On the screen. Right at the top, practically staring her in the face.

"Congratulations, you have been accepted to Generosity Exchange: Deutsche Lebenshilfe"

"This can't be real." The words snuck out before she could stop them, and even though they'd been quiet, they must have been louder than she'd realized because Chloe's head materialized just above the cubicle wall.

"What is it?" she hissed. "Good news or bad? Spit it out!" Her eyes searched Melody's face, widening before her very eyes. "Oh. My. God! It's good news, isn't it? You wouldn't look that freaked out if they hadn't accepted you, I know it!"

And then she was gone, reappearing just seconds later in the flesh inside Melody's cubicle, hugging her from behind and attempting to jump up and down. It was all very awkward, considering Melody was still sitting in her chair, still holding the mouse in her hand, and still staring blankly at the screen while Chloe maintained both her grip and her jumping.

"Do you know what this means?" Chloe asked, out of breath, when she finally gave up her physical celebration and stepped back so that Melody could turn and face her head-on.

Melody shook her head. She still hadn't been able to get a word out, between the mingled shock and confusion she was feeling. Was this something she was happy about? Was it even within the realm of possibility for her to accept the offer?

Luckily, Chloe was talking enough for both of them. "Well," she barreled on, "This definitely means that you and I are going to be having some very not-in-Michigan adventures. I'm thinking you should come visit me in London first and then maybe I'll come see you in Germany, and..." She paused, stroking her chin in thought. "Paris, for sure. And I don't know where else...Ireland? Iceland?" Her excitement level was ramping up again, evident in her widening eyes and rapidly increasing speaking pace. "We could go somewhere once a month, at least. Maybe even twice! I mean, it's Europe, Melody. You can get on a train and be in a new country just as quickly as we could be in Chicago if we left this office right now."

"That's a great point, Chloe." Melody had finally found her voice. "You should definitely do that. It actually might be easier if you make a list of all the places you *don't* want to go rather than the ones you do want to visit." She gave a weak smile, hoping to throw Chloe off the scent of how she had shifted the pronouns from "we" to "you" and get her friend back to her own cubicle, working on the list of all her travel destinations for the upcoming year rather than pestering Melody about being a part of it.

But Chloe wasn't so easily deterred. One of her eyebrows popped up higher than the other, and she tilted her head at Melody. "Why are you not excited about this?" She groaned then, before Melody could even respond. "Don't tell me you're thinking about not going. My goodness, Mel, that would be possibly the *most* boring thing you could do right now."

Melody maintained her silence, not quite meeting Chloe's eyes. How could she know what she was thinking if she couldn't have the silence and space she needed to figure it out? The more excited Chloe got, the more anxious Melody felt. All she really wanted was to be left alone, to get back to her work, and to focus on tackling something that she understood. She had plenty of projects waiting for her attention, and that was a better use of her time and energy than dreaming about spending her weekends traveling across Europe with Chloe.

If only she knew how to express all of that to Chloe.

Instead, Chloe rolled her eyes at Melody and stalked back to her cubicle, muttering, "You've got to be kidding me," plenty loud enough for Melody to hear.

Melody was in a daze the rest of the day, completing her work on autopilot. There had been an informational meeting in the afternoon for the participants who'd been selected for the Generosity Exchange program, but Melody was so dazed through it she knew she'd have to reread the handouts later if she actually decided to accept the offer.

Madeline Andrews, the director of the program, had been an impressive figure, commanding the room with a grace and power that were just about the only thing to break through Melody's haze of confusion and dissociation. As she led the presentation and explained the program, Melody felt a longing she couldn't explain. She longed to feel like she could belong to something like this. Like she could hear about a program, an opportunity, a way to take up space in the world and actually feel like she deserved to be a part of it. Instead, she felt so disconnected, like she was a mere observer watching all these people about to embark on the adventure of their lifetime.

What would it feel like to say "yes" to this chance that had fallen into her lap? How could she do that, when she looked at the group around her and couldn't find a place to slot herself into their mix? She didn't belong here—she was a little older than the rest of them, fresh college graduates that they were, and she was a homebody, while they all seemed to be excited, in the same way Chloe was, to travel and explore and meet new people and take up space everywhere.

On the other hand, she just wanted to do her work, to make her positive mark on the world, and to be told she was doing a good job at those things. And preferably to be home and in bed at a reasonable time, recharging her batteries in the comfort of her own apartment, catching up on reading and podcasts and all the finer things of life.

Just then, Madeline's voice cut through her thoughts. "Generosity Exchange is not all about fun and games, though. The partner institutions you'll be working with have selected some unique and high priority projects for each of you to work on, and the first order of business, the most important metric by which we will measure the success of this program, is its effectiveness in moving those projects forward." She peered over the top of her thick black frames around the room. "Therefore, if there is anyone here who is thinking this sounds like your chance to study abroad with a little more disposable income, put that thought out of your head. We *do* care about your work-life balance, but let it be abundantly clear that we are sending you abroad primarily to work. Your evenings and weekends are yours, but the time that you are in the office needs to be 100 percent focused on the objectives we're laying out now."

Something that felt like a silent groan rippled through the room, but Madeline's words perked Melody up. Maybe, just maybe, she wasn't in the wrong room after all.

·❤·❤·❤·❤·❤·

"I'm going to do it," Melody announced to Chloe over coffee the next morning. It was a Saturday, and the two of them had met up for coffee at the cafe in their favorite bookstore, as was the typical weekend plan for them. Nothing beat a cup of coffee that someone else made—why did it taste better?—and Melody had never actually managed to visit the bookstore without at least browsing the selection of new and used books—and usually going home with one of them. After all, how was she supposed to know what her plans were for the rest of the weekend if she didn't have a new book in hand?

Chloe took a lazy sip of her drink. "Do what? Trim half an inch off your hair? Buy two books instead of one? Give me a hint here, Mel. When you say a sentence out of nowhere, it helps if you remember that whoever you're talking to doesn't actually live inside your head."

Melody rolled her eyes. "First of all...rude. I have way more interesting things to share than trimming my hair and picking up an extra book." *Do I though?* she wondered, taking a quick mental inventory of something more thrilling that she'd done in recent history and coming up short. "Like how about this: I'm going to Germany." She sat back in her seat and waited for Chloe's reaction.

And she wasn't disappointed. With her jaw dropped to her chest, Chloe stared at Melody. "For real? Like...really? *Really* really? After the meeting yesterday and everything...you're convinced? This is happening?" Her expression remained skeptical, excitement seeping through only when Melody had nodded reassuringly at least twelve more times.

"Holy crap, Mel, this is amazing!" Chloe shook her head in disbelief. "And here I had been resigning myself to the fact that I was going to have to take this whole adventure alone, probably make a new English best friend to have all my memories and adventures and fun with...but you're doing it too! We're going to have so much fun together."

Melody gave a nervous chuckle. "Um...actually, we're going to be in different countries. Right, Chloe? So while I don't fully support your plan to replace me, I *do* think a local travel buddy might be a great idea for you."

Chloe was shaking her head vehemently. "No way, not missing my chance to travel and explore with you, baby girl. I'll be coming to see you in Dresden before you know it, and we'll figure out a plan for your first—of many, to be clear—trips to London when I'm there. And I'm thinking at least a weekend in Paris, maybe a little trip to Spain..."

And this time, Melody could humor her friend. There was no need to jump in and reassure her that she was actually going to be prioritizing work over travel...no. Chloe was excited, and Melody didn't need to be the one to rain on her parade. Besides, based on what Madeline had said, they both would have plenty of work to keep them busy.

The departure date for the Generosity Exchange participants was set for two weeks after the orientation program, far sooner than was comfortable for Melody. Considering that most of the participants were fresh out of college, the sense of adventure with the orientation group was strong. They continued to meet a few times a week, breaking into small groups based on the projects they had been assigned to.

The time flew by, between the orientation tasks that were added on to their regular responsibilities and the preparations that needed to be taken care of personally. Melody was grateful to find a subleaser for her apartment, something Felicity barely seemed to care about, and she'd been spending more time with her parents than normal to make up for the coming weeks and months that she would be gone.

Before she knew it, it was time to go. She had opted to take a rideshare to the airport with Chloe, having her tearful goodbye with her parents the night before rather than bringing it to the departures gate. It was never easy to make a big change like this, she knew, and yet still, those goodbyes and the pain she had felt at saying them nearly made her change her mind.

Chloe had known this would happen, Melody was pretty sure. What other reason could she have had for convincing Melody to ride to the airport together, arriving there with far more than enough time until Chloe's flight was scheduled to leave an hour after Melody's. When she had asked Chloe about it, she had simply shrugged and said she liked hanging out at airports. Melody suspected differently, though. Chloe might not admit it, but she cared about Melody more than she let on—enough, even, to inconvenience herself if it made her friend just a bit more comfortable.

The line to check in for Melody's flight to Frankfurt was long, but it moved quickly. "German efficiency," Chloe had said, with a knowing nod. "You'll have to get used to that."

Once Melody was checked in and her bags had been handed over, on their way to Frankfurt where they would be transferred over to her connecting flight to Dresden, it was time to get Chloe checked in for her direct flight to London.

"Coffee?" Chloe asked with a lightness that suggested that being free from her two large suitcases had, in fact, lifted a weight from her shoulders.

Melody shook her head. "Not yet. Let's get through security first and find something on the other side."

The process of preparing to go through the security line gave Melody equal amounts of anxiety and distraction. It was nice to have something to think about besides the fact that she was currently moving across the world—or at least across an ocean—but the pace at which she needed to take off her shoes, dig her laptop and liquids out of her bag, pat down her pockets, put everything in a tray and get in line to go through the metal detector definitely increased her pulse.

When the TSA agent waved Melody into the metal detector, she lost her last claim on dignity, hands over her head and pit stains on display for everyone in the area. "So much for traveling in style," Melody grumbled to herself as she caught a whiff of her own sweat. Her deodorant was no match for the stress and anxiety of this day.

There was nothing she could do about it now, though. Against all the travel-related advice she had been reading in her free time, Melody had not actually packed a change of clothes in her carry-on luggage. It turned out that packing for a year was a daunting enough task when you were just trying to make sure that everything important actually made it onto the plane, to say nothing about carefully choosing where every item went.

As a result, her carry-on luggage was piled high with the books that would have pushed her suitcase over the weight limit, toiletries—nothing that wasn't travel-sized had made the cut; she'd be shopping for German shampoo within the week—and a few odds and ends that had nearly been forgotten. Hair straightener, pens and notepads, her favorite travel mug...if TSA asked her to empty her bag, they were in for a real variety of boring items inside.

Melody and Chloe made it through the security line without a hitch and shuffled over to the nearest Starbucks once they had put their shoes back on their feet.

"How are you feeling?" Chloe asked, while Melody was studying the menu like she had never been to a Starbucks before and didn't already know exactly what she was going to order. Was it just the sudden awareness that familiar things—and a predominance of English words—were about to be in short supply that made her want to take it all in through her eyes?

She shook her head at Chloe, plastering on a smile. "Fine! I'm...excited, I think."

Chloe cocked an eyebrow. "Nervous?"

"No..." Melody shook her head. "I mean, yeah. Of course. But I'm telling myself that I'm excited."

"You can be both, you know. No need to pick just one."

"I mean, sure. I know that. It's just...well, I'd rather be excited than nervous. Only one of those feelings comes with doubting what the hell I'm doing here in the first place."

Chloe rubbed a hand on Melody's upper back. "I'll be here with you, making pretty much the same decision that you made. Okay? There's no need to wonder if you're making a huge mistake or to think about changing your mind now. You'd always wonder what you missed out on, anyway, and we can't have that."

The two of them stepped forward in line, closer to the register. "No, you're right," Melody agreed, smiling wanly at Chloe. "And I'm really glad you're here with me now. Did I tell you that yet?" She sighed. "I just wish you were going with me to Dresden, too."

Chloe laughed. "Not me! Nothing against Dresden, I mean, but I've got my own adventure in store for me. And let's be honest here. If you and I were going to the same city, it would be a totally different experience. Sure, we'd come away at the end of it even better friends than we already are. But we also might not have bothered to make any other friends or have any experiences beyond what the two of us already know we like. And I, for one, am not having that happen."

"You're right again." Melody shook her head. "I wish you weren't, but of course you are."

Melody had spent the flights feeling tired and wired, knowing simultaneously that her body was exhausted and that there was no real possibility of her closing her eyes and surrendering to sleep. There was simply too much going on around her. What if she missed something? A crucial update from the captain, a movie she hadn't watched yet, or—worst of all, perhaps—a meal?

As it was, she arrived in Frankfurt feeling like she was sleepwalking, floating through the terminal and through passport control as if her body and her mind were two separate entities and at least one of them was running on autopilot.

And it certainly hadn't helped that her ears hadn't fully acclimated yet after the pressure changes, making her stare blankly at the passport control officer as if she were listening from underwater or he were speaking a foreign language.

Because it hadn't been a foreign language. After she had blankly stared at him in response to his first question, he had sighed and held out a hand, repeating himself more slowly. "Passport, please."

Melody was too disoriented and tired to feel embarrassed, and she carried on that way until she was once again in front of a gate, waiting for her flight to depart. This last leg of her journey would last less than an hour, but she had longer than that to wait for it to begin boarding.

Melody closed her eyes and took a deep breath, taking a moment to listen to the sounds around her, and in particular, all the voices she couldn't understand. Of course, on the flight from Detroit there had been announcements in German and English, but it was only now, sitting in the airport with her fellow travelers, that she was aware of just how immersed she was in the new language.

It contributed to her dreamlike state, being surrounded by people speaking a language that she couldn't understand, apart from the absolute basics she suspected anyone could understand. *Gesundheit. Hallo. Sauerkraut. Frankfurter.* Melody shook her head at herself. Her knowledge would do her no good at all, and there was a very real chance she had overestimated just how international this new job was going to be. After all, weren't airports supposed to be international, too? And yet it certainly seemed as if everyone around her was speaking and understanding German and she was the only wide-eyed newbie who was completely and utterly clueless.

Melody sighed and sunk deeper in her chair. Freaking out about what a huge mistake she had made wouldn't do her much good right now, and yet that logic didn't help her stop feeling anxious. While it was true that she could turn around now and find a flight back to Detroit, even she had some sense of pride and couldn't imagine the grief and teasing she would get from everyone—Mr. Richards, Chloe, Felicity, and everyone in between. No, it was worth it to see this through even if only to spare herself that particular discomfort.

Digging through her purse, Melody dug out her phone and opened her email. She had been corresponding with Bettina Schmidt, the person who would be her supervisor in Dresden, and it was a reassurance to see that the messages they had exchanged had been in perfect English. *After all,* Melody reminded herself, *it's not as if anyone ever said that German was a requirement for this position or bothered to ask your current level. You are clearly overthinking this.*

And maybe she was. But she still downloaded the Duolingo app and popped in her headphones, determined to do as many language lessons as she could before she arrived in Dresden.

"Milch oder Tee? Wasser, bitte. Danke." Melody was mumbling the new phrases she had learned to herself thanks to the handful of lessons she'd been able to mainline on her phone. Still, she was a few minutes away from meeting Bettina Schmidt, and she couldn't quite see how knowing the language for choosing drinks was going to be helpful. At least it felt better than showing up completely empty-handed—or, rather, empty-headed when it came to German.

As she stepped out of the airport, a semi-familiar face greeted her with a smile and a wave. Melody had seen a professional photo of Bettina on the company website, and here she was now, in the flesh, waiting to greet her with a sign that read "Melody Critchfield" in handwritten capital letters.

"Ms. Critchfield! Welcome to Germany," Bettina stepped forward and held out her hand for Melody to shake it. "It's very nice to meet you in person at last." She looked at Melody's suitcase. "Can I take that for you? We're going to take the tram to your apartment, but it's not too far from here."

Melody shook her head. "Oh no, it's okay. I don't mind." But Bettina dismissed her with a wave of her hand.

"Please," she said. "I know how exhausting it is to travel internationally, and how much I appreciate it when someone helps me out. I promise I won't judge you for not being able to resist my offer. Plus, it's good exercise for me." And with that she took the suitcase, gestured to the sidewalk outside the airport, and took off at a good clip, Melody trailing along behind her.

When Bettina slowed down her pace to allow Melody to fall into step with her, she turned and smiled at her. "So," she began, "We will get you settled into your new apartment today and give you the rest of the afternoon to make yourself at home, find your way around a bit. You won't start in the office until Monday, but I thought you might enjoy meeting some of the team over the weekend. I've arranged a bit of a hiking trip for us tomorrow afternoon if you'd like to get some fresh air, stretch your legs, and get to know your new colleagues. I hope that's alright with you."

Melody managed to stop herself from widening her eyes in shock. "Oh! I didn't realize there was a lot of hiking to do here...I don't know if I really packed the right shoes for it."

Bettina looked down at the slip-on shoes Melody had worn for her travel day and pursed her lips. "If you have something else with a bit more grip, that would be good. What about your sport shoes? You did bring shoes for sport, right?"

Melody shook her head. "I...well, now I'm embarrassed to admit that I only packed with work in mind. So, I have plenty of professional and business casual options, but...not so much outdoorsy gear, I'm afraid."

"That's okay. You can buy something if you need it later, but for tomorrow at least, I can loan you some shoes."

She looked at Melody's feet then. "You're...what, a size 36? 37?"

"Um...maybe? Sorry, I looked up the shoe size equivalents once but now I can't remember. I wear a size 7 in US women's shoes, if that helps."

A firm nod from Bettina. "It does. That will work perfectly. It's settled, then."

And Melody supposed it was. Though there was a part of her that wanted to insist her new colleagues didn't need to go on a hiking expedition on her behalf, another—much smaller—part of her was curious about what the day would bring. Whether or not she would be able to keep up and not embarrass herself was something that remained to be seen, though she didn't feel as if she could turn down the invitation, not when she was the guest of honor.

By then, they had arrived at the tramline, Bettina coming to a stop and turning to face Melody with a smile. "Are you familiar with the layout of Dresden? If I tell you where our office is and where your apartment is, will it mean anything to you?"

"That's a great question," said Melody. "I've been looking at a lot of photos of the scenery, mostly of the really famous places like the Frauenkirche—"

"*Frauenkirche,*" Bettina interjected, her pronunciation vastly different from Melody's.

"*Frauenkirche,*" Melody repeated, earning a nod in response from Bettina. "And also...Neustadt? Am I saying that right?"

Bettina shook her head with a small smile. "Close. It's *Neustadt*. It means 'new city,' and that's the newer part of the city, unsurprisingly."

"*Neustadt*," Melody repeated. "It looked beautiful. Very cool and hip, actually. Though the old part of the city is beautiful too, just in a different way. I'm very excited about all of it, actually, and I can't wait to explore."

"Yes, we quite like this city of ours. And I'm pleased to hear that you've actually been doing your homework. I was concerned you might think you signed up to work in Berlin or Munich and didn't realize there were any other cities in Germany."

Melody shook her head. "It only makes sense to look up your destination, doesn't it? And it's my first time in Germany—in Europe at all, actually—so I tried to soak up all the information I possibly could."

"Very good. Well then, you might understand what I mean when I tell you that your apartment is going to be in the Neustadt, Bischofsplatz is your tram stop. And our office is on the other side of the river, the Prager Straße tram stop. After we get you settled in your apartment, I will show you around so you know how to get to work."

"Great! Wow, thank you. I...well, I'm even more excited about all of it now." Melody grinned, unable to refrain herself from expressing the joy she was feeling. This was really happening, and she was really about to live in the coolest part of the coolest city she'd ever seen. Not that she'd even seen Dresden yet, apart from the photos she regularly scrolled through on her phone. And not that she'd seen a particularly high number of cool cities in the decades she'd spent thus far on Planet Earth. Still. It was cool.

"Here we are," said Bettina as the yellow tram approached. The two women stepped on board, where Bettina punched a paper card in the machine before handing it to Melody. "We'll get you set up with a tram pass and the app, but for right now this ticket will do. Don't lose it."

Melody nodded as she pocketed the small ticket, sliding into a seat as the tram began to move. She enjoyed the views out of the window, first the open spaces around the airport and then the increasing number of buildings as they got closer to the city. Bettina was quiet, busy with her phone, and Melody enjoyed the moment to familiarize herself with the surroundings a bit.

Just as the movement of the tram was about to lull her to sleep, Bettina got to her feet, pushing a button. "This is our stop," she told Melody as she made her way towards the door. Melody followed her off the tram and onto the sidewalk, where she stopped and turned slowly, taking in the view. The buildings were just a few stories tall, the street level full of small shops and larger markets. She wanted to explore, to poke her head in the bakeries, the flower shop, even to wander the aisles of the grocery store and see what was different inside.

But there would be time for that later—Bettina was already off again, wheeling her suitcase in the direction of an apartment building. She directed Melody to a studio apartment on the top floor, its windows overlooking the neighborhood. "I love it," Melody breathed, taking in her cozy surroundings. It was small, but it was hers. There was a living space, complete with a couch, a table, and a small kitchen.

Bettina was particularly pleased with the kitchen. "This building is mostly for professionals on short-term stays. If you had come a little earlier, we might have been able to find you shared accommodation with the students, but..." She shrugged. "This is what was available on short notice. Do you like it? We can try to arrange something different, but it will take some time..."

Melody shook her head. "It's great. I've never lived alone, and this is just the perfect size for me. Really."

"Great." Bettina clapped her hands. "Shall we walk around the neighborhood a bit then? Show you the way to the office?"

As exhausted as she was, Melody nodded. If she didn't keep moving now, she'd probably fall right asleep, and everything she'd ever read about jet lag stressed the importance of adjusting to the new time zone as quickly as possible. It was no time for sleeping when she had a whole city to explore.

Outside, Bettina pointed out the best place to get fresh produce, the only bakery in the neighborhood that had earned her stamp of approval, and the tram stops for the different lines that passed near Melody's apartment. Before she even knew what was happening, they were back on the tram again, this time headed for the Deutsche Lebenshilfe office.

"Sit on this side." Bettina pointed to the vacant seat on the right of the tram car. "It's the best view, and you won't want to miss it. Trust me."

And she hadn't been wrong. As the Elbe, the river snaking through Dresden, came into view, the skylines of the city's oldest buildings framing it, Melody's breath caught in her throat. "Beautiful," she breathed, unable to take her eyes from the sight.

"It is." Bettina was transfixed, too. "You never get tired of that view. Or, if you do, I suppose that means it's time to move."

The two women walked in companionable quiet, Bettina pointing out buildings and historical sights as Melody snapped pictures on her phone. It all started to blur together, exhaustion and jet lag stopping her from fully taking in anything that she was hearing, and she hoped she would remember some of the facts Bettina had shared in the future when it didn't feel so much like she was sleepwalking.

Finally, Bettina had sent Melody back home when it had become clear just how quickly her energy level was fading. "Don't miss your tram stop," she had warned. "You'll wake up at the end of the line and it'll be a nasty surprise. Just go home, go right up to your apartment, and get some rest. I'll be there at seven tomorrow morning for our hiking outing. And I'll bring the boots for you, too."

"Thank you," Melody said with a smile, too tired to even react to the early wake-up time for a hiking expedition of all things. It was nothing she couldn't handle, not without one solid night of rest.

·❤·❤·❤·❤·❤·

As it turned out, Melody's assessment about a good night's sleep equipping her to handle whatever the next day would bring hadn't been entirely accurate. The hiking—she thought the area was called the Heide, but she had been too focused on keeping herself upright and putting one foot in front of the other to pay much attention to her surroundings—was good for stretching her legs and filling her lungs full of fresh air. But it had also made her even more aware of just how little time she spent on non-work activities, particularly anything remotely exercise-related.

"Do you do a lot of things like this?" she asked Paul, one of the accountants, while they were taking a break in the shade. "A lot of socializing outside of work, I mean?"

Paul shrugged. "Sometimes. Many of us like to hike, so we do that. Some of us like to bike, and we arrange rides together. It just depends what people like, I guess."

Bettina approached then, holding out a cup to Melody, which she accepted. "Is this not what your office was like back in America? What do you do for fun there?"

"I pretty much just work," Melody answered, taking a sip from the cup. The flavor of apples exploded across her tongue, along with a smattering of bubbles. "Ooh, what is this? I love it."

"It's *Apfelschorle*. Apple juice and sparkling water." Bettina frowned then. "But I'm concerned about your lack of hobbies. Work is not a hobby, Melody. And I certainly don't expect you to treat it like that. It's important for you—for all of us—to relax. At least to exercise and get some fresh air."

Melody waved a reassuring yet dismissive hand. "It's okay, really. I don't mind, and I really like what I do. My boss in Michigan said he might be sending me some extra projects to work on while I'm here, and I actually like the challenge of it. It helps me get better, if I keep myself fresh by always working on new things."

That statement was met with blank looks, so she plowed ahead. "I won't let Mr. Richards's projects interfere with yours, though. Don't worry about that."

"Of all the things you just said, that was not the one I was worried about," said Bettina, getting to her feet. "But to each their own. Come on everyone, let's get moving again. Ben!" She called ahead to a man at the front of the group, gesturing for him to get the group going. "Let's pick up the pace!"

As everyone fell into motion around her, Melody was still looking at the man—Ben, Bettina had called him. She hadn't seen him yet that morning, as large as the group had been, but now that her eyes were blessed with the sight of him, she couldn't look away. He was handsome, yes, but it went deeper than that—there was a magnetism about him that simultaneously had her aching to spend the rest of the day staring at him and wanting to run in the other direction and pretend he didn't exist.

"A crush?" she grumbled to herself as she rejoined the line towards the back. "You are ridiculous, Mel. And *so* unprofessional."

But the sheer force of will wasn't enough to push Ben from her mind. It was as if every time she tried *not* to notice where he was in the crowd, a part of her awareness was permanently dialed in to his frequency. Her attention was focused on Paul, on Bettina, or on one of the other friendly colleagues she had met...and yet, despite that fact, there was *still* a part of her brain that was tracking Ben's every move.

This had better just be jet lag-induced delirium, she thought. *And if not, then I'll just pray that Ben is in some remote department of the organization and I only see him once in a blue moon.*

Melody slept a solid nine hours that night, thanks in no small part to the 10,000 steps—and then some—that the Deutsche Lebenshilfe had completed on their hiking day. By the time she was heading in for her first day in the office, she was refreshed and ready to get to work, her fingers itching to be back on the keyboard.

After starting the day with the gorgeous view of the Dresden skyline and the Elbe from the tram, she entered the office ready with a smile for all the familiar faces that greeted her there. Even if hiking wasn't really her idea of a good time, she had to give Bettina some credit because it really *had* made Melody feel like she was already part of the team.

She followed the directions Bettina had given her on their previous tour, finding her way to the area of the office where the marketing team was located. Many team members were already there, getting settled in for the day, and she felt the briefest flash of being the new kid on the first day of school, searching for an empty desk while everyone watched.

"Right here," a deep voice called. "This one's free. You're sitting next to me." Her eyes followed the voice, finding it attached to her worst nightmare: the kind eyes and handsome frame of none other than her newly minted office crush, Ben.

She gave him a weak smile and dropped her things onto the desk, which really was *right* next to his. "Thanks," she said. "I'm Melody, by the way."

"I know," he replied, his smile just as devastating as she had feared. "It's nice to meet you. I'm Ben."

Melody nodded with a polite smile, then took a seat, busying herself with arranging the things she had brought—her best pens, her trusty notebooks—on her desk. She needed some sort of strategy if she was going to be working right next to her office crush, embarrassing as that phrase even was. Should she ignore the feelings, hope they would go away as she got to know him? She could try being friends with him, that could do the trick. She could use the unwanted feelings to fuel her to do her job even better than ever, let it create some sort of rivalry between them. Or...and this just might be the most farfetched of all ideas, she could act on her feelings, see if the spark she felt was mutual.

To acknowledge and act upon her attraction, turn to **page 40**

To put aside her attraction and focus on befriending Ben, turn to **page 287**

To channel her attraction into rivalry and competition, turn to **page 128**

266

Melody shook her head. "As much as I want this not to be the case..."

Ben's face fell, as if he already knew what was coming. "I understand," he said with a nod. "I don't like it, of course, but I understand it. We're about to be thousands of miles apart, and that's hardly the way a relationship should begin." His gaze dropped to the ground, a gathering of strength happening while his eyes were away from hers. "It was at least good while it lasted, wasn't it? And I'm not the only one who wishes we had more time together, am I?"

"Not at all." She stepped closer to him, her eyes searching his as she barely managed to stop herself from reaching for him. "You were the best thing that happened to me. And I don't just mean the best thing that happened to me lately...no, I can't think of anything better that has ever come into my life, shown me a new possibility, and flipped everything on its head. More than anything, I wish we could make this work."

"But couldn't we...?" When he saw no change in her eyes, in the expression on her face, any remaining hope left in the shape of his mouth, the light in his eyes was gone. "No, I guess you're right."

"I just mean...I wish with all my might that this program wasn't ending. That we still had all the time we were promised to figure out what we are together. What our future could be." Her mouth turned down at the corners, matching the tears that were starting to fill her eyes. "It's just so unfair."

Ben stepped closer and pulled her in for a hug, one that she immediately knew would be the last embrace they shared. That knowledge sparked the flow of her tears in earnest, and she didn't try to stop them. How could she, when saying goodbye to him was the saddest thing she could imagine doing?

When he finally released her and stepped back, his eyes were full of moisture and his cheeks were shining as he rubbed the backs of his hands across them. "I won't try to convince you to make it work," he said. "I know that would only cause you more stress and pain right now." He forced his lips up into an approximation of a smile as he caressed her cheek one last time. "Just...I want you to know how much you mean to me. And I want you to know that if you change your mind...if you decide you want to give us a try for real, well...I'll be waiting."

Melody shook her head. "No, you don't have to promise that. You should be happy, Ben. I want you to be happy, not sitting at home sad wishing I would change my mind."

His sad smile was breaking her heart. "With all due respect, you don't really get to tell me what to do now, do you?" He lifted her hand to his mouth and pressed a soft kiss across the back of her knuckles before releasing his grasp. "But I promise I won't wait for you forever. Is that good enough?"

"It has to be, I guess." She nodded, barely able to see him through the tears spilling from her eyes. "If anything could make me sadder than I already feel, it's the thought of you sad and alone and eighty years old, pining after the one that got away."

"Then I promise you that won't happen." His eyes searched hers. "I think I could have loved you." He shook his head. "No, I don't think. I'm quite confident about it. If we had been together for the rest of this year, the rest of the program, we would have been inseparable by the end of it. Fates tied to each other's and all that."

"I know. And I could have loved you, too." It was easier to say the words to him now that he was about to be gone from her life. A part of her had been growing to love him for far longer than she realized. "I was well on my way to it already."

She had hoped the words would make him feel better, the knowledge that he hadn't been alone in his feelings providing a comfort of sorts.

But Ben was no longer making any attempt to put on a happy face. "I think I need to go home alone."

Melody nodded back, no words coming because they would have been choked out by sobs, anyway.

He pulled her to him, his lips finding hers for one last kiss. It was salty, stained by the tears flowing down both of their cheeks. But even with that, it still felt like home, being pressed up against him like this. He was still comfort and warmth—no, *heat*—and home, even (or perhaps especially) when it felt like her heart was being torn in two.

Finally, he pulled away, and with a sad lift of his lips and a raised hand, he turned and walked away.

And Melody barely stopped herself from crumpling onto the sidewalk and dissolving into a puddle of tears.

As if in a daze, she made her way back to her apartment, walking the now-familiar path between Ben's home and hers as if she were on autopilot, not remembering even a single step of the journey when she finally arrived in front of her building. She slipped into her apartment, closed the door behind, leaned back against it, and slid down to the floor as the tears finally flowed unfettered, a sob escaping from her lips before she made it all the way to the floor.

The next day was a blur, Melody going through the motions of it in a daze of heartbreak and numbness. The goodbye with Ben was a raw wound, one that she kept poking and tormenting herself with by approaching it from different directions, all the thoughts and questions that were haunting her.

What if I made a huge mistake? What if being with him was my one chance at happiness and I threw it away rather than fighting for it? What if I change my mind and he's already moved on? What if I broke his heart so much that he'll never recover? Did I really choose my job, my stability, this thing that doesn't even love me back over Ben, of all people?

The questions persisted, the daze dulling all of her senses and keeping her barely aware of what was happening around her.

It wasn't until a few days later, a Monday, that Melody lifted her head up for the first time. It was the first day back at the EduPowerment office post Generosity Exchange, and Chloe was back in her cubicle next to Melody's.

As soon as Chloe came in that morning, she deposited herself in front of Melody, her look of frustration evaporating into concern as she reached for her friend and pulled her into a hug.

"Dang, girl," said Chloe into Melody's ear. "I was about to ask you where the hell you've been, loca, but judging by the look on your face, I'm not going to like the answer."

Melody pulled back from the embrace, sniffling as she forced a smile. "No, it's okay. It's good to be back to work, back to normal. There's been, frankly, an alarming amount of crying this weekend, so it's good to have the distraction." She grimaced at her words. "Not that work is a distraction. Work is good. Work is important." *Work doesn't love you back, though, does it?*

Chloe crossed her arms over her chest. "So that's why you didn't answer any of my calls? Too busy with all the crying?" She shook her head at Melody's stubbornness. "You know, that's usually the time when it's good to have a friend. I could have joined you. Comforted you, or at least cried along with you."

Melody frowned. "What would you be crying about? Did you get your heart broken leaving London, too?" What kind of terrible friend was she, that she'd been so wrapped up in her own drama that she'd barely asked Chloe about her feelings?

But Chloe just shook her head. "I mean, yeah, I did. But not by a person. Just by the city, really. Saying goodbye to her too soon. I'm so pissed at Mr. Richards for taking down the whole program. I've seen him do a lot of sketchy things, but this one really takes the cake. It's a new low, even for him."

Like a bad habit, Melody rushed to the defense of her boss. "I'm sure he wasn't trying to ruin all of our lives. Not everything is personal, you know?"

"Even when he's stirring up shit *this* much, you still can't bring yourself to say a bad word about him, can you?" Chloe shook her head. "Look around you, Mel. One man is to blame for all the things you see turned on their heads, all the jet-lagged people who are feeling sad and tired and disillusioned. To say nothing of your own heartbreak." She cocked an eyebrow at Melody. "That something you feel like talking about? I'm guessing it has to do with your little office fling with Ben?"

Melody felt herself bristle. "There was no *fling*, Chloe. There was something real, but it's over now, and it hurts a hell of a lot worse than ending any fling or leaving a really cool city you wished you had more time to check out." She turned in the direction of her cubicle. "And I don't really have the energy or the time to talk about this right now." Before Chloe could say anything in response, Melody had stalked away, not stopping until she was in the relative safety of her cubicle.

She knew, of course, that she shouldn't take her frustration and hurt out on Chloe. But it would have been a lot easier to do that if Chloe weren't saying stupid things about Ben and blaming everything on Mr. Richards, as always. Couldn't she get creative, for once? Find a source of blame for something—*anything*—besides their boss. *Zero points for originality, Chloe.*

Her fingers itched to pick up the phone and text Ben. She wanted to know how he was, what he was doing, what he had eaten for breakfast, what he thought about life after the Generosity Exchange program. But she couldn't, and she knew that. After breaking his heart, it was unfair to reach out to him. She couldn't treat him like a friend when they'd both already made it clear how much more they had wanted from each other.

And so, in one of life's most acutely cruel truths, the person who had played such a big role in her life and her happiness and occupied such a large amount of real estate in her heart had to become a stranger. Less than an acquaintance and far less than a friend, he was now someone she had to retrain her heart not to turn to in every moment that it wanted comfort.

Thank goodness for work, she thought. *It's literally the only thing I have going for me right now, and even I am aware of just how bleak that reality is.*

"Melody, you're here. Good. I need you, follow me." She jolted in her seat. She hadn't even heard Mr. Richards approach her cubicle from behind, so focused had she been on the knife twisting in her heart. She didn't even know what she had been doing when he'd looked in to her workspace, as there was nothing on her computer's screen that could even remotely be classified as work.

Heartbreak was the *worst* distraction, and she, frankly, didn't have time for it. She picked up her notebook and a pen and followed Mr. Richards back to his office.

"Right," he said, taking his seat and diving right in without so much as the barest of pleasantries. "We've got a massive mess to clean up with this whole Handout Exchange debacle. To get ahead of any bad press coming out about the program—you just know all the tree huggers and bleeding hearts are going to pin it all on me—we need to be decisive."

"Okay…" She was scribbling notes on the pad in front of her, fighting a losing battle against the urge to wonder why this particular task, which had nothing remotely to do with her job, was falling to her. Surely, Mr. Richards had his reasons and surely they would become clear.

"This whole network—" He spat the word like it tasted bad. "—of charities…we need to get ourselves out of it. I don't know why I didn't see it sooner, but it's clear now. This is not the right environment for EduPowerment. Too many bleeding hearts and too many sob stories. We need…you know what we need?"

It was clearly a rhetorical question, judging by the fact that he wasn't looking at her and didn't seem to be listening to her, but Melody still shook her head.

"We need to get out of this damn non-profit space. That's it. Change the whole EduPowerment model and incorporate ourselves. You can look into that, can't you?"

There weren't any words. Melody stared at him, mouth agape. "I…um, well…" There was nothing about this task that was remotely under the umbrella of Melody's responsibilities, to say nothing of the fact that taking EduPowerment out of the nonprofit space, turning it into a for-profit venture, went against everything she most valued about working there.

"I knew I could count on you," Mr. Richards said. "Have a plan on my desk by the end of the day."

He turned to leave, and that was when something snapped inside Melody. "No."

Mr. Richards whirled back around. "'No?' What could you possibly be saying no to? Lest you forget, I am the boss around here, missy, and I am not asking you if you are interested in taking on this project. I am *telling* you that it is now your responsibility. If you think this is somehow beneath you, then you know where the door is and you are welcome to show yourself to it." And before she could say another word or finish her train of thought, he had dismissed her and turned his attention back to his desk.

Melody fumed to herself silently as she returned to her workspace. What could she do? She had always done what Mr. Richards had told her to do, always justified his demands as being part of furthering the mission of EduPowerment, something that was more important than her own happiness.

But this was different, wasn't it? This went against everything about EduPowerment that was most important to her—sure, the mission would still be the same, at least she thought it would. But the lack of collaboration? Turning their education programs into for-profit businesses?

It wasn't that business couldn't be done well, couldn't leave a positive impact on the world. Melody was not naïve enough to believe that was impossible. But it was about the sense of foreboding she felt, the words Mr. Richards had used, and the implications of it all. Things were about to change fundamentally here, even more than they already had since he had taken over control of EduPowerment after his mother's death. Melody was now—or at least *soon*—about to face her moment of truth, where she would finally have to decide if enough was enough. If she could continue to justify Mr. Richards's demands or her lack of work-life balance or all that she had sacrificed to further the mission of EduPowerment.

And it wasn't as if there was anyone she could turn to right now, right when she most needed to talk it out. To work through what she was even feeling, let alone what her next steps should be. Ben was a world away, and he wouldn't want to hear from her. Chloe was in the next cubicle over, but the last thing she was likely to want to do at this moment was play Melody's workplace therapist.

No, she was on her own, and that knowledge made her feel the pain of Ben's absence even more acutely. If she had spent the last three months alone, she might still be in the habit of it. But she'd gotten used to him, darn it, and that made it all even worse. How dare he make her come to depend on him and then leave?

She shook her head at that thought. No, that wasn't what had happened. Ben hadn't *made* her depend on him any more than she had *made* him spend time with her. It had all unfolded between them so naturally that it was like a force of nature. Like caterpillars turning into butterflies or the leaves changing color before falling to the ground.

And it also wasn't as if Ben had just abandoned her, leaving despite all of her protestations. Like she had been a child, clinging to his leg on the first day of school, begging him not to go. He had wanted to stay in her life, to figure out how this relationship might continue between them. *She* had been the one to make that decision. To cut him loose.

That's what made all of this so unbearable: the fact that she had caused all the pain she was currently experiencing. She had been the one to end things with Ben. She had been the one to react to Chloe like a selfish jerk rather than being a good friend. And she had been the one to enable Mr. Richards's total lack of professional boundaries for all these years.

It felt like all she had now was this job, and she wasn't even sure if she was happy about that anymore. What had once been her dream career now felt like a cheap consolation prize.

For the first time since she'd started working at EduPowerment, it was time for Melody to take matters into her own hands. She opened her email account, digging around her old messages to find Jacqueline, the office manager's contact information. The fact that she'd never emailed Jacqueline before was an unwelcome reminder of all the vacation days she had never taken, all the days she had felt under the weather yet not used one of her precious sick days.

And without letting herself hesitate further, she fired off an email to Jacqueline, informing her that she had some personal matters to attend to and would be taking the day off. She didn't bother to let Mr. Richards know—sure, there was a pit in her stomach at that thought, but she wrote it off as an old habit that wasn't so quick to die off.

Soon, she would learn to stop caring what he thought. For today, at least, she just needed to get out of here.

She packed up her things with an unfamiliar speed, feeling a thrill at the awareness that she was leaving work early, stepping away from her responsibilities like a naughty student skipping their classes. She didn't even stop to tell Chloe where she was going—not that she would have wanted to hear it—before she ducked out of the office and into the crisp late fall day.

"Freedom feels terrifying," she said to herself, a layer of joy sprinkled on top of the utter despair she felt about her work, her friendships, her recently failed relationship. Leaving in the middle—okay, the morning—of the workday might be a small victory in terms of putting her own needs first, but it was far from a big enough step to turn her life around.

Because the fact was that everything sucked and nothing was going in her favor. Sure, she had put her own needs first for the first time in forever, but that just meant she was probably about to be fired on top of everything else that was already terrible.

And so, with that less than comforting thought in mind, Melody made her way to her apartment, fully intending to bury herself deep in her blankets, a veritable cocoon against the world and all its problems.

Melody stayed in her cocoon for a full day and night, emerging the next morning long enough to let Jacqueline know that she would be taking another personal day. The effort to send that email, to even dare tiptoe into her inbox where there were surely increasingly demanding and increasingly outraged emails from Mr. Richards waiting, was significant.

Sure enough, she saw his name there in her inbox more times than she could count, yet she resisted any temptation to open a message and expose herself to his ire. When the message to Jacqueline was sent, she closed her email and tossed her phone across the bedroom, where it landed on the carpeted floor near her desk.

It wasn't as if she needed to keep the device close—who was going to call or text her? Not Ben, not Chloe, and therefore not anyone that she wanted to hear from. Without those two in her life—or at least talking to her, as the case was with Chloe—what did she have?

Her job. The thing that she had prioritized above everything else and which now felt hollow and empty. The meaning she had found there before was lacking now, and she didn't know that she could ever get it back.

For the first time in her life, she understood the cliché that no one on their death bed regrets not spending more time at the office. She had always, on some level, believed that old adage only applied to CEOs of soulless corporations, people who were just working to make money. Surely, jobs that were actively making the world a better place were exempt from workaholism and the need for boundaries...or at least, that was what she had believed before yesterday.

Today, though, the world looked different. The shine on her job at EduPowerment had finally worn off, and along with it, her unquestioning support of Mr. Richards had vanished. And if her job wasn't there to ascribe the ultimate meaning to her life, then what was?

She couldn't lay any claims to being a great friend, judging by the state of her last interactions with Chloe. Felicity certainly wouldn't be nominating her for any "Roommate of the Year" awards. And as far as being a good girlfriend...well, that had practically been over as soon as it even started.

She was just Melody. Just herself, on her own, no ties to anyone that could define her. It was a terrifying thought, being that alone in the world, yet at the same time there was something like freedom wrapped up in it, too. She realized, for the first time in her adult life, that without a significant relationship or career to define her, she had only her own expectations to live up to.

Since saying goodbye to Ben, it had felt like nothing but endings and disillusionment. Yesterday, the grief had been acute—grief over her perfect job, her perfect friendship, her chance at happiness with a good man.

But for the first time, she was seeing it as the possibility of new beginnings. Just because things were falling apart didn't mean she couldn't put them back together in a way that was more beautiful than they'd ever been.

Melody left her room for the first time in 24 hours, plodding into the kitchen with a pen, a piece of paper, and the need for coffee and breakfast to fuel the breakthrough that was about to happen. She needed to figure out a few things about herself, and she needed to make a plan. And both of those things required food and caffeine to sustain her.

By the time she had eaten a plate of eggs and drunk two cups of coffee, Melody had brain dumped her way through the stickiest of feelings and come to a fairly simple conclusion: happiness.

The thing that she was seeking in her life was *not* meaningful work or a healthy relationship or even a close friend; it was happiness. Sure, all of those things could play a part in her happiness, but if she had learned anything in recent history, they couldn't be the *reason* for her happiness. If they were, her whole world would fall apart without them, and she needed her world to stand on a firmer foundation than that.

She needed to seek happiness, first and foremost, and then add other good things on top of it, like sprinkles on ice cream.

With a tired hand from all the morning's frantic scribblings, Melody moved to talking out loud to herself.

"But what makes me happy? I thought it was my job, but clearly that's not it. I had a lot of fun when Ben was with me...was that just about him? Am I running a fool's errand here, and the only answer to my happiness is a man that I sent out of my life?"

Even though it felt like there was some truth in that thought, she knew it couldn't be the sole cause of her happiness. Sure, love—*no, infatuation*, she reminded herself—was a hell of a drug, but even before things had gotten to that point, she had felt different. What had it been?

Melody snapped her fingers. "Fun." The word echoed through her empty kitchen. "Sure, I had fun with Ben, but maybe the key is that I had fun, period. I had a life outside of work, for once. And that's the difference. It's not just the presence of fun…it's the absence of a sole, obsessive focus on the least interesting thing about me: my job."

With that realization, the steps fell into place. Melody knew what she needed to do, and she got up from the table to get dressed and ready to head in to the office. Even though she wasn't working, there were a couple of very important items on her to-do list that were going to require returning to the scene of the crime—the crime in question being the hijacking of her happiness and murder of her desire to do anything if it wasn't in the best interest of EduPowerment.

Her first stop in the EduPowerment office was Chloe's cubicle.

"Hey," she said, poking her head in. "Can we hang out after you're done working?"

Chloe whirled around at the sound of Melody's voice, her eyes wide with confusion. "Mel? What are you doing here? Or…I mean, what were you doing not being here yesterday and today? What's going on?"

"Something that's been a long time coming, and I think you're going to like it," was all Melody said. "I'll tell you all about it, but first I need to make up for some lost time and be a good friend to you. I want to hear all about London and how you're holding up since you left. Want to come over? I'll make you dinner."

Chloe's smile was small but sincere. "Yes, please. I'd like that." Her eyes darted in the direction of Mr. Richards's office. "Does he know you're here? What's going on?"

"He doesn't know yet, but he's about to. We're going to have a long overdue conversation."

"I...*think* I like the sound of that?" Chloe's left eyebrow was raised just like her statement-turned-question.

Melody nodded once. "You will." She pointed at her friend. "Tonight, right?"

"Tonight. Looking forward to it."

Melody smiled at her. "Me, too."

Then she marched across the office, knocked once on Mr. Richards's door and let herself inside, where she found the man in question, sitting back in his chair with his feet up on his desk and a shocked expression on his face.

"What, you knock, but you don't wait for a response?" he asked, as he swung his feet to the floor and his chair squeaked with the movement.

Melody looked around his office with fresh eyes, realizing she'd never come in here of her own volition before. It was a nice space, with a great view of the park across the street, surrounded by tall trees. Far nicer than the cubicle she'd been occupying for the last few years.

"I needed to talk to you," she said, remaining on her feet despite the empty chairs facing Mr. Richards's desk. This conversation wouldn't take long.

"It's time for me to make a change. For too long, I've been putting this job before everything else in my life...my health, my relationships, all of it. And I'm done with that. We all need some balance, and that's my priority now." She met his eyes, her conviction strong. "And I refuse to be your errand girl any more. If you want to turn EduPower-ment into a for-profit company, that's someone else's job. Not mine."

Mr. Richards nodded once, his hands coming together on the table in front of him in a clasped position. "I see," he said. "And next in Melody's tour of delusion, I suppose you're going to be telling me you want a raise."

She shook her head. "I don't think you get it. I'm not telling you that I'm going to be doing *this* job differently. I'm telling you that I can't work for you any more. Effective today. Or...well, yesterday, I guess."

"Absolutely not." Mr. Richards was shaking his head fervently. "This is absurd, Melody. For one thing, the protocol if you're leaving is to give *at least* two weeks' notice. And for another, no one else has complained about this 'work-life balance' problem you're talking about." He lifted his fingers to make air quotes as he ridiculed her complaint. "This is just further evidence that hiring recent graduates is always a bad move. Especially female ones, since they inevitably end up moving on once they get in a relationship or have a kid."

Her jaw dropped at that. "Wow...sexist, much? No, the reason your employees don't stick around long is *not* actually that they're women or young or not committed to the cause." She crossed her arms over her chest, her weight shifting to one hip. "It's you, and it's this place. You run over people until there's nothing left of them and you have to start fresh with someone else." She gestured behind her to the larger office. "Your mother would be so ashamed of what you've done with this place." She shook her head. "Some of the blame for things getting this bad falls on me, that's for sure. But my responsibility is that I didn't set boundaries with you and I let you just pile more and more and more on to my plate. *Your* responsibility is everything else. And if you don't care to accept my resignation without two weeks of warning, then feel free to fire me."

As soon as the words were out, she knew she had to leave his office. While she had intended to quit, she hadn't meant to take it that far, taunting him into firing her. Melody had surprised herself, and even if it felt terrifying and like she might be burning her future career prospects to the ground before her very eyes, it was exhilarating.

Without another word, she stalked out of Mr. Richards's office and out of the building, only stopping when she got to the small grocery store near her apartment, where she picked up ingredients for her dinner with Chloe that evening.

When Chloe arrived, Melody met her at the door with a hug and a themed cocktail. "It's called an Apology Spritz," Melody said, passing it to her friend. "It's just an Aperol Spritz made with a lot of genuine feelings of shame and sorrow for being such a bad friend lately."

Chloe laughed and took a sip. "Well, it's delicious, so apology accepted." She followed Melody through to the kitchen, where the rest of her surprise was waiting.

"Oh no, it's not that easy," said Melody, with a shake of her head. "It took a lot longer for me to dig myself into the friendship doghouse than it did to make that drink."

She stopped at the table, gesturing for Chloe to take a seat. "And I really do want to make it up to you. I want to hear all about London. Your life, your heart, your dreams, your plans. I've asked so much from you lately and given you so little in return."

Chloe's eyes were wet with emotion as she smiled. "I...well, I want to say that you don't have to do that. But the truth is that I've been really sad lately. Felt really alone. And it would mean the world to me to talk it through with my best friend."

"Alright, then," said Melody, carrying over a bouquet of flowers—Chloe's favorite lilies—and some appetizers. "Then I'm all yours, and I'm all ears. And also, I hope you're hungry."

When the evening was over, Melody laid on her mattress, feeling satisfied—or at least almost satisfied—by all the changes the day had brought. She was on the right path to become who she wanted to be, even if she wasn't there yet. It would take some time, that much she knew, but she could trust herself to keep going, keep pushing until she got where she wanted to be.

There was just one person that she wanted to share this moment with, and she pulled out her phone to text him before she could think better of it.

"I know I shouldn't be texting you, but it felt wrong not to tell you. I quit my job today. I don't know what I'm going to do next, but I just know I'm going to try to be happy. I wish I'd realized this before we said goodbye, but hey...better late than never, right?"

She set the phone aside and stared up at the ceiling in the fading light. It might be too late—Ben's words about waiting for her might have turned into an empty promise after a few thousand miles of distance and a few days with a clear head—but at least he would know that he had left an impact on her. That she was better for having known him, and that his influence had helped her make the right choice for herself.

Just as her eyes were starting to drift closed, her phone began to buzz with an incoming call. It was probably Chloe, calling to tell Melody about something funny that had happened in the twenty minutes they'd been apart.

She lifted the phone to her ear without even checking the screen. "Hello?"

"Melody?" Ben's voice rang across the line, setting a swarm of butterflies in motion in her stomach. "It's me."

To get Ben and Melody through to their happily ever after, turn to **page 311**

To keep them apart and sad forever...well, read a different book. That's not an option in this story.

287

*J*ust ask him, Melody cajoled herself in her mind. *There's nothing wrong with a friendly cup of coffee, is there?*

Before she could stop herself, she was tapping on the entrance to Ben's cubicle, receiving a warm smile from him in return. "Hi," she said, with a small, awkward wave. "Any interest in a friendly cup of coffee?" She grimaced at her choice of words, reflecting her inner monologue rather than coming up with something cooler.

But Ben was already nodding and getting to his feet. "I'd love that. The friend *and* the coffee."

They fell into step together as they made their way to the kitchen, Melody craning her neck to meet Ben's eyes as he asked her about the projects she was working on, then listened intently as if the latest marketing campaign that had captured her attention was the most interesting thing he had ever heard.

While they waited for a fresh pot of coffee to brew, Melody asked Ben about his hometown, warming from within at the way his eyes lit up when he talked about both

Dresden and the village outside Izmir where he had spent his childhood summers.

And it was just that easy for the two of them to slip into a casual friendship. Melody knew it was like that sometimes—it wasn't as if it had taken her months of wooing to win Chloe over as a friend, after all. There was a part of her tempted to wonder if the easiness between them was a sign that they were meant to be *more* than friends, but she shoved that thought right back down from whence it had come. True friendship was a rare and beautiful thing, and it deserved to be treasured, with no less value than love and romance.

Melody and Ben made plans to do a little walking exploration of the neighborhood around the office after work, under the pretense of both of them getting to know it better when it was clear that only one of them truly needed the tour.

At the end of the workday, Ben was waiting at the entrance to Melody's cubicle when she turned to leave. She jolted in surprise, clutching her sternum to massage away the tension that had appeared there. "Where did you come from and how long have you been standing there?"

Ben hung his head in exaggerated embarrassment. "I'm sorry. I knew I should have announced myself. I swear I just stepped there, but you were so focused and clearly didn't hear me, so I just wanted to wait for you to finish what you were doing. Your...shut down routine, I guess?"

Melody nodded, swallowing peace with a big gulp, yet still finding her heart racing. "Yes, just the usual things, you know? Making sure there are no new emails, unplugging everything in case of a power surge, shutting down the computer properly rather than just closing the lid. Making sure my desk is nice and tidy, so I don't hate myself in the morning."

Ben lifted an arm to rub the back of his neck, looking a bit sheepish as he did so. "You're making me feel guilty for how I left things." He lifted a finger, biting his lip as he stepped back. "Wait for just a sec? I need to tidy up my workspace a little, too."

She smiled back at him. "I'm all done here, so I can come help. Seems like it's your first time, after all, and I don't want you to miss anything."

She followed Ben to his workspace, trying not to widen her eyes in horror at the sight of it. There were papers scattered everywhere, his computer was still on—and even displaying his desktop menu, if such a thing could be believed—and, all in all, it looked like he had just stepped away for a moment rather than leaving for the night.

The expression he gave her was like a naughty schoolboy facing his teacher without any homework completed. "It's bad, isn't it?"

Melody blew out a sigh. "If it works for you, it's fine, I guess." She gestured to the papers. "It would be good to tidy up all of this, unless, of course, you know where everything is?"

"Oh, I do. I promise there's a method to it. It's organized chaos." He started picking up the various notes and printouts. "This is a reminder to check in with Bettina about one of my old campaigns, these are some workshop materials I need to review..."

"Are they in any sort of order? Like, ordered by priority, I mean?"

Ben shook his head. "No, but they'll all get done. This is just the order they landed on my desk, and I'm planning to tackle it all in the morning."

Melody barely suppressed a shudder. How was he leaving with all of these things hanging over his head? If it were her, she'd stay longer just to clear these to-dos from her mind. But it was already becoming clear to her that she and Ben had very different philosophies when it came to work and that only one of them was likely to be haunted in their free time by unfinished tasks.

She stepped around him as he continued to stack the papers up on his desk, logging him out of his computer and shutting it down before unplugging it.

"Why do you do all of that?" he asked, nodding towards the computer.

She shrugged. "I just figured my computer needs to get some proper rest, you know? Like, be totally off for the night, not just snoozing." Her laugh was humorless, a little bitter. "At least one of us should do that."

Ben recoiled in horror. "You're joking, right? Please tell me you're joking. You...what? You don't sleep?"

"Oh, I do sleep, eventually. It just usually happens after I stress myself out about work for a couple of hours. Even if I don't bring my computer—and let's face it, I usually do that—I'm still jotting down notes and using my personal computer or phone to deal with emails." She cringed at her own words. "I know, I'm the worst. I promise, as I said it out loud, I heard how bad it sounded."

"It definitely did. So...are you going to try to change that? Or just try to be more careful about not saying it out loud?"

That got a laugh out of Melody. "Definitely the second one, but...I can *try* to work on the first one?"

"Fair enough then." He nodded his head in the direction of the door. "Shall we go, then?"

Melody nodded. "Sounds great."

As the two of them began to walk together away from their workspaces and towards the exit, she felt a flutter—butterflies, coming to life in her lower belly. *What a silly thing*, she thought. *Butterflies about a new friend? I mean, it's been a minute since I made a new friend, but this does seem like a bit of an overreaction, body.*

Walking around the area surrounding the office, they pointed out interesting shops to each other—a used bookstore caught Ben's eye, a stationery store caught Melody's—before ducking in to a café to sit and chat for a bit.

"So," Ben began when they were seated with two lattes in front of them. "Getting to know each other time. Siblings? Hobbies? Where do we even start? Can I just say, 'Tell me about yourself'?"

Melody shrugged. "I guess you can, even though that's the worst question ever. I mean, if I turned that back around on you, how would you answer it? Maybe if you go first, I'll have a better idea of what interesting Melody facts I should share."

"Okay, then," said Ben, more than happy to oblige her wishes. "My parents are both from Turkey, but they moved to Dresden before my siblings and I were born. We—my brother, sister, and I—grew up in Germany, though we spent our summers in Turkey, mostly. And I love to do outdoorsy things. Hike, have a picnic, go to the beach, ride a bicycle." He took a sip of his drink as he shrugged. "Pretty basic stuff, really, but that's the summary of Ben facts, I guess."

"I like it," said Melody. "And I think it's a great starting point. So, to address those same topics about me...let's see. My parents are both from Michigan, and so am I. I have one brother, but he's a lot older than me, so we weren't that close growing up. I really like my job, and well, it takes up most of my time and energy."

Ben nodded. "But what about fun? Or, if you aren't doing fun things now, what did you used to like to do?"

Melody winced. "Guilty as charged. I know work isn't a hobby. Back in the day, I did have some hobbies though, I swear. I was on the cross-country team in high school, and I did some running in college too, though I wasn't good enough to make the team. And I always like to do crafty things when I was younger. Knit, crochet, embroider." She shrugged. "That's about it. All I can think of now, at least."

"Got it. When was the last time you went for a run? Would that be something you'd like to do again?"

She raised an eyebrow at him. "Why do I feel like you're about to ask me to go for a run with you?"

"Ah, that's probably because I am." Ben smiled. "Why? Wouldn't you want to do that?"

"Oh, well...uh." Melody felt her cheeks heat as she looked down at the table. "I guess I don't actually have a good answer to that question. But I'm pretty sure I'm a way slower runner now than I ever was in high school or college." She shook her head, waving a dismissive hand at him. "I would definitely be slowing you down, and you wouldn't want that. It's okay. It was a nice thought, but we don't have to do that."

But Ben was shaking his head back at her. "No way. Look, I'm not really a runner. Yeah, I know I said I like doing outdoorsy things, but the vast majority of the time that's just me walking slowly on hiking trails and stopping all the time to take pictures of the scenery. I promise you're not going to be slowing me down. And even if you were—" He continued, plowing ahead before she could state her objection. "Even if you were, I wouldn't care. I think it would be a fun thing to do together, and that's it. Plain and simple."

"Plain and simple, huh?"

Ben nodded. "Sure. We'd get some fresh air, a little exercise, and time with a friend. What else do you need, except for maybe a really great meal at the end of it all?"

Melody smiled. "Now you're talking. Okay, mister. Maybe if you're going to convince me to lace up my running shoes for the first time in I don't know how long, I can take you out for a meal of your choice afterwards." She shrugged. "And I *may* be using the post-run meal as the motivation to get me out the door in the first place, but we don't need to talk about that."

They sat and chatted until it was time to clear their table and head back to their respective homes—past time, if you were going off Melody's typical weeknight work routine, but the time with Ben had flown by despite her best intentions to be home and checking her email by nine o'clock. When they parted ways, an awkward side hug exchanged in front of the cafe when Ben reached for a hug at the same time that Melody went in for a high five, they made plans to go for their first run. ("We can call it a jog if that makes you feel better," Ben had said, and it *had* eased Melody's nerves.) Melody would bring a change of clothes to the office the next day, and Ben would make a plan for what kind of meal they should grab for dinner.

"It's a date," he said, raising a hand to give Melody the high five she had missed out on.

His word choice, however, stopped her with her arm raised only to elbow height. "Uh...is it?"

"I mean, yes. Of course. What else would we call it?" Ben cocked his head at her, reading something on her face that had his eyebrows climbing his forehead. "It's...a plan?"

Melody nodded. "Sure, yes. Let's call it a plan. It's just...you know, 'date' kind of means something different. Not exactly the word you use for two friends hanging out, going for a run, and eating pizza afterwards. Side note: I really hope you choose pizza for your meal request tomorrow. But don't let yourself be influenced by me."

"I see," said Ben, still studying her face. "No, I did not mean to say that we are going on a date tomorrow. That is something that you should ask someone for, right? I don't know that much about American culture apart from what I see in the movies, which is surely only loosely grounded in reality, but in general, you should ask someone to go on a date with you before you call it a date. Yes?"

"Yes," said Melody. "In my limited experience, I can confirm that is exactly how it works. Or is supposed to work, at least."

"Good to know." Ben nodded. "I will remember that for the future."

Melody nodded back at him, forcing a smile. For whatever reason, she didn't particularly care to think about Ben asking someone out on a date. She already liked the thought of hanging out with him regularly after work, and she knew that if either of them were dating someone, it would probably cramp their style. Because, you know, in general, significant others wanted to spend time with you with some regularity, not just leave you to hang out with your work bestie. Or was Ben a work husband? She'd heard that term thrown around before, along with work wife, and always felt vaguely uncomfortable about it. Unless it was about Chloe. Chloe could be her work wife in a second. So what was different about Chloe and Ben, anyway?

"Okay then." Ben clapped his hands together. "I should go, and you probably should, too. I hereby promise to take your request for pizza into consideration. I can make no promises at this time about what tomorrow night's dinner menu will be, but I assure you I will try my hardest not to choose something gross or disappointing."

"Wow, thanks," said Melody, shaking her head as her grin spread. "That's so selfless of you. I'm sure you were craving gross, disappointing food, but just for me you would consider an alternative?"

Ben gave a nod that was so fake serious she only barely managed to stop herself from punching him in the arm. She knew enough about dating to know that was a classic flirtatious move and not something she needed to introduce into her brand new platonic friendship. "It's a hardship," said Ben, "But I'm sure you'll make it up to me somehow. And if you forget to, then I will gladly remind you."

Melody shook her head at him and gave a small wave before turning to head back to her apartment, enjoying the fading sunlight as she made her way home. Ben's final words hadn't been intended as flirtation, she knew...yet why did she keep wondering if they might be? And what that might mean?

From that day on, it was easy for Melody and Ben to fall into a regular friendship. They sat together at lunchtime—with Melody actually leaving her desk from time to time. They regularly shared a cup of coffee or at least prepared one for the other person if they couldn't get away from their desk. And they were often seen by their colleagues walking out the door together at the end of the workday.

It got to the point where Melody noticed the raised eyebrows and the pointed looks in their direction as they were leaving, but she shrugged it off. She didn't much care if her colleagues thought she and Ben were dating, and, in fact, she kind of enjoyed living in that little fantasy. Even if they were only together in the collective imaginations of their co-workers, it was a nice place to be together. Not that she was complaining about the state of their relationship as it stood.

Ben was a great friend and had quickly become her go-to confidant for issues at work. It wasn't like she had issues to talk about in other areas of her life, which was more a symptom of the fact that she didn't have much of a life outside of work, but at least when Mr. Richards gave her projects that were a little too much, Ben was the one she could turn to. Sometimes, he was even the one who would help her out. He would take time away from his projects to offer some input or an opinion when she needed a second set of eyes on a request from Mr. Richards.

And the requests had been constant. In fact, they had reached near peak levels. One day when Melody had received her sixth consecutive email from Mr. Richards with yet another new idea which required her immediate attention, but without sacrificing the work required on the previous five projects, she couldn't stop herself before she dropped her head onto her desk. It was probably the thudding sound that got Ben's attention and had him showing up at the entrance to her cubicle just a few seconds later.

"Is everything okay?" he asked, stepping towards her as his hand fell to her shoulder.

"Yeah..." Melanie sighed. "It's fine. It's not...well, it's nothing new."

Ben looked concerned. "Well, what is it? Something I can help with?"

"I don't think so?" said Melody, her voice raising into a question. "I mean, it's my job. I can't ask you to do my job for me."

"Why not? If it's causing you this much stress, I would love to help take some of that away."

"Yes, but I can't ask you to do that," she said.

"Well, good then, because I don't recall you asking. I just offered."

Melody was quiet for a moment as she scrolled through the series of emails waiting for attention. "Maybe you can help me with one of these. Just...just give me some ideas, I guess."

"Let me see," he said, coming closer, and leaning over her shoulder.

The first thing she noticed, which immediately distracted her from the particular message she was trying to find in her inbox, was the fact that Ben smelled terrific. How she had not noticed that yet was a mystery and likely had something to do with the fact that she tried her best to keep her distance from him. Of course they spent time together every day. But it was like there was an invisible bubble around him and an invisible bubble around her, too. And those bubbles kept them from ever crossing a boundary. If she was washing the cup in the kitchen, and he stepped forward to place a spoon in the sink, she would step aside and vice versa. If he was making a cup of coffee, and she needed to take a mug out of the cupboard, he would move his body so that they wouldn't accidentally brush against each other.

Melody didn't know exactly why the two of them behaved like that, whether it was because they were treating each other like school children who were afraid of cooties or just keeping professional boundaries in their relationship. Either way she'd never been tempted to cross that boundary, but now that Ben was hovering over her shoulder and she caught the faintest whiff of his clean, spicy smell, she knew she was going to want more of it.

But there was no way that could be enough to satisfy her craving. Craving for what, exactly? For free smells anytime she wanted them? Maybe. But for more than that? Well, that was something she couldn't let herself imagine.

She redirected her attention using her iron will to focus her energy from her nose back to her eyes, which had been staring blankly at the screen while her mouse's spinner wheel slid the contents of Mr. Richards's message up and down and up and down.

"Here," she said, pointing with her other hand at the screen. "It's this new project...well, it's not even a project yet. Right now it's just an idea, a twinkle in Mr. Richards's eye. But still, he wants me to come up with some potential marketing campaigns for it. This is how it works between us, you know? He shares an idea with me and I...well, I do my best with it. I work my magic with it to let him see it from all perspectives. By having the marketing messages, he knows what he would share with the board and what he would share with potential donors. And if it's strong enough, it makes it that far. And if not, it ends up in the bin next to his desk."

Ben turned and looked at her. *Wow, his face was close to hers. Gulp.* "Are you serious? He has you do all this work and then sometimes he just scraps it?"

Melody nodded. "More often than sometimes. I haven't figured out the exact ratio. I think it would be too discouraging if I did. But yeah, a lot of these projects end up in the recycle bin. Still, though." She sighed. "That doesn't mean I can phone it in, you know? I still have to give it my best. Treat every project like it's going to be the one that makes a difference and try to detach myself from the outcome."

Ben blew out a slow breath through pursed lips. "That's rough," he said. "He has a different way of managing than I'm familiar with, I have to admit."

"You're lucky," said Melody with a small smile.

"Maybe," Ben agreed. "That doesn't mean you can't be lucky too, though. Let me help. Forward one of these to me and I'll take a look at it. I'll do the best I can."

She looked up at him, smiling with a soft exhale. "I know I should say, 'no, that's okay. You don't need to do it,' but I really appreciate it. And I really need the help."

"Say no more," said Ben. "That's what I'm here for. I'm here to help you. And while it's nice that you appreciate it, and it's nice to hear you say thank you...it's not necessary. We're partners, you know, or at least we can be."

"I think we already are," she said with a nod. "And it's a great, great thing."

That evening, Chloe called again.

As Melody was relaying the events of the day, Chloe cut her short. "Hold on a second. You're telling me this guy just dropped his own projects to help you with yours because you were feeling overwhelmed? Or wait, let me correct myself—because Mr. Richards was being a nightmare, per usual?"

"He's not a nightmare," said Melody. "He's just...well, he's got a lot of ideas and some of them are actually really good."

"Yeah, yeah. I don't need a Mr. Richards apology tour on his behalf. I get that he can't be inherently evil, doing the work that he does and all that jazz. It's just...well, you know the way he treats you is only slightly better than the way he would treat a low-end kitchen appliance."

That got a laugh out of Melody. "A low-end kitchen appliance? What a...what a weird thing to say."

She could practically hear Chloe shrugging on the other end of the line. "Don't tell me it's not accurate, though. I mean, you buy a cheap blender at the grocery store, right? And then you treat it like it's a Vitamix. You're surprised when it burns out and stops working, but then you just go buy a new one, you know?"

"Hold on a second," said Melody. "Is that what you think is happening here? That he's overworking me because it's cheaper to have me than...what? Someone better?"

Chloe sighed. "I am not saying that anyone exists who is better than you. Or who cares about this job more than you do. I'm simply saying this. You, my dear, are absolutely positively underpaid and overworked and not appreciated the way that you should be."

"Ah. So. You know, the usual."

Chloe's laugh was humorless. "Yep. It is the usual and I will continue saying the usual things to you until...well, until you hear them, I guess. Until you make a change. Until you stop cosigning your own destruction, your own burnout."

"Right," said Melody. "Well. If it's just that, then can we...I don't know...move on? I'm kind of tired and not really up for this conversation right now."

"I'm shocked. Truly." Chloe's tone was deadpan. "But yeah. So tell me more about how Ben saved your bacon today."

A smile spread across Melody's face. "It was...brilliant, actually. Not just the work that he did. I mean, that was great. I sent it right along to Mr. Richards and I couldn't think of anything that I would have added to it or taken away from it. It was just exactly the way I would have done it. But I don't mean that just that part was brilliant. I mean...well, it feels so wrong to say this, but...it felt pretty wonderful to have somebody rescue me."

"He did not rescue you," Chloe interjected. "He did one little project, took one little thing off your plate for you. And it was a perfectly reasonable thing for a team mate to do."

"Oh, yeah? Well, as far back as I can recall, you never did that, so..."

Chloe let out an exasperated sigh. "Are you freaking kidding me right now? The reason I didn't take on any extra projects was because I already had my own and more than enough to do with them. And because I don't want to enable this twisted relationship of yours with your boss. So. Just because Ben's helping you now, don't...don't think that the job is better than it is, you know? Don't keep putting up with the nonsense for longer than you should."

Melody shook her head even though Chloe couldn't see her. "And here we are, again, back at this topic. It's like there's no avoiding it, is there?"

"Well fine then. If you don't want to talk about work and being taken advantage of and all my favorite go-to topics, then why don't we talk about how special and wonderful and nice and handsome your friend is?" She leaned so hard on the word "friend," that Melody could practically hear the air quotes around it.

"He's just a good friend," said Melody. "I promise. Not so good that he's about to replace you, so, you know...don't get jealous or anything. But, you know, don't get any other ideas either. We really are just friends. Plus, it's temporary, you know? When the program ends, we're going to be thousands of miles apart. So even if I wanted it to be something more, it couldn't possibly be."

"Oh, that's interesting," said Chloe.

"What is?"

"The fact that you're already explaining to yourself, justifying to yourself, why it can't be more than a friendship. It seems to me that if you weren't interested in him on some level, then you wouldn't have even had to have that conversation with yourself. Right?"

Melody was quiet, thoughtful. "You're right," she finally admitted. "That's not totally a normal thing to think about a new friend, is it?"

"Not in my experience, no," said Chloe. "It's not really helpful to look at anything in terms of its end date, is it? I mean, if we had known that you and I were going to be parted for a year, would that have made you pull back from our friendship? From getting too close just because, you know, things were about to change?"

"Of course not," said Melody. "It's not a big deal, anyway. And anyway, at the same time that Ben and I are going to be separated, you and I are going to be reunited, and everything will be back to normal."

"Yeah, but...I mean, you know it's going to be different, right?" asked Chloe. "This whole experience, this whole year...it's not nothing. It will change things. For you. For me. For Ben."

Melody sighed. "Yeah, I get that. I'm just saying you and I are going to be back in the same office. Working side by side."

She heard Chloe grumbling on the other end of the line. "Not if I have anything to say about it."

"What's that?" Melody felt her pulse pick up. "What's going on? Are you thinking about not coming back or…or what?"

"I don't know what I'm thinking of for myself," she said. "I just know that one of my greatest wishes is to see you spread your wings, get out of there, and go someplace where you will actually be appreciated."

"Huh," said Melody. "And here I thought you would just love being coworkers and cubicle mates for as long as we both shall live."

"Oh, no matter what happens, you're not getting rid of me. That's just a fact. But, you know, if you and I were both working our dream jobs and we didn't see each other at work every day, that wouldn't be so bad, would it? We'd still be together. We'd still have plenty of fun. We just wouldn't have work drama and office politics to complain about."

Melody scoffed. "And what would we do without that?"

Chloe's tone was stern, serious. "We would be just fine. There's a whole life outside of work frustrations, I promise."

"Hmm. Well, you'll have to tell me more about that sometime," said Melody.

"You are impossible, you know that? You could just find out about it for yourself."

"We'll see. I just might do that."

It turned out that Melody had the opportunity to find out about life outside of work even sooner than she would have anticipated. The next day at work, Ben poked his head in her cubicle early in the morning.

"Hey," he said, greeting her with a wide smile. "Any chance you're free tonight? After work I mean?"

"Uhh." Melody hesitated. That was always such an awkward question, wasn't it? If she said that she was free and then he offered something like helping him move a couch to a new apartment, she'd have no way to back out of it.

He seemed to pick up on her hesitation and he put his hands up. "I'm not trying to trick you into anything. I just...uh yeah, you're right. That probably wasn't the right way to ask. If you are interested, I would love to invite you over and make you your first proper cup of Turkish coffee. If you're available today, we could do it today and if not, maybe a different day?"

"Oh!" Melody smiled, warming to the thought. "That...that actually sounds really nice. I would love it. Thank you."

Ben's smile stretched even further, further than she had known was possible. "Great. I'm really looking forward to it."

"Me, too."

*To continue the story, turn to **page 8***

306

Her heart won in the end, and she gave an exasperated sigh. "No, you beautiful human. No! I don't want to be away from you. I don't want to forget about you. And I even understand why you're acting like this. You're scared." She shrugged. "I'm scared, too. I'm trying to do the right thing, I guess. I don't want you to do something impulsive just to be near me and sabotage your whole career, you know? And I'm not prepared to do something impulsive like that, either."

He stepped closer, hands coming up to caress her cheeks. "So you don't really believe the universe is conspiring to keep us apart?"

She shook her head, her eyes filling with tears. "Of course I don't. How could I? If anything, I could be persuaded to believe that the universe conspired to bring us together in the first place." She blinked once, slowly, freeing a few drops to slide down her cheeks. "I certainly don't understand why it's got us in this position now, but..." Her eyes lifted to meet his. "We can figure it out, can't we?"

He nodded, smiling for the first time that morning. "We can. I know we can. I can't see the path forward right now, but I'm sure there is one. There *has* to be."

"Okay." She hesitated, studying his face like the map for the path he was talking about might be hidden in his eyes. "Just promise me you aren't going to quit your job and move across the world permanently just so we can have a shot at being together. I don't think even the best relationship could handle that kind of pressure, and I don't want you throwing away your career on my behalf."

Ben gave a soft scoff. "I promise not to make any impulsive decisions *today*. How's that?" He shrugged. "But I can't promise not to make a grand gesture. Who are you to decide that my career is worth more than my happiness? Or that I couldn't be perfectly happy living and working in Michigan with you?"

"Those are some big questions," she said. "And we can talk about them later. It's just...it's not the right moment, is it? We need to at least deal with this mess."

"You're right." He nodded. "And what a mess it is. I can't believe the program is over practically before it even had a chance."

"You and me both."

"Well, how about we have one last evening hanging out? A little company during packing...before the airport tomorrow." He blew out a slow exhale. "It's really going to be tomorrow, isn't it?"

Melody nodded. "Sounds like it. Mr. Richards is itching to get things back to normal as quickly as possible. And it looks like everyone else is on board with that, too."

"Okay, fair enough, then," said Ben. "I better..." He tipped his head towards his workspace and all the tasks waiting for him there on this most busy of days.

"Yeah, me too. We'll talk later." She squeezed his hand and then got back to work.

After work Ben and Melody went home together, taking the steps a little more slowly than normal, knowing that it was the last time.

"So I have to ask," he said. "I was going to wait, but the question has been weighing on me all day."

"What question?"

"I guess the question is...what's the verdict? Do we stick it out? Try to make this work long distance? Or is it all feeling like too much now?" He gave her a sad smile. "I know what you said this morning, but that may have come along with all the big feelings of the day. I just want to make sure we're on the same page before...I don't know...before I make any big declarations or anything like that."

She was quiet, looking down at her feet as they continued to walk. "It's definitely been on my mind," she said with a nod. "How could it not be? You know? And I've been weighing the pros and cons, of course. Of both options."

Ben exhaled through his nose, the weakest laugh she'd ever heard come out of him. "Well, I'm curious to see how I measured up on the pro con chart," he said, a hint of bitterness in his tone.

"It wasn't...it's not about whether *you're* worth it," she said. "It's about all the other things. You know? What do you think about the long distance relationship? I mean, there's a lot of other factors there, you know. Obviously, the goal is for it not to be long distance forever. And if we're going to close that distance, then we have to think about your career, my career, your family, my family..."

Ben stopped and turned to her, his hands coming to her shoulders. "Melody, no. That's...you're getting way too far ahead of yourself, aren't you? I mean, that's like..."

"I know," she said, sadly. "It's like I'm talking about marriage or something. And it's not that. It's not that I'm thinking about whether we're going to be together forever or not. But I guess I'm just thinking about the challenge and the pain of a long distance relationship and if it's going to be worth it, or if it's just going to be kicking the can down the road. You know? The pain that we might feel parting now...well, it might be more manageable than the immense pain we would feel six months from now if we tried to make this work and it didn't."

Ben closed his eyes, taking a deep breath. "I understand," he said finally. "And I respect that. I respect the hell out of your mind. The way you put it to use in situations like this where...well, I know my heart and my feelings are all over the place." He gave her a small, sad smile. "You're the only one of us bringing any amount of reason to this decision."

She shook her head back at him. "If you want to call it that."

"What else would it be?"

"Well, it might just be my own fears trying to steer me away from what I really want." She shrugged. "Who's to say?"

"So." His eyes searched hers. "What's the answer to it all, then? What do your mind and your heart say?"

To tell Ben that they need to end things, turn to **page 266**

To tell Ben that they will figure it out together, turn to **page 96**

311

Ben's voice on the line was a balm to her soul. "This is great, Melody. I know it feels scary, especially making such a big change, but..." He sighed. "Well, I'm just so relieved. That place wasn't good for you, you know? And I'm glad you see it. The whole world is open to you now. You can do anything you want."

She ran her fingers along the bedspread, tracing its pattern. "I guess that's one way of looking at it. It feels pretty overwhelming to me right now, I'm not going to lie." She blew out an exhale. "But there's a little part of me that thinks it's all going to be okay."

"Of course it is. Mr. Richards doesn't run the whole world. You could find another job in a heartbeat. The question that matters is what do *you* want to do next, not who can you bend over backwards to accommodate?"

"It might sound stupid, but I want to be happy."

"That doesn't sound stupid at all. I think it's a great starting point. So that's what you need to figure out, isn't it? What will make you happy?"

Melody was quiet for a long moment, finding her next words. "I was happy when we were together. But it's not fair to put that on you, to make all my happiness depend on your presence."

"No, you're right. I was happy with you, too. But I don't want to be in the kind of co-dependent relationship where my happiness is your responsibility, or yours is mine. Do you?"

"Absolutely not. I think I'm just getting out of a co-dependent relationship with Mr. Richards, and more than anything else I want, I don't want to do that again. Not with you."

"Okay, then." She could hear the smile in Ben's voice. "But you *do* want to be with me?"

"Of course. That was never the question. I mean, sure, I had my moments where I was too afraid for my own good, too scared of how real this thing between us had the potential to be..."

"But now?"

She lifted her chin. "Now I know I want it. No matter what. Even if it's complicated and long-distance and time zones are hard to navigate."

"Good." He blew out a long sigh. "That's really good. Now all you have to do is figure out what you want, where you want to be...and I'll take care of the rest."

"What do you mean? It's not that simple, Ben."

"Sure it is. Just figure out what's going to make you happy and where you're going to do that, and I'll find a way to be there. I want to be where you are, Melody, and if you want me to be with you, there's nothing that will stop me from figuring that out."

She was already shaking her head. "But no, Ben. No. We can't do that. I can't ask you to uproot your whole life to be near me. That wouldn't be fair to you, and weren't we just talking about how that's not a good foundation for your happiness?" She felt the emotions welling in her throat. "I'm not enough of a reason for you to be happy. I can't even make myself happy, so how can I do that for you?"

"Melody." His voice resonated into her bones, cutting through the anxiety bubbling under the surface. "I'm not asking you to make me happy. I'm just asking you to let me be near you. I can do my job from anywhere—Bettina wouldn't have a problem with that. And I have my hobbies already, the things that bring me joy. Books, hiking, baking...I can do those things anywhere."

Her emotions were flowing freely now, and Melody sniffled as she wiped her eyes. "Is it really that easy? It can't be that easy."

"It is, Mel. I've found what makes me happy, the little joys in my life. Now you find yours, and then when we combine our forces, we'll truly be unstoppable."

Her laugh was wet with the tears that were still flowing. "Okay. I can try."

"You'll do better than try, Melody. If I know you at all—and I am sure that I do—then you're going to nail this."

"Okay." A pause. "I love you, Ben."

"I love you, too."

For the first time since her school days, when summer vacation and spring break were full of long, lazy days to do whatever she wanted, Melody was free. She didn't need to go anywhere—*because she didn't have a job anymore,* she reminded herself, tamping down the anxiety that came along with it—and the day stretched ahead of her with potential. There were so many opportunities to find that joy she was looking for that she almost didn't even know where to begin.

She started with coffee. Breakfast. Picking up a novel off her shelf rather than something related to her personal or professional development. A slow stroll around the block to admire the bright leaves that were still on a few trees, the holiday decorations and twinkly lights that a few eager neighbors had started displaying.

There was no one thing that sparked an epiphany in Melody about where her happiness could come from. A good cup of coffee didn't mean she should devote her life to roasting the perfect bean or pulling the perfect espresso shot. An appreciation of her neighbor's landscaping didn't mean she should take on an apprenticeship with the team that did the local yard work. Reading a good book didn't mean that she should become a librarian or open a used bookstore...even if there *definitely* was part of her intrigued by the idea of having her own bookstore/coffee shop and all the romantic dreams that entailed.

As she returned to her apartment and unlocked the door, she remembered what Ben had said about the things that brought him joy. They weren't things that he did for any particular end result—except for the baking, she suspected, because the end result of that hobby was always delicious—but simply because he enjoyed the process. And maybe that was the key—enjoying the process. Pausing in the middle of something, in the middle of *anything*, to appreciate what you were doing.

With that thought in mind, the day took on a different light. Rather than looking at her home, her meals, her chores, her neighborhood through the tired eyes, the lenses that had seen them day after day and grown accustomed to them, she tried to see it all for the first time. To appreciate what she had in this moment rather than wondering what was missing that might be the secret ingredient to her happiness.

Very soon, she found herself smiling a lot more than she had since being separated from Ben. There was so much to appreciate, so many ways in which she was already living a blessed life, rife with opportunities for happiness. All she had to do was pay attention and tap into what was already there.

It turned out, though, that being grateful for everything and everyone that crossed your path was exhausting. Or else, all the years of too much work, too much stress, and not enough sleep had caught up with Melody. Either way, she found herself falling asleep on the couch in the early afternoon, settling in for a luxurious nap with no responsibilities—apart from figuring out what she was going to do with her life—hanging over her head.

A few weeks into Melody's new life, she received an unexpected email from Madeline Andrews, director of the Generosity Exchange.

Dear Ms. Critchfield,

As you are no doubt aware, the fallout from the recent Generosity Exchange cohort has had severe professional implications for the leadership at EduPowerment. In the subsequent debriefings about what went wrong and what could be improved upon in the future, your name was mentioned a number of times, both in terms of your commitment to the mission and ideals of EduPowerment and your skill and ingenuity. It seems that most of the work for which Mr. Richards took credit was, in fact, completed by yourself.

My colleague, Bettina Schmidt from Deutsche Lebenshilfe, and I would be very interested in interviewing you for a position in the new and improved Generosity Exchange Consortium. The salary is competitive (far more so than your previous role, I don't mind telling you), and the position would be fully remote.

Please let me know your availability. I'm looking forward to speaking with you soon.

Regards,
Madeline Andrews

Three weeks later, Melody was on a plane to Dresden, not-so-patiently approaching the final descent. Though the time had passed since she had last seen Ben, it hadn't passed quickly. It had been equal parts missing him and wishing he were closer, along with settling in to her new reality and routine, easing in to her new responsibilities at Generosity Exchange with a much healthier balance between work and the rest of her life.

Now, it was the first week of December, and Ben had invited her to join him in Dresden. The Christmas markets he had told her about would be starting up just in time for the First Advent, and she was eager to find out what that entailed. But not as eager as she was to see Ben.

And though the time between the plane landing, exiting into the terminal, reclaiming her bag, and making her way out of the airport stretched on for an eternity, teasing her with the sweet reunion that was awaiting her, it did end. And it ended in the best possible way, with Melody running into Ben's arms and him picking her up, twirling her around in a circle, and never letting her go again.

Well, that wasn't entirely true. He had to let her go from his embrace so that he could step back and look at her, take her in fully, and then pull her close to him again for another embrace, a kiss, the cycle repeating. But if he never let go of her heart again, if he held onto it for the rest of his days, well, that would be just fine with her.

She leaned in to the kiss, relishing the familiar smell of him, the taste of him. She had thought she had known what she was missing, but Ben in the flesh was even better than she remembered him being. Even sturdier, even more comforting, even more enticing.

"I missed you so much," she said when they finally parted.

He was stroking her cheek and looking at her with warm affection. "Not as much as I missed you."

She raised an eyebrow. "I wasn't aware it was a competition."

"It wasn't. Competitions have winners, and I'm pretty sure we were both just in agony." He smiled. "But it's over now, right? You're here, and I'm not letting you go." He threaded his fingers through hers, his thumb caressing the back of hers.

She smiled at him. "It is. I'm here now." She lifted her shoulders before dropping them back down. "And I have no idea what happens next, but..."

"But you know just as surely as I do that we're going to be together for it?"

She blew out a deep exhale as her face split in a smile. "I mean...yeah. I don't know how that works, but...yes. Please."

He pulled her to him again, his lips against hers before she finished her sentence. "Then all we have to figure out next is...where do you want to go from here?"

Bonus: Ben's POV

I t shouldn't be this big of a deal, he knew, inviting a woman over for coffee. But Melody wasn't just any woman, was she? From the first time he had seen her, she had pinged on his radar like she was there to stay. Like no matter how much he might not want it, might even think it was creepy, he was always going to be aware of her presence.

And it had been true. Every room he had entered, if Melody had been there, her eyes were the first ones his had found.

Even when he was talking to someone else, with her just at the very edge of his peripheral vision, his entire body was aware of her. No matter how much he focused his attention on the conversation he was having, part of him—more than half of him, it felt like—was with Melody. Aware of her, tuned in to her, wishing she were the one he was with in that moment.

So if he was going to invite her to come over for Turkish coffee tomorrow, then he needed to make it the best darn Turkish coffee experience she had ever had. Never mind the fact that there was every possibility she had never actually had a Turkish coffee experience, which would by default make this one both the best and the worst.

"You know what that means, then," he said out loud to himself, as he picked up his favorite cookbook. "Bake your feelings, Ben. The way to someone's heart is through their stomach, right?"

He found his favorite recipe, the apple tart he'd mastered as a teenager, the first time he'd discovered he had any proficiency in the kitchen. And as he peeled apples, prepared the crust, and assembled all the components, he gave himself a pep talk.

"No matter what happens, it's going to be fine. Whether she feels the same way about you or not, at least you'll be out of the agony of not knowing. If she doesn't feel the same way..." He shrugged, playing it off. "Well, that will be a bit awkward, but the program won't last forever. At some point, it will end and you'll both be put out of your misery."

He stopped mid-peel, as the next thought occurred to him. "And if she *does* feel the same way..." He blew out a long exhale. "Well, that would really be something, wouldn't it?" It was too good to even imagine what life could be like if Melody Critchfield reciprocated his feelings. If he could touch her, hold her, share all the things with her that he'd been bottling up deep inside. If this thing between them wasn't just in his imagination, then it was likely to really be Something, with a capital S. Not a fling, not a fun way to pass the time while they were in the same space, but a game changer. A life changer.

It was a restless night for Ben, the smell of the tart filling his apartment like it was about to be put up for a real estate open house. His mind was consumed with Melody, playing over every possibility the next day contained, as if by thinking through them all, he could prepare himself for any inevitability.

As he got ready to go to the office the next morning, he gave himself one last long look in the mirror. "It's going to be fine. She's going to say yes." He shrugged. "Well, I don't actually know that, and neither do you. It's going to be whatever it is, and she's going to say whatever she's going to say. But no matter what that *it* is, it will be okay." It wasn't the peppiest of pep talks, but it did the job and Ben was soon on his way in to the office.

When he saw Melody there, leaning over her workspace as she arranged her things on her desk, his heart skipped once in his chest. He would never get tired of seeing her, never grow accustomed to the shock that went through his system at the first sight of her each day. Weekends were torture, being away from her, and he had never been more grateful for Mondays than he had become as a man infatuated with Melody Critchfield.

It felt like it took ages for the opportunity to present itself. It wasn't as if he could march right up to her and invite her over for Turkish coffee. What would she even think of that? But as they went through their normal routines, fell into the rhythm of working alongside each other and sharing their pleasant—and occasionally barbed—banter, he relaxed just a bit. Her presence, even though it put every part of his being on high alert, was also a balm to his soul.

Being around her was joy and peace and comfort and sheer thrill, all wrapped up in one.

"Would you—" He blurted out the question before he could think better of it, before he could stop himself. "Would you like to come over for a cup of Turkish coffee? I'll make it for you, in my apartment, I mean."

He felt his cheeks heat at the awkward delivery, fighting to suppress the blush he knew was flaring across his face for her viewing pleasure.

And then, miracle of miracles, she smiled and nodded. "I'd like that very much."

Author's Note

I had so much fun writing this story and keeping track of all the different threads, even if at times the sheer number of loose ends was overwhelming.

At the beginning of the year, I had no plans to write this book, but the idea took root when I learned a number of other romance authors were launching Kickstarter projects in February. It started with a daydream, wondering if I could launch a project with them, and then the idea quickly built from there. I told myself I'd do it only if Kylie Sek, who had been on my list of dream cover designers for ages, was available, and she quickly became a dream collaborator, designing this cover and all of the other goodies that went along with the Kickstarter.

If you enjoyed this book, please consider leaving a review, as that is one of the best ways to support indie authors like me. Reviews left on major retail sites (wherever you bought this book is a great start!), The StoryGraph, GoodReads, and BookBub will help other readers discover this book, too.

To stay updated on other works in progress, please visit my website at kcmccormickciftci.com and subscribe to my newsletter. I send out monthly updates on upcoming releases, books I'm loving, and other recommendations.

Acknowledgements

This book was an extra special undertaking, possible thanks to the support of a number of Kickstarter backers, credited below.

Regina D.

Danika Bloom

Mahi Mistry

My Queen, Jane McCormick

Becca

Jayna, Austin, and Kohen Schmid

Madeline Tipton

Anthea Sharp

Lainey Davis

Jessie Katz

Sarah Daniel Martin

Cousin #1

Sarah Woodson

Nancy Paul

Ember Leigh

Karen & Dan, lovers of talent

Carmela

Laurie M
Jordan Spence
Eron Wyngarde
Jay Ishino
Sydney Moore
Victoria E
Marla Bradeen
Mikaeli R.

About the Author

KC McCormick Çiftçi is an English teacher turned romance writer. She spent the majority of her twenties living and working abroad, collecting the experiences that inform the stories she tells. She enjoys telling multicultural and international love stories through romantic comedy and women's fiction. She lives in Turkey with her husband and a herd of cats.

Prior to diving into the world of romance, KC published two self-help books for intercultural couples, *Loving Across Borders* and *The K-1 Visa Wedding Plan*. Both are available wherever books are sold.

For updates on upcoming releases, behind the scenes news, and all my favorite book recommendations, visit kcmccormickciftci.com (or just point your phone camera at the QR code below).

Books by KC McCormick Çiftçi

Austen in Turkey

Pride, Prejudice, & Turkish Delight

Sense, Sensibility, & the Mediterranean Sea

Home (Abroad) for the Holidays

Christmas on Inishmore

Intercultural Relationship Self Help

Loving Across Borders

The K-1 Visa Wedding Plan